DAWN'S
GRAY STEEL

A NOVEL ABOUT SHILOH:
APRIL FIFTH THROUGH EIGHTH 1862

Daniel F. Korn

Author's Tranquility Press
MARIETTA, GEORGIA

Daniel F. Korn/Author's Tranquility Press
3800 CAMP CREEK PKWY SW BLDG 1400-116 #1255
Atlanta, GA 30331
www.authorstranquilitypress.com

Publisher's Note: This is a work of fiction. Names, characters, places, and incidents are a product of the author's imagination. Locales and public names are sometimes used for atmospheric purposes. Any resemblance to actual people, living or dead, or to businesses, companies, events, institutions, or locales is completely coincidental.

Ordering Information:
Quantity sales. Special discounts are available on quantity purchases by corporations, associations, and others. For details, contact the "Special Sales Department" at the address above.

Dawn's Gray Steel/Daniel F. Korn
Paperback: 978-1-959197-84-3
eBook: 978-1-959197-85-0

DEDICATION

No one writes something like this without having help along the way, and I would be remiss if I did not express some appreciation for those who helped. First, I must thank fellow educators Gail Fowler and Mike McCoullough, who took the time to read various parts of my manuscript and offer vital suggestions. Gail, a master history teacher, spent many an hour meticulously reading, checking, and penciling in corrections, as well as offering suggestions on the material. Mike, who is a superb librarian and researcher, spent much time assisting me in finding sources of information as well as taking the time to help critique the research and writing. Their assistance was invaluable, and I am proud to call them my friends.

To professors Dr. Mary Corey and Dr. Lynn Parsons of the State University of New York College at Brockport, for their assistance in completing this novel. Both took the time to read my original manuscript and offered encouragement and subtle suggestions. I thank you both for your help, not just for this, but to Dr. Corey for helping me as her student, to gain valuable insight into the teaching profession and for her encouragement of me to complete the project, and to Dr. Parsons for his incredible knowledge of the Civil War and his willingness to push me as a student to expand my own horizons. Thank you for your time and assistance.

To school principals Susan Hustleby and Dr. Bryan Setser, both of whom I have had the pleasure of serving under as a member of their respective teaching faculties. Both offered strong encouragement in my pursuit of excellence in my writing. Susan never hesitated to push me when I needed a nudge. Bryan took time during his pursuit of his doctorate to help guide and critique me in my own work towards my master's degree which this book became a part of. Having been born and raised in Corinth, Mississippi not far from the Shiloh battlefield, Bryan proved to be an excellent sounding board for my ideas. Their professionalism is a shining example for all in the teaching profession, and I am proud to call them my friends as well.

My parents Fred and Nancy Korn (Gardner) were always strong advocates of my desire to learn. My mother was always taking us to various programs and museums, and constantly encouraged me to "learn more." She still to this day looks for ways to encourage my love of history, sending me various newspaper articles that she has clipped from various sources to send to me. She has always been there when I needed her. My father always pushed myself and my brothers to always do better, and to give our very best, no matter what we were doing. All his life he lived what he preached to us, an ethic of hard work and perseverance. Although he was not a well-traveled man, he did enjoy listening to my tales of where I had been, and what I had seen. He died long before I finished this, but I believe his hand has been there to guide me along the way. My mother was fortunate to meet a good man some years later. My stepfather Raymond Gardner is the hardest working man I have ever known. He is a true "man of the soil" and delights in his incredible ability to make things grow. I love them all for the example of hard work and responsibility they set for us. I thank you for helping to install in me the desire to learn, read, and experience those things that led me to write this.

My in-laws Lyeth and Pat Henderson have certainly done their share to help. My father-in-law, Lyeth, loves to go to historical places, airshows, and reenactments with me. It was suggestions by him after a joint trip to Gettysburg that pushed me to re-enter the teaching profession. It was the best advice he ever gave me. Both he and my mother-in-law Pat have demonstrated their love, support, and encouragement many times along the way. Thanks guys!

To my children Gena Marie and Michael Raymond, for making life interesting for their dad. My daughter Gena sees life in her own special way and has no problem expressing herself on almost any subject. It was she who found my unfinished manuscript and hounded me to "finish what you started." Mike has a tremendous sense of humor and is my co-conspirator in doing Revolutionary War reenacting. It fills me with great pride to have my son participate along side of me in making history come to life. Both of them have also helped me to see many things through their eyes. I am a fortunate parent to have two such interesting people for my children, and I could not love them more.

My wife Cheri must have a special place in heaven reserved for her. She has had to put up with a great deal over the years as I have struggled with writing this. It has been a long journey, with many stops along the way and she has consistently expressed her love and encouragement. She has always understood that "trips" would include stops at battlefields, museums, cemeteries, and other historical places all along the way, and never wavered in her support of her husband's desire to "do this." I simply could not have done it without her. She is the best. She truly is my heart light.

To all the others along the way, you all know who you are. Thanks!

PREFACE

Some of the greatest works of fiction ever written have to deal with the Civil War. Stephen Crane's *The Red Badge of Courage* and Michael Shaara's Pulitzer Prize winning *The Killer Angels* are but two that quickly come to mind as having set the standard for others to follow. There have been many other prize worthy works throughout the years, so it was with some trepidation that I entered this field, a mere novice in the field of writing historical fiction.

I had often noted that the majority of the Civil War fiction that I read had to do with the eastern theater of the Civil War, and especially, the immortal Robert E. Lee, his Confederate Army of Northern Virginia, and their heroic encounters with the Union's Army of the Potomac. Also, I had realized that many people simply were not aware of the fact that while in the *east* the Confederate South was usually winning, at least in the early years of the war, this was not the case in the *west*. It was with this knowledge that I decided to write a work of fiction regarding the first great Civil War battle of the west, that being the April 1862 battle on the shore of the Tennessee River at Pittsburg Landing in south-central Tennessee-Shiloh.

Shiloh was one of the earliest major battles of the American Civil War. It was a battle that saw a deadly combination of strategic chance-taking, tactical genius, blunders, and luck. Creative spirit, the ability to face the storm and not flinch, make necessary adjustments and sacrifices on the fly, cruel happenstance, and luck, both good and bad, were all factors in the horrific struggle between two huge amateur fighting forces that took place around the Shiloh Meetinghouse that started on that Sunday morning in April 1862. Shiloh's hallmarks of sheer tenacity, dramatic blunders, and bloody ferocity would mark her as one of the most bloody displays of armed conflict to ever take place on the North American continent, a throwback to the conflicts of the Middle Ages of Europe, to a time where knight fought knight in a general melee. However, none of those armored warriors could ever have realized the destructive power of a rifled musket or a modern artillery piece. It can be said that Shiloh was a medieval battle that used medieval tactics but was fought with modern weapons.

Dawn's Gray Steel is the story of those bloody days. It tells the tale of Shiloh through the eyes of the commanders who led the forces competing against each other. For the North, you have the stubborn Ulysses S. Grant, the excitable William T. Sherman, Benjamin Prentiss, and their various supporting players. For the South you have the quixotic Albert Sidney Johnston, the mercurial Pierre Gustave Toutant Beauregard, Braxton Bragg and their supporting cast. All of these men had their own story and Shiloh would be a defining chapter for some, and the end of the story for others.

I have tried to define all the events as they actually happened. The story is written in the language of the time, and that language, as best as I can tell, is quite accurate. Most of the actions and comments of the characters are accurate as to what they did and said and are based on the actual reports by the individuals concerned. Where necessary I have filled in with what I believe would have been appropriate comments and actions by the various individuals as I have come to know them so as to best tell the story. I have done my best to at least give the reader a glimpse into the "other" half of the war. I hope you enjoy it.

Dan Korn

CONTENTS

JOHNSTON

Mitchie's Farm
April 5, 1862: Noon

Nothing had been accomplished. General Albert Sidney Johnston sat and fumed as he watched, watched the precious morning hours dwindle down to nothing.

Rain. It had rained incessantly throughout the night and into the morning. A heavy, soaking rain, one that had turned the dusty, red Tennessee clay into a soft, clinging, gray mud. A mud that molded to Johnston's soldiers' bedraggled clothes and made their homespun uniforms even grayer in appearance. A grayness that matched the day's own as the would-be troops tried to shake the heavy Tennessee mud from their boots as they filed into line.

Time. So much precious, irreplaceable time had passed. Six hours had come and gone since Johnston and his second-in-command, the colorful Louisiana-born Pierre Gustave Toutant (P.G.T.) Beauregard had arrived upon the scene.

Johnston had expected to find the troops in ranks, primed and cocked, ready for combat, anxious to meet the enemy. Instead to his dismay, what greeted his disgusted gaze was an unorganized and undisciplined mob. A mob that believed themselves, soldiers. A mob that thought itself capable of licking anyone else, as if war was nothing more than just another street brawl.

Johnston rode angrily up and down the clearing, his impatience mounting with each step that Fire-Eater, his big, thoroughbred bay took. He had never been known for a sweet temper, and the prancing mount, sensing his master's unhappiness, was doing nothing to help the situation, Johnston having to pull the reins constantly. Now as the big bay whinnied and tossed his head, Johnston's temper boiled over. This delay was someone's fault, and Johnston wanted answers.

"Where's Bragg?" Johnston demanded of Beauregard. "I want some explanation for these delays." Beauregard said nothing, merely pointing down to the end of the clearing where General Braxton Bragg, commanding general of the Second Corps of Johnston's Army of the Mississippi, huddled with his staff beneath the dripping branches of a large oak tree. It was Bragg who commanded the right wing of this army.

"Let's go, General." Johnston hauled on Fire-Eater's reins and headed for Bragg's command post, Beauregard and the rest of their staff trailing behind.

The dyspeptic Bragg, poring over maps with his staff, appeared to be lost in thought as Johnston rode up. Johnston wasted no time, quickly dismounting from Fire-Eater. Tossing his reins to a waiting orderly, Johnston quickly stepped over to the oak to join the war council and catching Bragg's eye Johnston spoke.

"General Bragg, what seems to be the problem?"

Bragg noted the water dripping from the brim of Johnston's hat. "Problem, General Johnston? What problem?"

Johnston removed his soaked hat and wiped his forehead with a big bandanna. He replaced the hat on his head before replying.

"Why are your troops not deployed and ready to go? Why are they not on the march?"

Bragg grimaced. "Oh, well, I am missing one full brigade, General. They have not arrived yet."

Johnston frowned, the pot that was his temper beginning to boil over. "Well, where are they, General?"

"It's somewhere back there." Bragg airily replied, waving his hand and gesturing in the direction of the road Johnston had just ridden down. "I am trying to locate it now. I've sent riders. We will find it. They can't be a far."

Johnston's eyes turned hard. "You don't know where they are? How could you lose them, an entire brigade?" His words were clipped, the tone, harsh.

Bragg looked up again, then leaned forward, his hands flush on the map-covered table. His face flushed with anger and surprise. "General, I am sorry, but these things will happen. After all, these are not experienced troops that we have here. Their commanders are learning their jobs, just as their men are. I promise you. We will find them, General Johnston, sir." Bragg stood up, stiffly at attention, his arms at his side, fists clenched. His dark eyes snapped with anger.

Johnston, his nerves stretched thin, his mind tired with frustration and lack of sleep, felt the lid coming off the pot. Snapping his watch open, he stared at the face of the timepiece, then quietly announced.

"12:30." He angrily snapped the watch closed. He looked out from under the tree at the dripping sky. Then, his temper giving vent to his feelings, he exploded.

"12:30! This is perfectly puerile! *This is not war!*"

Bragg, Beauregard, and the others immediately backed away, realizing nothing they could say would cool Johnston's explosive mood down. Studiously avoiding eye contact with their frustrated leader, they all looked to their own activities, Bragg and Beauregard looking again to the map, the others stepping away, knowing it was far better to appear busy then to set Johnston off even further.

Johnston stalked back out into the rain over to Fire-Eater. Mounting the animal, he snatched the reins from the startled orderly. "Well, somebody needs to find those troops! General Beauregard?"

"Sir?"

"You and your staff will please stay with General Bragg and complete whatever preparations are necessary for this attack!" Leaving the astonished Beauregard and Bragg behind, he gave the spur to his horse, and galloped away.

"Well hurry up, go with him!" Beauregard snapped, causing the rest of Johnston's escort to scramble to mount and ride, hurrying to catch up with the angry army commander, now many yards down the road.

Johnston continued his gallop, then thinking better of it, slowed Fire-Eater down to an easy canter, his staff catching up, but keeping behind, no one daring to ride up to his side. Johnston's thoughts turned back to thinking about the battle plans. They had sat in Bragg's bedchamber two nights earlier, working into the wee hours of the morning of April 3, laying out the plan. His mind drifted to the thoughts of that night. Thoughts of himself, weary from lack of sleep, his mind feverish with plans on how to best to destroy an enemy that now enjoyed basking in the reflected glory of a string of victories. An enemy that had captured the Confederate Tennessee strongholds Forts Henry and Donelson only ten days apart, winning for their conqueror a new nickname, a play on the winner's name.

When the besieged Confederates inside the surrounded Fort Donelson, knowing their chances of survival were slim, asked for terms of surrender, they thought they had reason to believe that the federal army would be magnanimous in victory. After all, their commander, Brigadier General Simon

Buckner, had thought that his old West Point classmate and friend, Brigadier General Ulysses S. Grant, commanding the federal forces, would be lenient in his surrender terms. Instead, Grant had been anything but lenient, stating that the only terms he would offer to his old friend was immediate and unconditional surrender. The disgruntled Buckner had no choice but to surrender, and twelve thousand Confederate soldiers found themselves prisoners-of-war, and a new federal legend was born. Next, "Unconditional Surrender" Grant's Army of the Tennessee had taken Nashville, thus securing the major southern city for the federal cause. Then, Grant's swaggering troops had continued along the Tennessee River and were now camping at Pittsburg Landing, a short march from Memphis, Tennessee. This was almost certainly Grant's next target. Johnston's ruddy face turned even redder as he recalled Confederate president's Jefferson Davis's latest telegram. The Confederacy's leader had made it known in no uncertain terms the depths of his displeasure about the recent turn of events in the western Confederacy and had insisted that Johnston do something before it was too late.

The fifty-nine-year-old Johnston was an imposing presence. In appearance, the six-foot-one-inch soldier was the epitome of a noble Southern aristocrat. His good looks blended well with a powerful personality. He was a gifted intellectual but lacked mental discipline, often allowing his passions to rule both his mind and his actions. His personal courage was well known and above reproach. Despite all this, so far, his tenure as a department commander had been a disaster. His distress at the twin losses of Henry and

Donelson and the resulting criticism had piqued his anger. The twin disasters had resulted in Johnston being forced to withdraw from Kentucky and to have to relinquish middle Tennessee. No, Johnston was looking for one master counterstroke to regain what had been lost. Johnston made no excuses for himself, knew he had made mistakes, and accepted the responsibility of his actions. Now he was determined to correct those mistakes and had listened fervently as both Beauregard and Bragg had argued that now was the time to strike.

"This is a grand opportunity to strike, General." Beauregard had argued. "Our scouts have learned that Grant's (now a major-general) Army of the Tennessee is now camped in a loose grouping, about three miles wide, and occupying the high ground inland from Pittsburg Landing. Their lines generally face west, with the swamps and lowlands of Owl Creek to their north, and the Little Creek marshes on their south flank. I propose that we place our troops in such a way as to attack and drive the entire federal army away from the Tennessee River, and into the Owl Creek bottoms, where it can be destroyed in detail." Stopping for a moment, Beauregard handed Johnston a telegram.

"General, this tells us that the federal troops are preparing to move out and attack Memphis." Johnston took the telegram, his eyes scanning the contents as Beauregard watched. The telegram did say just that. "Old Bory," the troops affectionate nickname for Beauregard, continued on with his plea.

"Now is the moment to advance and *strike* the enemy at Pittsburg Landing. He is fat. He is lazy. His defenses are poor. He does not suspect! Now is the time! Now, General, *now!*"

Johnston had to agree, especially since Bragg was in loud agreement with Beauregard. Bragg had thundered his opinion to Johnston.

"Now or never, General! It has to be now or *never!*" Bragg emphatically agreed. Johnston could only nod in acceptance of their impassioned pleas and gave the triumphant Beauregard instructions to draw up march and attack plans. That had been two days earlier. Now . . .

"Why did I say all right to Bory's plan?" Johnston fumed. "These boys aren't ready for a complicated plan like this. "For what Beauregard had designed, was a plan of attack based on Napoleon's battle plan for Waterloo.

"Well, all I can hope is that this "Waterloo" doesn't boomerang against us the way Bonaparte's did on him. I should have given him directions that are more precise."

Johnston continued in his musing, now silently to himself. *I should have remembered what the weather was like in April. It's not much different here from Kentucky.* For Johnston had been born in Kentucky fifty-nine years before. He had gone on to West Point and then served in the federal army. Resigning his commission, he had moved to Texas, and served under Sam Houston in the Texas army. He had returned to the regular army when the Texas Republic joined the United States, and then fought in the resulting Mexican War. He had continued to rise in rank and was serving as a brigadier general in California when the Civil War began. Despite the best efforts of the federal high command, Johnston had turned down the offer of higher command in the Union army, deciding to cast his lot with the rebellious states, and returned to Texas. Jefferson Davis had immediately offered him a full generalship in the Confederate army, which Johnston accepted. He had assumed command of the Western Department of the Confederacy in September 1861 and had been fighting an uphill battle ever since.

It was now easy for Johnston to see how Beauregard, in that first flush of triumph, had drawn a plan far more suited for Napoleon's elite shock troops, so far more used to discipline and order were they. A plan that was completely unsuited to the rough, tough, and undisciplined Confederates under Johnston's command.

We can still pull it off! Johnston mused, in his mind reviewing the plan. He could see the two roads that ran from Corinth, Tennessee up to Pittsburg Landing. The two roads resembled a string bow, leaned sideways, and curved up, with the two opposing armies at the top and bottom of the bow. The lower route, through Monterey, was the string. The upper route through Mitchie's Junction was the bow. Bragg and Breckinridge with their troops were to travel the string, Hardee and Polk the bow, in that order. Hardee was to reach Mickey's that night. Then at three o'clock in the morning he was to pass on and form into battle line in the fields stretching beyond Mitchie's. Polk's troops were to wait while Bragg's marched up the Monterey Road and cleared the junction at Mitchie's. Then Polk was to follow Bragg into position, clearing the way for Breckinridge in turn. They were to give each other room so as to not delay each other, yet at the same time keep their files well closed, keeping proper spacing in the ranks.

Well, so much for those plans. Johnston thought. If all had gone according to plan, the attack would have been well under way by now, and we still haven't finished the damn march yet!

Beauregard had been forced to push back the entire plan by a day. The men were simply not ready for such grandiose designs when it came to implementing the attack. Now delay after delay with the inexperienced troops, complicated by the uncooperative weather, continued to force Beauregard to make further changes in the timetable of operations, and to push the planned attack even further back.

Things sure looked more promising yesterday before we left Corinth. Johnston mused. The interlude spent at the "Rose Cottage" home of one of Corinth's leading citizens as his planning staff had prepared the battle plan had been most pleasant. His deep blue eyes gleamed as he remembered how their lovely hostess, Mrs. William Inge, had begged Johnston to allow her the honor of preparing some sandwiches and cake to take with them on their quest.

"No, Mrs. Inge, we soldiers travel light!" His response had not stopped the good-hearted belle, who had managed to outfox him anyway. She had taken advantage of the opportunity to do it while Johnston's attention was diverted as he conversed with his chief aide, Major Edward Mulford, slipping some sandwiches and cake into his coat pockets before Johnston had ridden away from the mansion. His smile broadened as he remembered the fair lady, waving good-byes with her lace handkerchief, her face glistening with a mixture of tears and expectations, as the Confederate army had marched off. However, his sour mood returned as he remembered his comments to Mulford.

"Yes, I believe I have overlooked nothing, Major." Johnston had commented.

Yes, nothing. Except the damned weather.

And now, this. Two days of rain. Two long, dreary days of rain, mud, and more mud. Two days gone. Two days of opportunities lost forever.

"Look at them." He sighed. "They are just a bunch of rain sodden would be warriors. Not one of them knows for sure of what he is supposed to do. I should have listened to my own counsel. These boys need more training; hell, three-fourths of them never have heard a shot fired in anger. I should have been more careful." Johnston looked up at the dripping trees, the drops falling onto his face. Shaking his head, and wiping his face, he exclaimed to the wet sky. "But if I can't use them, if I don't do something, there won't be an army much longer. And those boys over there yonder won't have anything to stop them. Nothing to stop them at all!"

Johnston angrily shook his head, the reverie over. The sharp crack of musket fire was coming from the side of the road. Troops were yelling, gesturing, and shooting at something on the edge of the woods. Feeling alarmed, Johnston reined Fire-Eater up and gestured to a young junior officer who was standing next to the road.

"Lieutenant, are these your men? Stop them from all this hollering. The *enemy* is just beyond those woods. Order your men to stop, clean, and reload those weapons. This practicing of marksmanship on *rabbits* just merely alerts the enemy to our presence!" Johnston's face was a mask of rage.

"Yes Sir. Immediately, Sir!" The young officer scurried off.

"General!" Johnston looked around to see Munford barreling down on him.

"General, we have found them, General Bragg's missing troops."

"Where?"

"Up the road. Mitchie's intersection. They are stuck behind another division, General."

"Well, let us go get them unstuck, Major." Johnston tapped Fire-eater gently into motion, and followed Munford down the muddy road. It was a short ride to the crossroads where two large groups of soldiers were angrily shouting back and forth. The filthy soldiers, spotting the officers as they rode up, backed up, quieting down as they did.

"Gentlemen, can somebody please tell me what the cause for all this commotion is?" Johnston angrily exclaimed.

A grime-speckled private, his beard dirty and unkempt, his feet, blocks of mud, walked out in front of the group and spoke. "Well General, Sir. Begging your pardon, but we'uns are supposed to be movin' on up, but you see, Sir, we all got started a little late, what with the rain and all. We got ourselves caught up behind the damned bishop's division, uh, begging your pardon, General. Now these here boys refuse, just refuse to let us by!" The angry muttering behind him began anew. Johnston held up his gloved hand, the muttering trailing away.

"Who commands this division?"

"General Ruggles, Sir." Replied the same mud smeared private.

"Where *is* the general?"

"Over there, General. Near those trees." The soldier pointed to a figure standing next to a tall thicket of trees.

Brigadier General Daniel Ruggles was a curious figure in the Confederate Army's command structure. A stern New Englander, his background and domineering disposition made Ruggles unpopular with his subordinates. A West Point graduate and Regular army soldier, he was considered a strict disciplinarian who held himself aloof from the volunteers. His clerk was sometimes required to sleep at night on top of a writing table so as to be ready to write orders at a moment's notice. Now Ruggles was looking off into the woods. He turned from his inspection of the woods to see Johnston riding toward him. Ruggles face darkened as he spied the look on Johnston's face.

"General Ruggles, sir, what is the reason for all these delays, General, if you don't mind telling me?" Johnston's voice was filled with ice, his blue eyes flashing with fire.

"General Johnston, Sir, my sincere apologies for the delay." Ruggles sputtered. "I must report that my officers have reported shots being fired ahead of them."

"Shots, General?"

"Yes Sir, General. I have sent out scouts to see if we are engaged with the enemy, but they have not returned as of yet."

Johnston sighed. He glared down at Ruggles. When he spoke the ice in his voice, had become even colder. "General Ruggles, there is no engagement in progress. Those *shots* your officers heard were those of our own troops, probably target shooting. Troops that are green and are being led by *officers* as green as they are!" Johnston's face now resembled a fiery thundercloud, his words, bolts of lightning. "Troops who think that the only way to check to see if their powder is wet is to fire their weapon!"

"General, I am sorry. I was not aware . . ."

Johnston cut him off. "Oh, never mind, General! Time is fleeting. Now because of one brigade, your division is lagging behind General Bragg's corps. Now, if you please sir, if you don't mind, would you please hurry them up? Hurry, man, hurry!"

Turning away from the humiliated division commander, and looking up to the sky, Johnston ignored the man's continued attempts at an apology. The sun was barely visible through the remains of the rainstorm. Johnston angrily noted that the day was rapidly beginning its descent into afternoon, and thus, toward nightfall. Gesturing to another of his aides, Colonel Preston, Johnston pointed down the road.

"Come Colonel, let us get these men aside so as to let poor General Ruggles and his lost brigade pass. Now, please men, hurry. Let us hurry. We have already lost much precious time." This last comment was followed with another angry look at the demeaned Ruggles. There was no response from Ruggles.

"Sir, yes sir, General." Preston replied.

Shuffling at first, then more quickly under the commands of their officers, Polk's lead division was moved off the road, and Ruggles' troops lined up on the road, ready to march. General Ruggles had quickly mounted his horse and had moved to the head of his column, studiously avoiding any eye contact with any of Johnston's party. Quickly issuing the order to move out, his column began to march down the road, deeper into the woods, his men marching fast, if only to keep from seeing Johnston's temper flare once again at their hapless commander. Johnston ignored them, his only concern now the time. Again, he eyed the sky, and checked his watch.

Two o'clock.

Hurry, men, hurry.

Now Polk's lead troops began their march down the road. A young officer, new and full of his mission, all prissy and fresh despite the rain and mud, rode ahead of the column and headed for Johnston. He stopped in front of Johnston, saluted, and handed a message to Major Munford. Munford scanned it and then turned to Johnston.

"General, General Polk's compliments sir, he wishes to inform you that they have just received this message. It is a telegram from his Excellency, President Davis. The courier is to wait for any reply, sir."

"Thank you, Major." Johnston took the proffered telegram. "Captain, if you would wait, please, one moment. I hope it is good news."

Silently he thought. *I need some right now.* He read silently.

General Albert S. Johnston Commanding, Army of the Mississippi

April 5, 1862

General;

Have received your telegram dated the 5th, and am in agreement with your plans to attack the enemy. I hope you will be able to close with the enemy before his two columns unite. I anticipate a victory.

Signed,

Jefferson Davis

I hope so, Mr. President. I hope so. Turning to the courier, Johnston spoke.

"Thank you, Captain, but there will be no reply." The courier saluted and rode off. Turning back to the still mounted Preston, Johnston motioned for him to dismount with him and to follow Johnston.

"Proceed with your business, gentlemen. I wish to speak to Colonel Preston alone." The others nodded and watched as Johnston and Preston walked a short distance away into the clearing. The others began scurrying about on the business of the Army, keeping a respectable distance away from the two men. Johnston stopped and sat down on a log. He removed his hat and motioned for Preston to sit down next to him. Both men sat, motionless and silent, Johnston watching the passing troops on the road, absorbed in his thoughts, Preston, sensitive to Johnston ways, sat quietly, waiting for the other man to say what he was thinking. Both watched the passing troops, now on the move and headed for their respective destinations. Johnston pulled out a bandanna from his shirt pocket and wiped his face. Replacing it, he then spoke.

"Bill. This business is taking too long."

Colonel William A. Preston, Johnston's close friend, confidant, and brother of Johnston's deceased first wife, grimaced a reply. "Yep, I know, General, I know. But what else can you do?"

"I never should have agreed to Beauregard's plan. I think sometimes he still thinks he thinks he's still in Charleston, still the conquering hero." Johnston was referring to Beauregard's victory at the beginning of the war, when troops under Beauregard's command had bombarded the massive stone fortress known as Fort Sumter into rubble and forcing the federal troops to surrender the island fort, launching the war and making Beauregard the toast of Charleston, and of the South.

"Ah Bill, but it's too late now. We will just have to do our best to drive the Yankees into the swamps. We have to do this now before we lose everything, and the men get discouraged."

"Well now, General. I don't think that's going to be a problem." Preston smiled. "These here boys are just spoiling for a fight."

"Bill. It's not a question of whether they have the will or not. You know as well as I do that all those boys out there all think they can whip the Yankees all by themselves. No one doubts their fighting capabilities. I know they can all shoot the eyes out of a squirrel at a hundred yards. It's that squirrels don't shoot back! It's their training I am worried about. It's about learning to follow simple orders. It's about learning to do things *right*, quickly, without having to explain *why*. This is no game, Bill, and too many of this army think that all they have to do is throw their hats out there, and the Yankees will run for it!"

Preston spoke. "Ah, Albert, you know any southern boy can whip five Yankees by himself." Preston smiled at his joke.

"Yes, well that's just what those Yankee boys down that road thinks they can do to us, too. You know Bill, those boys have not done too badly for themselves. Grant is no fool. Oh sure, he might like the bottle occasionally, but he's no drunk. Taking Henry and Donelson the way he did made him a hero and gave him that damned nickname! *Unconditional Surrender* Grant. Who would have thought it back in the old army? There was never a clue that he could be this back in the old California days."

"I'll bet old Buckner would like to hit Grant over the head with that moniker, especially since they were so close in the old days. What with Buckner being in his wedding and all." Preston laughed.

"Yes, well war does have a way of changing things, Bill. I guess old Simon found that out the hard way. Just remember one thing though, Colonel. Sam Grant is no fool. He won't panic when things get a little rough and the lead starts flying."

"What about Sherman?" Preston was referring to Brigadier General William Tecumseh Sherman, a division commander of Grant's as well as Grant's friend. "You know they say he is crazy."

"Bad press will do that to a man. But who says he's wrong about that newspaper quote where he said that the North will need two hundred thousand troops to subdue the Mississippi River valley." Johnston stood up and put his hat back on. "Hell, I hope he's right! I hope those fools in Washington really believe that! Maybe the northern newspapers might start screaming more about the cost of this war. Hell, I wish they thought that they needed twice that much. We sure haven't done much to make them feel that way, at least not out here in the west." Johnston walked back toward the road, Preston getting up to follow, the quiet moment of familial intimacy over.

"You know Colonel, I doubt that there is anything wrong with "Cump" Sherman's mind. If there were, he sure wouldn't be leading troops for Grant, no sir. No Colonel, the only thing I can hope for is that Grant *thinks* we're discouraged and ready to quit." Johnston grinned. "I just want a chance to enlighten him."

"Well, I hope you're right, General. We may see soon. Here comes Munford." Munford rode up with a grin and a splash.

"Wet enough for you, Major?" Johnston quipped, seeing the mud splashed all over his aide's boots and uniform.

"Yes sir, General. It is indeed." The sopping wet Munford grinned. "General, I beg to inform the General that General Polk's corps is about all passed through, and General Breckinridge's boys are on the way next. Oh, and General Beauregard requests your presence. He's still up ahead with General Bragg. I believe he wants your approval on his plans."

"What time is it, Major?"

"Sir, it's almost four o'clock, sir."

Damn, too much time is being wasted. Well, I suppose there is nothing we can do about it. Might as well go and see what Pierre is thinking up now. But it's really too late to make any major changes. Johnston looked at Munford and spoke. "All right, Major. You go and hustle General Breckinridge's division along. Report back to me when they have arrived and are in place. I'll be up with General Beauregard."

"Yes sir!" Munford snapped off a salute and galloped down the road from whence he came.

Damn, it will be dark soon. Johnston thought to himself, looking up into the afternoon sky. He noted the shadows growing longer as the dark sun dipped further toward dusk. The woods around them grew darker as twilight grew closer.

I never should have listened to Pierre's plan. Delays, delays, and more delays. Damn the rain! Damn this infernal mud! Damn the need to hurry! Another day wasted! Damn!

Yet hurry we must. Hurry and attack.

But not today, no, not today. Tomorrow will have to be the day.

"What time is it, Colonel?" Johnston asked Preston.

"Just about four thirty, General."

Johnston sighed, once again looking at the lengthening shadows creeping across the woody, muddy fields. He turned to Preston and spoke.

"All right Bill, let's ride up to the front of this mess and see what General Beauregard has for us."

"Yes sir." Both men mounted their horses.

Spurring Fire-Eater back into the quagmire of a road, one thought continued to lay heavy on Johnston's weary brain.

Hurry, men, hurry. Hurry, but not today. No, no attack today.

Damn, not today.

SHERMAN

Shiloh Church
April 5, 1862 Afternoon

DRILL. Brigadier General William Tecumseh Sherman believed in it. His new soldiers, the men of the Fifth Division, Union Army of the Tennessee needed drill and lots of it. Since the troops were Sherman's, they got drill. Daily drills with its accompanying fatigue, duty, and discipline were all necessities, and by God, Sherman was just the man to drill that discipline into them. Drill, drill, and drill some more.

Those that wrote of Sherman often spoke of his eyes. Eyes that showed bright with a half-wild expression. An expression some blamed on Sherman's excessive smoking. It appeared to be a fact that the man was never without a cigar, as the constant cloud of smoke around him could attest to. A redheaded, gaunt skeleton of a man, Sherman always looked like he needed a shave. The man gave the appearance of being an anxious man of business, which he had once been, rather than that of a soldier. His energy level was known to be prodigious, for he often worked twenty hours at a time, and expected his staff to keep up with him. It was not unknown for him to be dictating messages at any hour of the day or night, much to his staff's chagrin. He slept little, drank powerfully, and was indifferent to dress or fare. He appeared to live on bread and water, (and his constant cigars), and expected others to do the same, (except for the cigars.)

When concerned about some matter, he would worry at it until the juice was all wrung out of it, like some old pug dog and his bone. Therefore, it had been no surprise, when earlier in the war, Sherman had made the mistake of saying that the North would need two hundred thousand men just to subdue the Confederate forces occupying the Mississippi River valley, only to see it splashed all over the newspapers. It had convinced some in official Washington of his "nervous anxieties," forcing his recall from command, amid cries of "Mad Sherman." Only the intervention of Grant and Henry W. "Old Brains" Halleck had saved Sherman. Halleck's position as department commander of the western theater, army operations had provided the clout necessary to get Sherman reinstated as a brigadier general in Grant's Army of the Tennessee. It didn't hurt Sherman either to have a United States Senator for a brother. (The Honorable John Sherman of Ohio had twisted a few elbows on Capitol Hill to help his younger sibling.) It also did not hurt Sherman to have served admirably as a commander being with Bull Run. Now Sherman was determined to overcome those past complaints and build himself a new reputation.

When Sherman's green division had first, arrived at the river docks of Pittsburg Landing back in March, they had been ordered to set up camp there, near the shores of the Tennessee River. Sherman had decided to move inland instead, some four miles, and had set up camp near a crossroads and a one room log church erected by Methodists a decade earlier, and now unoccupied. Sherman's Fifth Division occupied the advance position of the Army of the Tennessee. Sherman's left flank was held by one brigade, which was commanded by Colonel David Stuart. Stuart's brigade was anchored on the Shiloh and Owl Creeks, both of which were lowland swamps. The other three brigades of Sherman's Division were McDowell's, Buckland's, and Hildebrand's, each man a colonel in his own right. These three other brigades stretched to the right of Stuart's camp. Thus, Sherman's division covered the main approach to Pittsburg Landing via the Corinth Road. A scant six hundred yards or so to the south, another division, the Sixth, also made up of inexperienced troops, occupied the woody ground bordering the Ridge Road. These men were so new that they had just barely drawn their muskets. Their commander, crusty Brigadier General Benjamin M. Prentiss had been an Illinois lawyer and was a combat veteran of the Mexican War. Together, these two green divisions made up the front lines of Grant's army.

Immediately to the left and rear of Sherman's camp were camped the five brigades of Donelson veterans, which made up the First Division commanded by Brigadier General John A. McClernand. Their tents covered the fields along the Purdy Road. Next to McClernand was the Fourth Division of

South Carolina-born Brigadier General Stephen A. Hurlbut. Like Prentiss, Hurlbut had also been a member of the Illinois bar prior to the war. Behind their camps and backing up to Pittsburg Landing's bustling docks, was the well-trained Second Division previously commanded by Major General Charles F. Smith. Smith had suffered a leg injury (which would become infected and prove to be fatal) prior to the start of the campaign and had turned command of the division over to Brigadier General William H. Wallace, another Donelson veteran. Major General Lew Wallace and his Third Division were camped some six miles down the river at Crump's Landing. The Union gunboats' *Tyler* and *Lexington* cruised the Tennessee River, their heavy cannon a comforting presence. Altogether, Grant's Army of the Tennessee numbered about forty-eight thousand men. It was one of those strange twists of fate that all the inexperienced troops, those that made up the bulk of five of Grant's six divisions, and had never seen combat, were in the front most lines, while the combat experienced veterans either camped in the rear or were miles away. All five were bivouacking in the narrow triangle bordered by the muddy creeks that ran into the Tennessee. No trenches, earthworks, or rifle pits had been dug. In fact, even the picket lines were often within yards of the camps, on the edge of the deep Tennessee woods, thus giving those on picket duty little time to holler a warning, if deemed necessary. When Sherman had suggested to Grant that perhaps it would be a good idea for the troops to dig some trenches and rifle pits, and set up some defenses, old crusty General Smith had loudly exclaimed that by God, he wanted nothing better than to have the rebels come out and attack, saying that they would whip the rebels to hell. Sherman had tried to press the argument only to have Smith shout him down. Smith argued that the tough westerners that made up the bulk of Grant's army were there for a fight, and if "they began to spade it might give the boys the impression that we feared the rebels." After all, Smith concluded, this army's slogan was to fight "man-fashion," and stand up to the enemy's fire like the British at Waterloo. Smith would have none of that "defensive" talk, and Grant concurred with his advice, leaving Sherman to have to agree with the two more experienced leaders.

Now Sherman's camp was set upon a knoll, hard by the one room log church. Shiloh Meetinghouse was until recently where itinerant churchmen had preached their own version of hell and damnation, complete with fire and brimstone. Their half-literate congregation, the dirt farmers of west Tennessee, had listened to the wild-eyed preachers calling upon them to defend the South as if it was God's special creation. They claimed that it was a Paradise on earth, and that the forces of darkness through their agents, (abolitionists) were threatening the South's idyllic way of life. The aroused farmers had listened as the men of God had berated them to be avenging angels, and protect the South, their loving Mother, against the barbarians from the North.

"A place of peace indeed." Sherman muttered to himself. The irony of it all being that was indeed the meaning of Shiloh. Yet somehow the sleepy church, nestled in among the yellow blossoms in the Tennessee glade, seemed like a safe haven. No, nothing like Waterloos' Flemish countryside, filled with ancient stone villages among the open fields. It was almost easy for Sherman to forget that those avenging angels were out there *somewhere*, and perhaps spoiling for a fight.

When the newspaper correspondents attached to Grant's army asked Sherman, what he thought the chances were of a southern attack on the federal lines, he had replied that they were in great danger. Yet, when pressed by the newspapermen as to why he didn't communicate his suspicions to Grant, Sherman had exclaimed; "Oh, they'll just think I'm crazy again!" So, he kept his own council. Yet, he really didn't expect an attack, believing that Beauregard would not want to over extend himself from his base of operations. He did not know that Johnston was on the scene and spoiling for a fight. So, Sherman continued to drill his green troops.

Grant had made a field inspection two days prior, and it had gone well. The troops had plenty to eat, their health was good, the army doctors having little to do, and morale was high. Spring had burst forth gloriously, the days sunny and warm, the nights deliciously cool for sleeping. That is, until today's rains, anyway.

Everything seems all right. Sherman mused. Now if I can just get these boys ready to move on Corinth. We're just waiting for Buell, (Major General Don Carlos Buell and his twenty-thousand-man Army of the Ohio), to arrive. Then we'll be ready to move out. No, I think everything is all right. This army is in no danger here. Now if I just could convince some of my officers of that!

Some of these youn

g pups are worse than old grannies! They're worse than I ever was, myself. Sherman chewed on his cigar ferociously, spitting out the specks of tobacco, and wiping his lips with his dirty shirt sleeve. He was indifferent to that, and the specks that had fallen onto his blouse. He looked around the camp, still seated on his old stool near the campfire. The staff was busy with camp work, no one bothering him in his thoughtful mood.

All the commanders are inexperienced, most still just learning their jobs, just like their men. Most are good boys, quick on the take, but there are some that just don't seem to get it. There's that one youngster in particular that sees danger every time a leaf moves on a tree. Appler. Colonel Appler and his 53rd Ohio regiment. Good boys. Just not sure about their commander. Still can't figure how those boys made that man a colonel. He's about as high strung and jumpy as a man can get. Why, to listen to him, the whole reb army is camped right outside his tent flap, just waiting for the right moment to strike. Hell, and they call me crazy!

It was just this past Friday that fool colonel lost seven men on picket duty to gray back cavalry. Then he went and sent a company out to look for his missing detail and ended up drawing enemy fire. I still have to chuckle when I think about his report. What fool officer of his was it that when they were challenged told their challengers that they were the advance guard of the Army of the United States? What reply did they expect except for that blast of musket fire they got in their faces? Damn fools. The rebs must have been in those trees, one of those damned scouting parties Beauregard likes to send out to keep checking on us. I'm not surprised that our boys came flying back, just like a pack of geese fleeing at the sight of the hunter. Well, they'll know next time not to do a fool thing like that again. I just took Appler's report and filed it away.

Didn't even bother sending a report down to Sam (Grant) at headquarters. He already knows that the rebs are sending out cavalry patrols, but he's attaching little importance to them. They're just more of a nuisance than anything else really.

No, sir, no, I'm not going to let those "Nervous Nellie" stories get started again. No more "Wild Willie" Sherman quotes for the newspapers. No sir. Besides, I've got plenty to do already, what with reorganizing the Army's artillery and cavalry. Good old Sam. He knew enough to keep me busy.

And there's all that transfer paperwork to do. I wish we didn't have to let some of these veteran boys go someplace else. They know the ground. They know the enemy. These new boys don't know these rocks and hills.

Well by thunder, I'll just keep on drilling these greenhorns till I get every detail burned into their brains. They'll know their jobs before I'm through. Then when they finally see the elephant, (a veteran term for combat that harkened back to the great Carthaginian general Hannibal's time), they will be ready.

"General?"

Oh, time to go back to work.

Sherman shook himself free of his daydreaming and looked up from under the brow of his hat. Young John T. Taylor, lieutenant and Sherman's aide, was standing there, a respectful distance away, but watching Sherman. Lieutenant Taylor worked hard to keep up with Sherman but had yet to see combat. Waving the ever-present cigar, his face wreathed in a pungent cloud of smoke, Sherman spoke.

"Well Lieutenant, don't just stand there a gaping at me, what's on your mind?" Sherman gestured to the empty campstool next to him.

Taylor sat down, a sheepish look on his fresh face. "Well sir, it's about all these reports we keep getting about enemy contacts. You know, these cavalry reports . . ."

"Scared, Johnny?"

"Oh, no sir!" Taylor shook his head emphatically. "It's just that, well, you know . . . I've never actually seen action yet, General, and . . ."

"And you're wondering if I think that the reports are real or not, or just Johnny Reb trying to spook us?"

"Well, yes sir, General, I am. I mean, well . . . are they . . .?" Taylor sheepishly grinned.

Well, are they? Sherman mused. There's no question something's out there. Whether or not it's more than just marauding cavalry lurking about, is anyone's guess. I've seen the skirmish reports. I've got Buckland's and McDowell's contact reports about reb skirmishers hitting our picket lines. Those reports we picked up from the questioning of reb prisoners. It all adds up to make me think that there may be one hell of a big rebel army somewhere out there. But it could still be some of their typical Southern bragging. They sure haven't done much to stop us yet. Still . . .

"General?"

Damn, there I go again!

Sherman lifted his head back up and pushed his hat back on his brow.

"Sorry Johnny didn't mean to do that. Bad habit. It is possible that the reports are real, just possible. However, I don't think that there is anything to get yourself all in a lather about." Sherman stood up, dropping the remains of his cigar to the wet ground, watched it sizzle in the newly falling rain for a long second, then started to walk toward a group of men drilling, Taylor jumping up to follow him. Sherman stopped at the edge of the clearing, the recruits just a few yards away. He and Taylor watched as the drilling continued, the drilling troops and their junior officers painfully aware of Sherman's presence, even as they barked out their commands. They did not stop the drill even when the rain became more persistent, knowing that Sherman had issued a standing order for marching and command drills, even in inclement weather. Sherman watched with unblinking eyes, then shook his head, lighted another cigar, and then turned back to Taylor.

"No, John, we've got some boys probably spooked by birds, who think they see rebs out there eating breakfast."

Sherman took another look back at the unhappy recruits, then turned to the officer in charge. "Good work, Captain. Keep 'em at it." He then turned back to Taylor. "But I don't think they know what they're talking about." Sherman headed back toward his tent, Taylor following.

"You mean like that sergeant from the Seventy Seventh Ohio?" Taylor asked. "The one you wanted arrested because he was spooking the other men in his regiment?"

"Well, I'm sure Captain Mason handled the whole matter all right." (The company commander had quietly pocketed the arrest order and had taken matters into his own hands. The overzealous individual had lost his stripes, and the matter quietly dropped.)

"Uh, General, shouldn't we inform General Grant of our present situation?"

"What situation, Lieutenant? Besides, we've nothing solid to report. Relax. Besides, I believe it's time for a drink. No, on second thought, send General Grant a message that all is quiet here. Then we'll have that drink." Sherman began to step into his tent, Taylor following him in.

"General, why don't we march out and hit the rebels in Corinth?"

Sherman turned and smiled at Taylor. "Don't worry son, you will have all the fighting you want before this war is over. Now, Lieutenant, you just go take care of that message to General Grant. You know what to say."

Taylor smiled back, his youthful face betraying his eagerness. He snapped off a salute to Sherman. "Yes sir. I will take care of it, immediately, General." Taylor stepped out of the tent, and a moment later, Sherman heard the sound of departing hoof beats.

A good boy, Johnny. Sherman thought to himself. But young, so damned young, and inexperienced, just like most of these boys, and their officers. Most of these boys are fresh from their schoolhouses in Ohio, or Illinois. They treat their officers just like they were their schoolteachers, (which, in truth, many had been before the war). They steal liquor, books, and clothing with equal fervor. Trouble is, when those schoolteachers- turned- officers try to enforce discipline, their ex-students just threaten them with defeat at the next officers' election. And the ones that weren't schoolteachers were politicians in the past, and those characters fear punishing subordinates, less they offend voters back home. By thunder, it does make for an interesting time of things. Trouble is, the undisciplined westerners have got to learn, they have to knuckle under to what is necessary, the discipline it takes to do things in the army.

Sherman frowned at his recollection of one incident. An Indiana regiment had done a fine job of undermining its major's authority. The officer had some of the regiment's privates thrown in the stockade for stealing clapboards from a barn in order to make beds. For days afterwards the sorry officer had heard nothing but yells of "cla-aa-aap board!" Eventually the humiliated major had released the prisoners and offered a public apology to his troops. Everyone had laughed, thinking it was all a big joke.

"He should have busted their whole company." Sherman grumbled to himself. "They still think discipline is a joke."

They really do think that. Recruits don't seem to mind a man being forced to parade through camp with a big knapsack of rocks on his back, but they sure do protest profusely about a fellow soldier being hung up by his thumbs. They understand and even approve the reasons for drumming deserters out of camp, one side of their head all shaved clean, that big old sign hung around their neck for all to see. Hell, they think that's just fine! It's a big laugh to them. They still think it's funny to watch offenders get mounted on a mule backwards, and get themselves paraded around camp, with that big old sign telling the world what they did ignominiously hung around their neck. Sherman grinned at that. Hell, I guess I can see why they'd laugh at that, too!

We got too damn many of them getting sick. Influenza, bronchial ailments, pneumonia, and diarrhea still affect the camps. Tennessee quickstep, that last one. I heard some old grizzled veteran call it that just the other day. You would think that farm boys who spend so much of their life outdoors would have better immune systems, but no sir, not these boys.

Of course, there are some other, more personal-type ailments some of these lads are getting their first exposure to also. Damn!

What was it that one old Minnesota colonel told to do about the "clap?" Oh, yeah, that's right, when they complained that the hospital wouldn't (or couldn't) do anything to cure their ailment, he told them to try red-hot pokers, for it was a sure cure. Sherman winced at the memory. Yes, and for other things as well. Inexperience, it just caused problems.

Take yesterday's little fracas. Buckland's old regiment, the Seventy-Second Ohio, lost a picket outpost to Confederate cavalry. Buckland reported the incident to me and then sent some infantry out to investigate. I sent out some 5th Ohio cavalry boy to check it out. Major (Elridge) Ricker's a competent commander usually and I figured he'd get the straight facts. Then that thunderstorm hit and got things all messed up. When Ricker finally caught up with Buckland's boys, he found them tangling with a regiment of a reb calvary. Old Elridge, he sure knew what to do, slipping around and flanking the gray backs. Sure, caught them by surprise. Chased them a good piece, our boys just potting away at the rebels with their new carbines. The rebs apparently retreated, staying 300, 400 yards ahead of his men. Ricker had excitedly described the chase, his men caught up in the heat of the moment, until they rode over a small knoll and run smack into a Confederate battle line, just bristling with artillery and ready to fight. At least Ricker's losses were neglible, only losing one trooper. Poor soul rode right into the rebs, and still would have got away, Ricker said, if the damned fool hadn't tried to shoot it out with the rebs and got himself shot. He still might have made it back if they hadn't got hold of his leg and pulled him off the horse. The rest of

Ricker's men had turned tail and skedaddled back to safety in the Union lines. They had brought back with them twelve gray-coated prisoners. Ricker sure was surprised to see me waiting with two infantry regiments drawn up in battle line.

Buckland had tried to explain to Sherman what had happened, explaining how his men had gotten into their situation in the first place. Sherman had angrily cut him off, replying that Buckland and Ricker could have drawn the entire army into battle.

Ricker had attempted to continue the explanation. "General, the enemy's force was quite strong. There were at least two regiments of infantry and a large calvary force there. That's two thousand men backed up with one or two batteries."

Sherman had silently scowled the two officers into silence, his cigar wig wagging in his clenched jaws. "Oh . . . tut.tut! You militia officers get scared too easily. No, this is simply Beauregard attempting to rattle us and as such I will treat it. Now take your men back to camp." He told them to send their prisoners to General Grant's headquarters.

Sherman had later sent a report to Grant, telling him that it was his opinion the whole thing really was nothing. Grant accepted the report that there was nothing to get excited about.

But that was yesterday. Today there were more incidents occurring.

Damn, I could use a drink. Sherman turned and started back toward his tent, only stopping at the sound of the approaching hoof beats. Lieutenant Taylor had returned, wiping his sopping face and saluting all in one motion as he dismounted. Sherman returned the salute and spoke.

"Well John, did you get that message off?"

"Yes sir, General."

"Grant have a reply?"

"Just to carry on with our present operations, General."

"All right, fine. Well, John, I promised you a drink, but I think maybe we should take a little ride and check on the troops. Let's saddle up."

"Yes Sir. Whatever you say General." The two men mounted their horses and headed south toward the outside regimental lines, Sherman's headquarters being close to the Shiloh church. They had not ridden far when Taylor spotted the hell-bent-for-leather rider headed for them, coming from the direction of the front lines. "General, I think that's one of the 53rd Ohio's officers coming."

"Damn! Now what?" Sherman chewed down hard on his cigar, as the excited horse and rider pulled up beside Sherman. The rider, a young lieutenant stammered, "The Colonel wishes to report a large force of the enemy is moving in on our camp, and he wishes to know what further directions you may have, Sir?" The lad, sweat pouring down his face, finally stopped to catch his breath.

"Sherman said nothing. He just stared at the out of breath soldier. Then, his temper flaring, he exploded. "Further instructions?" Sherman bit off, the cigar smoke blowing out of his mouth as he spoke. "By God, I'll give him further instructions!"

Sherman spurred his horse forward, leaving the surprised officer standing there dumbfounded. Sherman continued his tirade. "It's time to straighten out this situation once and for all!" Sherman headed toward the field where the Ohio regiments were posted. "Show me where your colonel is!"

Damn fool! Thought Sherman. Damn incompetent amateurs! The whole Army is full of men like this. Yet I know it can't be helped. Volunteers can never be expected to behave or react like regular troops until that greenness is replaced by experience. Combat's the only answer to that question. Still, these clashes have to mean something. Even though I really don't trust all these reports, some might be true. Damn, I wish these boys weren't so green, or so young. I'll have to put starch in these boys' backbones.

"General, there's Colonel Appler." Lieutenant Taylor spoke, pointing to a group of officers standing on the edge of the woods, near the Rhea Field, which was south of the 53rd 's camp.

Colonel J.J. Appler, commanding the Fifty-Third Ohio, was standing some distance from the road, alternating looks at a map and into the dark scrub oak of the forest in front of him. The thirty-one-year-old former probate judge had his back to the road and didn't notice Sherman's group arriving as he continued to gesture toward the woods. His excited gestures accentuated his conversation with his staff. Sherman sat his horse and impatiently waited for Appler to notice him, glowering at the small group of officers. Appler finally turned and saw Sherman sitting there. Appler saluted, speaking as he did, his Adam's apple bobbing up and down. His taunt face betrayed his fears.

"General Sherman Sir, we have just come into contact with a large enemy force." Appler hopped around, his arms flailing about like windmills as he spoke. "Sir, we must prepare for their attack. They're lining up in the woods out there, hiding in the woods. What are your orders, General?" Appler stopped his prancing and now stood still in front of the still mounted Sherman, who sat his horse, not saying a word. Appler spoke again. "General, we need to know what your instructions are." Appler's voice trailed off.

Sherman sat his horse, his hot stare piercing the woods, plumbing the dark depths for unseen dangers, then turned his gaze upon the discomforted colonel. Then jerking his reins on his horse, Sherman turned back to the road, staring over his shoulder at Appler, freezing him with his eyes even as he spoke, his words laced with acid.

"Colonel, take your damned regiment back to Ohio. Beauregard is not such a fool as to leave his base of operations and attack us in ours. There is no enemy nearer than Corinth." Appler's regiment, drawn up in ranks, exploded into laughter. Sherman rode away, leaving the shamed face Appler staring after him in humiliation.

Appler may be crying wolf, but the rebs are out there, Sherman thought. The rebs are out there, but they won't attack. Not here anyway. Not now. Not us. Not here. Beauregard won't do that. I'll send Grant a report when we get back.

Dusk was beginning its approach. Looking up at the darkening skies, Sherman mused some more. No, they won't attack our position. The rebs may be a bit saucy, but they won't push hard at our pickets. No, they will not attack us here.

Sherman peered hard at the darkening woods, trying to plumb their depths, searching the deep bushes, and trying to find what secrets were hidden in the wet green blossoms of the early April foliage. Lieutenant Taylor rode silently beside him. Sherman finally breaking off the inspection, and glancing over at Taylor, spoke.

"Johnny, I think it's time for a drink." Sherman smiles at his young aide.

"Yes, Sir General, that sounds like a good idea." Taylor replied.

"There's De Hass." (Lieutenant Colonel Wills De Hass, commander of the 77th Ohio, was standing near the road.) Sherman said. "Let's join them." Waving ahead to De Hass, Sherman called out. "Good evening, Colonel. How are you?"

De Hass smiled at Sherman, saluting as he did. "Good evening, General. Would you care to join us for some evening tea?"

"Just as long as it's not coffee, Colonel." Sherman returned the salute with a grin and swung from his horse. "The Lieutenant and I could use a drink right about now." Spotting Colonels Buckland and Hildebrand seated at the fire, waved them back down to their seats. "Hope's you boys don't mind the company if I join you."

"Not at all General. Please join us. We're just having a free exchange of ideas here" Buckland replied.

Accepting with murmured thanks, a dented tin cup, Sherman sipped with a smile. He looked around at the officers huddled around the campfire. The night air was cooling off rapidly as the darkness deepened. He noted the unspoken questions, the flames of the campfire illuminating their dark faces. Questions that weren't spoken, but nevertheless were being said.

"Well boys, what's the topic of conversation this evening?" Sherman sat down on a stool, smacking his lips as he sipped from the cup some more. *Ah, this is good whiskey* he thought to himself. *Let's see what they've got to say.* He lighted another cigar.

"Well General" The speaker was Major Ben Fearing, De Hass' second-in-command. He gestured around the fire. "We were all just wondering what your thoughts might be about the, ah, well, what I mean Sir is whether or not you think there's any concern about the rebels attacking us?"

"Attack us? Here?" Sherman said incredulously. "Nonsense." *I hope anyway.*

"Well begging your pardon General Sir, but there are enemy troops out there." De Hass pointed toward the now deep black woods beyond the campfire. Night had fallen and the stars were beginning to make their appearance through the thinning clouds.

"Yes there are." Sherman gestured with his cigar. "But I'm positive that those contacts are merely scouting parties from Corinth. General Beauregard is just trying to feel us out." Sherman took another sip from his cup, finishing it. He continued his explanation.

"No boys, those troops are just scouts, scouts that are here to keep an eye on us. They just want to see what we're up to. For the rebs to do anything else would be crazy. And you know, I'm supposed to know something about that." He grinned, the others chuckling at his joke. Buckland and Hildebrand grinned nervously.

Sherman stood up and waving the others back down onto their seats he began to pace around the fire, puffing as he did on his cigar. The other officers watched him intently, silently noting his nervous pacing. They were remembering earlier rumors about his sanity. Sherman noticed them watching him.

Damn, I have got to be careful about this stuff! Otherwise, those stories will start up again. "Crazy" Sherman is at it again. Sherman stopped his pacing and stood there puffing on the cigar. De Hass spoke again.

"Well General, I hope there is no one crazy out there" De Hass laughed.

No, they haven't forgotten, Sherman thought. By thunder, I have to be more careful about things like that. Otherwise, the stories will start up again. I have to watch the pacing around too. I noticed Johnny was watching me real close too. I got to be careful. No slip-ups.

"Well Colonel, it should ease your mind to know we expect Buell should be here within the next forty-eight hours or so. When he gets here that will give us one hell of an army. When that happens, we will march right on down through the rest of Tennessee right into Mississippi, take Corinth and drive the rebs right out. The rebs should be pretty demoralized right about now. They know we're coming right after Corinth (Mississippi). They're probably trying to get themselves ready to try and stop us, not preparing to attack us. No sir."

Sherman spoke positively and firmly, conviction flowing from his mouth, yet he sensed that not all around the fire agreed with his sentiments. Looking up at the now star filled sky, the embers in the sky twinkling to match the glow of the fire, Sherman forced himself to display calmness for all to see. He looked back down into the glowing embers of the fire, and then around again ath the officers huddled around the fire. He gestured with the now empty cup.

"Throw another log on the fire boys. Let's have some more of this "tea." The others chuckled again, someone handing Sherman the bottle. He poured some more into his cup, handing the bottle around again.

No. He thought, No. They won't attack us. Not here. Not now.

Not here.

BRAGG

Pittsburg-Corinth and Bark Road Intersection
April 5, 1862 5:00 P.M.

Major General Braxton Bragg was in a foul mood. It had taken the better part of a day to get all his divisions into proper lines. Ruggles tardy division had finally arrived and joined the rest of the corps in formation. Precious time had been lost, time that was now lost forever. Now Bragg had been summoned to a meeting with Beauregard at Bragg's temporary headquarters, and the veteran soldier was not amused.

The bushy eye-browed Bragg was a North Carolinian by birth. He had graduated from West Point like so many of the other Confederate Army officers had, and had seen extensive action against the Seminoles in Florida as well as combat with Winfield Scott down in Mexico. Bragg had resigned his commission in 1859, and had become a successful planter down in Louisiana. When Louisiana had seceded, Bragg joined the cause, accepting an appointment as head of Louisiana's military forces. Now Bragg and his ten thousand men made up the right wing of Johnston's army.

Bragg was known to be a good administrator, but also to be something of a martinet. His Second Corps was probably the best disciplined troops in the Army of the Tennessee. Johnston had appointed Bragg Chief of Staff, in part because of his reputation for good administration, but also to instill badly needed discipline in the inexperienced troops. Bragg had worked hard to do so, imposing several draconian methods in order to improve discipline. Unfortunately, not all the corps had responded well to his program. Polk's rough and tumble Kentuckians and Tennesseans, they whose loyalty was somewhat suspect to begin with, had never taken to Bragg's style. Now this entire army had to get together, get together and fight the enemy.

Braxton Bragg looked like a volcano on the edge of eruption. He had not been feeling well lately, and his often-nervous stomach had been acting up. All the recent days of turmoil had not helped Bragg's stomach concerns, nor had it improved his disposition. Now Beauregard had called for this meeting.

"As if I don't have enough to do already." Bragg grumbled; his tender stomach's miseries not helped by his horse's uneven gait over the muddy road. He rode toward his headquarters, his edginess increasing with every step the horse took.

Beauregard sitting on a rock just off the road, was surrounded by his aides, all talking and gesturing at the same time. Beauregard had also been ill of late, quite ill, and was still recovering. He was looking at a map, seemingly oblivious to all the commotion around him, when Bragg rode up.

Pierre Gustave Toutant Beauregard was a man small in stature but possessing of a muscular build that would have befitted a physically much larger man. His deep olive skin was perfectly accentuated by a superbly trimmed jet-black mustache. The overall effect lent itself to a strikingly handsome man. Born just outside New Orleans, Beauregard had grown up speaking French, never learning English until he was a boy of twelve. His Gallic culture espoused merrymaking, grand living, and the maintenance of honor, mixed with superb manners. Beauregard was the epitome of this culture, and when you mixed in the customs and traditions of the deep plantation South, what you had was one of the most colorful and volatile characters of this, or any war.

Beauregard, like Bragg, was a graduate of West Point, and had also seen service in old Mexico. His military experience only enhanced his martial bearing. Some saw him as vain, obnoxious, and pompous; others thought him chivalrous, even glamourous. They admired his inspiration in speech, his grave military bearing, and his deep devotion to the Confederate cause. His reduction of the defenses of Fort Sumter, and his part in the victory at Manassas had made him a popular hero to the South. The masses had conferred upon Beauregard the nickname: "Napoleon in Gray," and he intended to live up to his nickname. Bragg did not share in the high esteem so many others held Beauregard in.

"Well, General, are we feeling any better?" Bragg asked sarcastically.

Beauregard looked up, noting the storm clouds building in Bragg's eyes, but made no attempt to be amiable in return. The Tennessee quick step was running rampant through the army, and Beauregard, having been one of the victims, was in no mood for Bragg's sarcasm.

"Well General, all these delays have not helped at all, nor have they helped our cause. Have they?"

Bragg stiffened, then swung down from his horse. He stood there facing the small group of officers, slapping his gauntlets into his palm, his bushy face contorted with anger. Before Bragg could utter an angry retort, Beauregard, noting the tense looks on the collective faces of his staff, quietly spoke.

"Gentlemen, would you please excuse General Bragg and me? I wish to speak to him alone." Beauregard stood up and motioned to Bragg to follow him. Bragg walked away from the road to a low stone fence bordering the oak woods, Bragg following along. Beauregard sat down on one of the larger rocks and gestured for Bragg to join him. Bragg did so, but said nothing, waiting for Beauregard.

Beauregard, took of his kepi, and mopped his face with a large red bandanna. He looked at Bragg, still sitting there silently, his moody face watching Beauregard. Bragg still said nothing, content to wait for Beauregard's explanation for the summons.

"General, I believe we have a problem." Beauregard slid the bandanna back inside his uniform coat as he spoke. "I believe that too much time has elapsed, and too much noise has been made. I believe that there is absolutely no chance of our forces being able to complete our attack as planned. I have sent General Polk a message requesting his presence to discuss this with us. Therefore, I ask you, General Bragg, what is your opinion of the present situation, sir?"

Bragg looked at Beauregard, and then stood up, straightening his coat as he did. He stood there for a long moment, his arms crossed, turning to stare at the dark woods.

"I fully agree with your analysis of the situation, sir." Bragg's voice was icily cordial. He continued to look at the dark woods. His ears were pricked by the sound of troops in the woods, the noise of their movements echoing through the clearing. There was a drum playing in the distance, the beat clearly audible. "The delays have been many. Too much time has been expended in getting the troops into proper formations. On top of that the men think they are on some kind of lark, a picnic of sorts! There has been a total lack of, no, a *wanton* disregard for secrecy by the troops, what with all the yelling and discharging of their weapons." Bragg now turned toward Beauregard, his face reflecting the anger seething inside. Bragg continued to speak, his words clipped and hot.

"Why General, my men are not even properly, provisioned. Many still have not been properly armed yet. They're still carrying the weapons they came to us with! Sir, I must protest. I am sure that the enemy knows we are here, *sir. They must!*"

Beauregard's sleepy blood hound-like eyes opened wide, his ire stirred by Bragg's last words. "I agree with you, *General.*" Beauregard's voice was beginning to reflect the anger in Bragg's. His hands fluttered like birds as he spoke. "But tell me, General, how is it your men have run out of food? They were to draw rations for *five* days, and it has only been *three*?"

"The General knows that my boys are unaccustomed to being in the field and have not learned to properly conserve." Bragg hotly retorted. "Besides, I feel that they would still have enough if my men weren't forced to stop to let General Polk's troops pass around us, sir!"

Easy. He's got a point. Beauregard thought. "I must agree with you, General. There is no excuse for General Polk's troops blocking yours. On top of this, General Cheatham's division is *still* not in position, and Breckinridge's troops are still far to the rear." Beauregard turned away and motioned to one of the officers lurking in the coming darkness.

"Captain Brown, please ride to General Polk's camp and find out when he can join us? We need to make a decision. Then find out who is playing that blasted drum and *order* him to stop!" The distant drum roll had continued through their entire conversation.

"Yes sir, General. Right away." The officer saluted, and quickly left. Beauregard turned back to Bragg and continued to speak. "Yes, General, I agree. Surprise is everything. And with this infernal racket, surprise is *impossible*! I should also tell you that it was just brought to my attention that there was a clash yesterday between our cavalry scouts, and Yankee infantry." Bragg's heavy beetle eyebrows flared at this news. "We lost several troopers in the encounter. We must assume that they were captured, and probably interrogated. So, we must now assume that the enemy knows from where we came, and that we are here. So, surprise is now gone." Beauregard suddenly stood up and pointed to the road. "Ah, here comes Polk now. The bishop has arrived."

Major General Leonidas Polk was also a North Carolinian who had emigrated to Louisiana. A West Point graduate who had left the Army to enter the seminary, Polk had become the first Protestant Episcopal Bishop of Louisiana. He had joined the Confederate army in 1861, eventually becoming a corps commander under Johnston. "Bishop" Polk presented an eminent image when he donned his cleric's robes. Now instead of trying to save men's souls, he was trying to send them to their Maker.

Beauregard waved a salute in return to Polk's. "Welcome General. Please join us. I believe, gentlemen, that there is now coffee prepared on the fire. Let's all have some. It is becoming quite damp, and cold, and I am sure we can all use some."

Polk swung down from his horse. His clean-shaven face, so unusual in this army, was handsome even in its irritated state. Polk carried himself with all the gravity of a member of the clergy. Polk and Beauregard had differences before, and Polk was not in a mood for levity. He accepted the proffered cup, murmured his thanks, but said nothing else, waiting for Beauregard to speak, the Creole-born Beauregard having moved over to a camp table, where he put his mug of coffee down on it. Beauregard did not disappoint him.

"Well, General. What seems to have been the problem with your troops?"

Polk's face registered surprise, then resumed a placid look. He drew himself to his full height, looking every bit the cleric in the pulpit. He then spoke, the bishop delivering a sermon, Beauregard, Bragg, and the others a not so willing congregation.

"General Beauregard, just what is that supposed to mean? Of course, my men were late! So also, would any troops so delayed, delayed and forced to stop, stop, stand, and just wait. Wait while another division's troops took their own sweet time getting through the crossroads at Mickey's." Polk stopped for emphasis, his stately gaze coming to rest upon Bragg's stone face, then continued his thought.

"*Any* troops, sir."

Beauregard, angered by Polk's smugness, angrily retorted. "Nevertheless, General Polk, the situation is a disaster. A disaster, sir! It is already ten hours past the time I planned for the attack. *Ten hours, sir!*"

"General, that is not unusual in a war." Polk's calm face belied the anger in his voice. He looked toward the heavens, as if to find divine solace and inspiration in their starry depths.

"It doesn't make any difference, General, that it is not so unusual to happen in war. Here, under these circumstances, it is an unmitigated disaster. *A disaster*! No gentlemen, I am afraid I will have to propose to cancel this entire movement of the army and return back to Corinth. Our attack is no longer an option, particularly because we have lost the element of surprise. And that, gentlemen, I believe we have completely, irrevocably, *lost*!" Beauregard slammed his fist down on the camp table for emphasis, spilling the contents of the cup over the table.

The others stood in shocked silence, Bragg's beetle eyebrows arching in disbelief, Polk, his arms crossed, merely stared in anger at Beauregard. Both men knew that Beauregard simply did not have the authority to cancel the plan, not with Albert Sidney Johnston around. Only Johnston could make *that* decision.

"Captain Brown?" Beauregard turned to the officer he had sent to find Polk. "I gave you an order to find that damn drum and have it silenced!" Beauregard gestured in the direction of the still beating drum. "Why was my order ignored? Don't you know that it could alert the enemy to our presence here?"

"But General, I have been waiting to report, sir." Brown replied. "That drum is not one of ours. It's in the enemy camp." Silence all around followed his statement. Then, Beauregard pointed toward the distant sound.

"Well gentlemen. That should take care of any lingering doubts any of you may have. If we can hear them this clearly, *they most certainly can hear us!*"

With this last statement, a definite chill had fallen over the little group, a chill that the hottest fire could not warm. Darkness was coming, and with the night's arrival, would end that day's opportunities. All were aware of this, but only Beauregard seemed ready to call it all off.

"General Beauregard, with all due respect, I think you are wrong." Bragg snapped.

"So do I." Polk added. "If we go back now, my boys will be as demoralized as if they were whipped in a fight. No, General Beauregard, sir, I must protest your proposal." The cleric spoke as if from the pulpit, his words ringing through the descending darkness. Beauregard glared at Polk, angry with the condescension evident in Polk's voice. Before Beauregard could reply, Bragg spoke.

"Well, here comes Sidney Johnston now. He had to make that decision anyway. It's time for him to get involved in this."

Johnston had ridden up as Bragg finished, just in time to hear most of the stormy words being uttered. He had spotted Beauregard's wild gestures as he approached the camp and had quietly approached the meeting. Now, having caught the tail end of the discussion, he dismounted, and walked over to the campfire conference.

"Well now, gentlemen, what seems to the subject that has brought on such a heated discussion?"

Johnston looked at each man in his turn, his gaze finally coming to rest on Polk. Polk turned away to the campfire, stooping down to pick up a cup and handing it to Johnston, then picking up the hot coffeepot, noted Johnston's silent assent, and pour some of its contents into Johnston's cup. Only when the cup was filled did anyone speak, Polk breaking the silence.

"General, perhaps General Beauregard should be the one to tell you what we have been discussing." Polk spoke quietly, but his words were firm.

Johnston turned to look at Beauregard. He noted how deep were the depths of the shadows already, the darkness growing deeper. Beauregard's aides were busy setting up the night's camp, the hustle and bustle all around them. Campfires were beginning to sprout here and there, beginning their assault on the Tennessee night's chill. Johnston sipped from the cup, the hot contents steaming in the cool air, then spoke.

"Well General, what is it?"

Beauregard did not reply. Instead, he bent over and poked at the fire with a long stick, stirring the flames. The glowing embers sent sparks flying into the air, a glow that reminded one of the fire flies, flitting around the campsite. He refilled his empty coffee cup and took a long sip from it. Then, as if fortified to do battle, he turned to the taller Johnston and spoke.

"General Johnston, I must humbly request that we leave this place. It is now . . ." Beauregard paused and glanced at his watch. "Ten hours, no, *more than* ten hours past the time this attack was to be launched. There has been delay after delay in getting all of our men into line for battle." This last was accompanied by a glare at Polk, now sitting on a tree stump. Polk immediately began to rise, only to sit back down to Johnston's quiet admonishment.

"Later General, later. Let General Beauregard finish." Johnston stared down at the shorter Beauregard. "Continue, General."

"Thank you, sir. In addition to those delays, I've already spoken of, there has been too much noise, and thus, General Johnston, sir, we have lost the element of surprise. *Too much noise.* Sir, I cannot emphasize this enough. Surprise has been lost, and that, General, was crucial to our plan."

"Now General, how do you know that this is the case?" Johnston's voice was soft.

"General Johnston, sir, my comrades here can attest to this themselves. While we have met here, we could plainly hear the beat of the enemy drums, right in this place." Johnston looked around. The others nodded their agreement at this last statement. Beauregard then continued to press his argument.

"Sir, it is quite plain to me, that if we can hear their drums, the *enemy* must certainly be able to hear our gunfire, our men and their yelling, their hollering, our mistakes. In addition to that, General, I must inform you that it has been reported to me that we have lost several cavalry scouts, these men being captured in a clash with federal infantry last night. I am sure that by now the enemy must have interrogated those boys and have at least some ideas of our location. They must know we are no longer in Corinth."

"So what do you think this means, General Beauregard?"

"General Johnston, it means the situation has changed. Therefore, sir, I must propose that rather than chance a complete disaster by following the plan and commencing this attack, that instead we return to Corinth and make a new plan. I must insist on this General, I must insist! There is no element of surprise!" Beauregard slammed the empty mug onto the map table. "Now they will be entrenched to the eyes, and it would be a slaughter, sir, a terrible slaughter!"

Silence. Johnston's eyes had never left Beauregard during the Creole's impassioned speech. Now, he looked into the fire, his eyes searching for answers in its glowing crater.

Patience. This is the time for these men to express their thoughts. Johnston lifted his eyes, his gaze landing on Polk, still seated on his stump. All right, Bishop, now's your chance.

"Well General Polk, what do you think?"

Polk slowly and majestically drew himself to his feet. He rearranged his uniform and cloak, looking as if he was about to address one of his many congregations. He first looked at Johnston, his roommate those many years back at West Point, then allowed his gaze to slowly sweep across the rest of the assembled war council. Beauregard shook his head and moved away from the group and the now roaring fire. Polk began to speak, his hands grasping the lapels of his uniform coat, the resonance of his deep, pulpit voice echoing through the clearing.

"General Johnston, my comrades and I are here for a fight. My troops are in good condition, and they are eager, yes eager to come to grips with the enemy. They hunger for combat. I have spoken to each of my divisional commanders, and they are in complete agreement with me. We have left Corinth to go into a fight, and, as I said before to General Beauregard, to leave this place without one would be as demoralizing, perhaps even more so, than if we were to get whipped in combat. These men came here for a fight. They are ready to tear into the enemy as a tiger would tear into raw meat. They are ready to attack, and *beat* the Yankees, and what's more, they *believe* they can do it." Polk clapped his hand to his chest, covering his heart. He knew how to play the dramatic moment.

"Sir, they are ready to smite the enemy, to avenge the losses at Henry and Donelson. They are ready, sir. They believe it. I believe it. I believe they are ready, General, yes, I believe in their fighting spirit. Sir, I believe we will win a glorious victory." Polk raised his arm, the outstretched hand pointing toward the sky. "General, *God* will watch over this army in its quest. We are destined for this day. We *must* continue. To victory, sir, to *victory*!" Polk stopped, the homily over. He sat back down on the stump.

Well, I really didn't expect any different from the Bishop. Johnston thought to himself, a small smile evident on his face. *The man sure can deliver a sermon.* His gaze traveled to Bragg, who was watching Beauregard, who was still walking outside of the circle of firelight. Johnston looked over at Beauregard, but in the dark could not make out the man's face clearly.

Probably doing it on purpose. He doesn't want us to see his reaction to their words. Johnston spoke.

"General Bragg?"

Bragg's eyes never left Beauregard. He spoke quietly, but with strength in his voice.

"General Johnston, I agree with General Polk."

All right. That's these two, but I want one more, just to be sure. Turning from the others, Johnston beckoned to an aide, Lieutenant Thomas Jack.

"Lieutenant, please go and find General Breckinridge, if you would please. Please inquire as to the condition of his corps and ask if he would be so kind as to join us here."

"No need to, General. Sir, I believe that is him coming now. And I believe, that is General Hardee with him, General, sir." Jack pointed down the dark road, illuminated on the fringes by the now numerous campfires. Breckinridge was riding down the trail, flanked by Hardee.

John C. Breckinridge was a man of reputation in both the North and the South. The Vice-President of the United States under President James Buchanan, Breckinridge had been unsuccessful in his attempt to claim the White House for himself in 1860, losing to Abraham Lincoln. Now the Kentuckian had "gone south," joining the Confederate cause. He had helped raise troops for the Confederacy, had accepted a brigadier general's star in the Confederate Army, and now commanded Johnston's Reserve Corps. The tall, handsome, mustachioed Breckinridge had never led troops in combat.

Major General William J. Hardee was a West Pointer, class of 1838, and a career soldier. His military experience included service in both the Seminole and Mexican wars. He had resigned his commission as a lieutenant colonel to join the Confederate Army and had accepted a commission as a brigadier general. Now, he was a major general, and commanded the Third Corps in Johnston's Army of the Mississippi. His corps was in the van of the army, the first in line, and would be the first to strike the enemy. A former West Point commandant, he was known as a good soldier, and strong student of tactics, having written an excellent manual on the subject.

"General Johnston, please forgive my tardiness if it is, but I have just learned of this council." Breckinridge spoke with a salute and a flourish, a true, polished, politician. Hardee's salute was short and crisp, a soldier's salute.

"There is no need for apology, General." Johnston returned the salutes, smiling as he did. He liked Breckinridge.

"We were just discussing whether to fight here or withdraw back to Corinth."

"Withdraw?" Breckinridge was stunned. "But why? The enemy is there to fight, not to run from!" Hardee nodded his approval of the statement.

"Well, I believe that General Polk and General Bragg are in agreement with you. However, General Beauregard is of the strong opinion that the enemy knows we are here and will be thoroughly prepared to receive an attack from us." Johnston replied, sipping from the coffee cup as he did. His eyes were still on Breckinridge.

"General Johnston, with all due respect to General Beauregard." Breckinridge nodded toward Beauregard. "I must agree with General Polk and General Bragg. A retreat? Oh, no sir, that would simply not do."

Well, that's three. Johnston turned his back on the fire and walked out into the darkness. He stood silently, sipping on the now cold coffee. He grimaced at the taste and poured the remaining contents of the cup onto the ground. The others stood silently, awaiting his words. He turned back to face the others, all but Beauregard still grouped around the fire.

"General Breckinridge, how are your provisions?" Johnston's eyes were burning, reflecting the heat of the fires inside of him, the warrior weighing his options.

"In ample supply, General." Breckinridge smiled. "In ample supply."

"And you, General Hardee?" Hardee stood and met Johnston's gaze with his own. "What do you have to say to all this?"

Hardee did not hesitate. "General Johnston, my boys are in line and ready for battle." He then smiled at Johnston, one warrior to another.

That's four. Johnston nodded, and looked at Beauregard, still standing alone, an island unto himself. The others made no move to join him.

Well Pierre, you lose this one. Johnston turned to Bragg and Polk. Both had their own small smiles, the light of the flickering flames dancing on their faces. The flames reached higher into the sky, the sparks one with the stars.

"Gentlemen, we shall attack at daylight tomorrow." Beauregard stiffened, started to say something, then stopped, curtly nodded, and turned away. The others also nodded, then saluted and quickly mounted their horses to return to their respective commands. The war council was over. It was now time to prepare for the upcoming morning's events. Johnston watched them all ride away, then turned to look at Beauregard. The Creole was standing on the edge of the clearing. Johnston watched him for a long second, sighed, then turned and walked over to the waiting Fire-Eater. He stood by the horse, looking at the string of campfires that stretched along the road, the army settling in for the night. The fires looked like a string of luminescent pearls, glowing against the black velvet backdrop of the night woods. Johnston mounted Fire-Eater, and slowly rode him over to where Beauregard stood, stopping a few feet short of the man.

"General Beauregard, please make the proper dispositions for the morning attack. I plan to be near the front to help direct it. Please prepare the plan so that Hardee's men are in the front wave. The other corps, as we have discussed, are to follow in succeeding waves. Make all the necessary arrangements. I wish you to coordinate all the operations from the rear. Oh, and please have all commanders informed that there are too many campfires. There should only be one per company. No sense in telling the enemy our true size." Johnston spoke quietly. There was no reason to raise his voice. He knew Beauregard heard him.

Beauregard turned and looked at Johnston mounted on his horse. He slowly raised his arm and saluted Johnston.

"Yes, General Johnston. I understand. All will be ready, sir."

Johnston said nothing, but returned the salute, and pulling on Fire-Eater's reins, began to ride down the road. He looked at his staff officers, sitting their mounts, a respectful distance away.

"Gentlemen, our decisions are made. Please all ride ahead and see that all is in order at our camp. That is, all of you except Colonel Preston and Major Munford. Colonel, you will accompany me. Major, ride behind and stay close."

"Certainly, General. It is my honor." Preston rode up. "Yes sir, General. It sure sounds like we are ready to go." Preston smiled Johnston.

"Yes, I believe we finally are." Johnston smiled tiredly. It had been a very long day, and it was not over yet. He looked back at Beauregard, who was still standing by the road, watching them. Johnston noted the dejection in the Creole's posture, his once grandiose plans having hit a snag. Johnston turned back to Preston, and spoke, his voice at once tired yet filled with emotion.

"I would fight them if they were a million."

JOHNSTON

Mitchie Junction
April 5, 1862 7:00 P.M.

Albert Sidney Johnston was in a quandary. He had just seen his second-in-command do a complete one hundred and eighty-degree turn from just hours before. Beauregard had been one of the strongest advocates for a fight. Now, "Old Bory" was calling for them to retreat to basically just run away. To run, even before they truly had a chance to even try to get at the federal army. Johnston was deeply concerned by this. He rode silently, alone with his thoughts, Preston at his side, but a yard or so back, Munford keeping his distance a few yards further back. Johnston suddenly looked back at Preston and motioned for him to join Johnston.

"Colonel, please come up beside me."

"Certainly, General." Preston drew his horse up beside Johnston. Munford continued to keep his distance. Johnston bent over, and spoke softly, his words meant only for Preston's ears.

"Well Bill, that was quite a scene. I'm not sure I've ever been a part of a discussion quite like that before."

Preston understood that Johnston had deliberately been informal in his speech. "Can't say as if I've ever been either, Sidney. I was glad to see the others all come down the way they did, wanting to fight."

"Bill. I meant what I said. I *would* fight them, even if they were a million. The Yankees may have put themselves into a trap. They can present no greater front between those two creeks than we can. The more men they crowd in there, the worse we can make it for them. We can drive them just like rats right into the river and pile them one on top of the other. That's what I need the others to see. Polk is a true soldier and friend. He sure likes a tussle. I'm not worried about Hardee. He likes a good fight. Breckinridge wants to make a good impression, but the others, they worry me."

Johnston turned on his horse to look back at Munford, who was carefully keeping his distance from Johnston and Munford. Johnston motioned to Munford to join them.

Major, my apologies, but would you please ride ahead and find Doctor Yandell, (Johnston's personal physician). Tell him I want to see him. Then find Colonel Jordan." (Colonel Thomas Jordan, Johnston's adjutant general and old friend.) "Ask him to join us. We'll be here on the road."

"Yes sir, General, immediately, sir." Munford spurred his horse, and passed the two officers, his horse speeding up to a fast trot.

"Let's stop here, Bill. Let us walk a bit." Johnston reined up Fire-Eater and dismounted.

"All right Sidney, as you wish." Preston called over to a small group of soldiers, clustered around a campfire close by, telling them to hold their horses, and to send Yandell and Johnston to them when they came looking for them. Johnston had already walked to the edge of the woods, their depths' dark and menacing. Johnston turned and looked back at the campfires of his army. Those that still burned looked like a series of fireflies along the road. At the sound of Preston's approaching footsteps Johnston looked back at him and spoke.

"Yes Bill, I will fight them. I would fight them if they were a million. Like I said, they cannot present a greater front between those two creeks than we can. Let them try to, because the more they crowd in there, well, the worse we can make it for them."

"Bill, I want to tell you something which I desire to be remembered. I shall tell no one but you and perhaps Munford, but I do not wish that what I say to be forgotten. It may become very important someday."

Preston heard the note of quiet intensity in Johnston's voice. "Certainly Sidney, what is it?" He waited for Johnston to continue.

"Bill. They wish me to withdraw the army without a battle, without a fight! Well, I would like to know your thoughts, what is your opinion?"

Preston was stunned. The closeness of their relationship was known, but Preston was still, just a colonel. This was Johnston's decision to make. Preston could not believe that after the campfire conference, after polling the army's commanders, after telling Beauregard to make plans for a dawn attack, that Johnston was still, at this late moment, actually reconsidering his decision. Preston gathered his thoughts, then spoke, his words calm, but strong with passion.

"General, a defeat is preferable to that. This army cannot be withdrawn without a fight, and still be kept together. They will become disheartened and just melt away. It is true that as a trained fighting force they are raw and somewhat undisciplined, but their heart is great. It is the heart that matters, and they are most eager, most eager for a fight, General."

"General, I have been around these boys and their campfires. I have mingled freely with them. I have spoken with them. I *know* that if anyone can do this thing with such an undisciplined army, it is you, and now is your time! Now is the time. They . . ." Preston swung his arm around, pointing out into the darkness. "They are ready for the fight!"

Preston stopped, his words still ringing in the still night air. He stared at Johnston, who was now squatting on his haunches. Johnston's eyes glowed like a cat's in the reflected firelight, but he made no reply. He made no sound, just drew lines in the dirt with a stick. Finally, he dropped the stick, and stood up. He began to gaze again, perusing the black woods. The air was filled with the sounds of night, the early spring crickets chattering away in the darkness. Minutes passed, the tension of the moment growing as Preston waited in concerned silence for Johnston's response. Finally, Johnston turned and looked at Preston. He straightened his shoulders, stood tall, the tired look gone from his handsome bearded face. He spoke, the excitement evident in his voice.

"There is still a matter worthy of consideration, Colonel." Johnston motioned for Preston to have a seat on a nearby overturned tree. Johnston sat down, Preston joining him. Preston picked up a stick, pulled out a small pocketknife, and began to whittle on the stick, as Johnston continued to speak. "There is the fact that we have lost a day. We know that Buell, (Union General Don Carlos Buell), is supposed to be marching an army as large as our own to join up with Grant. If he has not gotten a case of the "slows," Buell should be joining up with Grant very, very soon. The force we plan to attack is, right now, larger than ours, better armed, and, from all reports, better anointed then ours is. Let us suppose we attack that force and find that instead of fifty, sixty thousand federal troops, there are ninety, even a hundred thousand blue troops waiting for us. What do you think of our chances of success then?" Johnston stopped. Even for him, that was a long speech.

Preston said nothing. He stopped his whittling, turning the stick over in his hand and inspecting his handiwork. He then looked over at Johnston and smiled.

"Well Sidney, I guess we're going to find out if you say go. It is all up to you, General."

Johnston stood up and began to pace. "There's Lick Creek on my right. Owl Creek is on my left. These two creeks effectively protect my flanks. I have men enough to cover my front, and the more they try to crowd into that small space between us and the river, the better for us and the worse for them. No, it is time. It is time, I believe, time to I think beyond any doubt, to hammer them! I have given orders for an attack tomorrow morning at daylight, and I intend to hammer them, Colonel!"

Johnston stopped. He walked away from Preston, who sensed that the discussion was over. Preston stood up, and quietly walked away, knowing that Johnston probably wanted to be alone with his thoughts, and to keep an eye out for Jordan and Yandell.

Johnston sat down beneath a big oak. He closed his eyes and let his mind drift. Drifting, drifting to back, before the war. Back, back . . . to California.

The decision to leave the federal army had been made in San Francisco. It had not been easy. The federal government's attempts to keep Johnston on the side of the Union had proven fruitless. When Johnston's adopted state of Texas seceded and joined the Confederacy, the native Kentuckian had felt that he had no choice but to go with

Texas. The trip first from San Francisco to Los Angeles, then across the desert eastward bound was arduous for Johnston and his party, all Confederates-to-be. Their journey through Arizona and New Mexico had not been easy, especially since they were dodging both federal patrols looking for them, and marauding Apaches. Finally, after the long trip they reached Texas and the newly born Confederacy, and Johnston received some news. It was in Texas that Johnston was surprised to hear that he was now a general in the Confederate Army. In his ears rang Jefferson Davis's hopeful words.

I hoped and expected that I had others who would prove to be generals. But I knew I had one, and that was Sidney Johnston.

"General?"

Johnston opened his eyes. Colonel Jordan was standing there.

"You sent for me, sir? My apologies for disturbing you."

Johnston waved off the apology. "That's all-right Tom. I was thinking about California and those last few days in the Old Army."

Jordan, who had served for eight years in the Old Army on the Pacific coast, smiled in remembrance. "Those *were* good days, General, good days."

"Yes, they were, Tom." Johnston replied. "Win, (Winfield Scott Hancock, who had gone with the Union), threw a farewell party for all of us that were leaving. We sang, danced, and toasted each other all evening. I will never forget Hancock and Lew Armistead crying and hugging each other as they said goodbye to each other. Lew was going south, too and Hancock was not happy about it. The two of them were hoping they'd never have to face each other, yet you knew that they would both do their duty if it came to that."

"Yes, I am sure that it was hard on old friends, General."

"Ah Tom, it was . . . but the hardest moment was when I asked Mrs. Johnston to sing some of the old songs."

"Well Sidney, your wife does have a lovely voice."

"No one could sing *Kathleen Mavoureen* like she did that night. There wasn't a dry eye in the place." Johnston sighed over the distant memory, pleasant as it was. "I need memories like that, especially to counter ones like those that the United States government gave me regarding my replacement." The last words were bitten off with contempt. Johnston had not forgotten that the federal government had secretly replaced Johnston as commander of the Department of the Pacific in April 1861, and had sent his replacement, Colonel Edwin V. Sumner by steamer under an assumed name. The whole thing had left Johnston in a rage and seething for revenge.

"I will never forgive what they did to me, Tom, nor shall I forget it!" Johnston spoke with vehemence, the memory stirring up thoughts of anger.

"Sorry General, forgive me. I did not mean to upset you." Jordan spoke soothingly. "Was there something special that you needed? Was there something, specific you needed me for?"

Easy, easy, Jordan is on your side. Just relax. "It's all right, Colonel. It's all right. No, but thank you. I guess there is nothing after all."

Sensing that his commander's mind was again drifting away, Jordan knew it was time to leave. "Well General, with your permission, I will take my leave." Johnston nodded assent. "Thank you, sir. Good night, sir." Jordan saluted his goodbyes, and left, leaving Johnston to return to his silent dreams.

Johnston continued to stare off into the darkness, his thoughts continuing to unwind. Yes, Jefferson Davis thought he had himself a real general. Well, Mister President, I guess now is the time to prove it. But first, I have to do something about Beauregard.

"General?"

Looking up, Johnston saw his personal surgeon, Doctor D. W. Yandell, standing in the firelight, his black medical bag held against his side.

"General, you sent for me, sir?" Yandell's face wore a concerned look.

"Yes Doctor, thank you for coming so quickly. I am in need of your medical expertise in a certain matter." Johnston deliberately kept his voice low, not wishing anyone else to hear.

"Are you ill, General? How may I be of service to you?" Yandell walked over to Johnston and began to open his bag.

"No, Doctor, it is not I." Johnston waved his hand. "I am fine, thank you. No, this is another matter. I am concerned about a fellow officer's health, and what I need is an expert's opinion, a medical opinion. Please, sit." Johnston moved over on his stump, making room for Yandell.

"Whose health, General? Is this a member of your staff?"

"Yes, Doctor. I am concerned about General Beauregard's condition." Johnston replied. He stood up, waving Yandell back down onto the stump. Johnston rubbed his back, frowned, and began to pace.

"You see, Doctor, I am concerned that the good general is not showing his customary zeal and confidence, especially with the enemy so close. You must understand, sir, that I have given General Beauregard a great deal of latitude in planning and directing this campaign, a great deal. Yet now, at such a crucial moment, he demurs, and the burden of decision, that which is the decision to fight or retreat, is now solely mine." Johnston stopped his pacing and turned to look directly at Yandell.

"So you see Doctor, I suppose that what it is I am asking you is this. Do you have an opinion as to the health and *fitness* of General Beauregard? I ask you this as a medical man."

Yandell stood up. He said nothing but walked over to the now dying campfire. He peered closely into the softly glowing embers, as if looking for an answer as he tried to gather his thoughts. Johnston said nothing, giving him time, and knowing the man would not be rash in his conclusions. Finally, after a few minutes, Yandell looked up from his contemplation of the fire, and spoke.

"General Johnston, with all due respect to both you and General Beauregard, I must state that it is my considered medical opinion, that General Beauregard is still unwell." Yandell stopped, waiting for Johnston to comment. Johnston said nothing, merely nodded for him to continue.

"Based on what I know, it is *possible* that the general's health has been somewhat, compromised, and thus, may have affected his thinking. However, sir, it is also my considered medical opinion that the general's health will improve with *time*, and thus, so also will his thinking." Yandell stopped. He had nothing more to say.

Johnston closed his eyes. God, I am tired. I want to rest. I need some sleep, badly. But no rest, not yet at least. I still have things to do. He opened his eyes and turned to Yandell.

"Thank you, Doctor, for your advice. That will be all. Oh, please send Colonel Preston to me if you would be so kind." Johnston saw that his orderlies had finished erecting his tent and started to walk toward it. He then stopped and looked back at Yandell. "And, Doctor, not a word of this conversation to anyone. Good night."

"Certainly, General. Not one word. Good night, sir." Yandell saluted and stepped off into the darkness. Johnston stepped into his tent, closing the flap behind him. He sat down on the waiting camp cot, and began to pull off his boots, then thinking better of it, stopped. He closed his eyes, and began to let his mind drift again, seeing the picture of the enemy caught in the vise of two creeks, his army tightening the screws on the captive force. The rustle of the tent flap stirred him back to lucidity. Preston was standing there.

"Colonel Preston." Johnston spoke quietly, his voice tired, but firm. "Please see to it that all corps commanders are informed to make sure that all troops are to be sure to be completely deployed. Then men are to sleep with their weapons in line of battle. There must be no misunderstanding."

"Yes sir, General. All troops deployed, in line of battle, with their weapons at their sides. No misunderstandings. Yes sir. I will take care of it." Preston saluted, and started to leave, only to stop at the sight of Johnston upraised hand. Johnston stood up and walked back out of the tent into the night air. A great stillness had settled over the Confederate camp. Johnston stepped further out into the evening light, looked up, and pointed at the stars.

"Bill, it is time I put my trust in the iron dice of battle. The eyes and hopes of eight millions of people rest upon us. Oh, and one more thing to tell them. Commanders are to emphasize to fire low. We don't want the boys to be overshooting now, do we?" Johnston chuckled, a smile on his lips, that didn't quite reach his eyes. He then abruptly continued his instructions.

"Soldiers are not to break ranks to strip or rob the dead. Anyone who does, or who attempts to run away, on any pretext, *is to be shot on the spot!*" Johnston slammed his fist into his open palm, in an accompaniment to those last words which were clipped, and hard.

"Yes sir. I will give them your orders. I will tell them. All of it, General." Preston responded, excitement mixing with some fear in his voice. "I will make sure they understand."

"That's all, Colonel."

"Yes sir." Preston saluted. He quickly moved to his waiting horse, mounted, and took off to deliver Johnston's commands. Johnston now stood alone in the great blueness of the deepening night. He watched as the stars continued to wink on, one by one, paling the dim sickle of the moon. The warrior stood, the stars bathing him in their surreal glow, as if anointing Johnston with their unearthly fire. His eyes flashed with the reflected glory of their brightness, then deepened as if they had absorbed the beams, until his eyes glowed like the coals of the evening fires of the camp. He whispered, his words meant only for those watchful eyes in the sky, the spirits of the warriors gone before him.

"Tomorrow. Tomorrow, out of dawn's gray steel we will rise to make the enemy feel the steel of our own bayonets. And I will lead them."

Tomorrow.

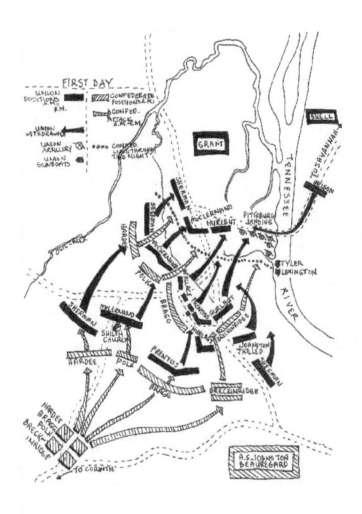

BEAUREGARD

Headquarters, Army of The Mississippi, Pittsburg-Corinth Road
Sunday, April 6, 1862. Dawn

I have to try once more. There must be some way to convince him. He must understand that there can be no element of surprise. With all the noise of last night they must have heard us. They must have!

Dawn was breaking and Beauregard was in the saddle headed for Johnston's camp. Fresh and rested, Beauregard's mind still chewed on the campfire conference. Somewhat the superstitious soul, he was wearing for luck the flat-topped kepi he had worn at Manassas. The hero of Fort Sumter had not lost any of his previous night's conviction that an assault on the Union lines was doomed to failure.

It's quiet now. Beauregard took a deep breath of the rain-washed air. It's quiet, quiet as a Sunday morning should be. Like church, it's a good kind of quiet. After all the rain we have endured lately today looks like a good day. The kind of day you want to have if you have to fight. Not too hot, and clear. But not today. No, they have had too much warning, and they're probably entrenched now, dug into their teeth. I must convince Sidney of this. Too many good men will die if I don't. No, not now. Later. Someplace else. Not here, not today.

Beauregard spied Johnston and his staff grouped around the small campfire of Johnston's camp. The early morning's fare of dry crackers and hot coffee was rapidly disappearing. Daylight was beginning to filter in through the trees, filling the glade where the camp was with a soft light, a light that illuminated the mists in the woodlands surrounding the Army.

Johnston and his staff had already been out, scouting the terrain well before dawn. They had ridden up to the Y formed by the junction of the Pittsburg-Corinth and Bank roads earlier, scouting ahead to see what they could. This was where Johnston had decided to place his battlefield headquarters.

Johnston stood drinking his morning coffee. He was resplendent in a finely tailored uniform and sash, his legs covered to his knees with high shiny black cavalryman boots, and the whole thing topped off with a wide brimmed soft black hat with a sweeping plume adorning it. He looked up and greeted Beauregard with a smile.

"Good morning, General. Care to join us for some crackers and coffee?" Johnston gestured toward the bubbling coffee pot, sitting on the morning coals. "It's fresh."

"Is it real?" Beauregard grinned, remembering the time somebody had given Johnston a cup of brew made up of scorched sweet potatoes, wheat, and rye. Johnston had never forgotten or forgiven for that. It had been quite the scene.

Johnston grimaced in memory of the same incident. "Nothing but." He replied.

Beauregard smiled. "Thank you, sir. I will." He accepted a cup, inhaling the heat, and sipping the steaming contents. He felt the heat pass through his being, it feeling good on this cool morning.

"A good morning, eh General?"

"Yes." Johnston smiled. "A good morning to fight." Beauregard said nothing to this.

"General Beauregard, I have decided to make a little change in our plans."

Keep calm! Beauregard's heart leaped at Johnston's words. *Wait, listen, but don't overreact.*

"What sort of change, General?"

Johnston smiled. He stooped over the fire and refilled his coffee cup. Then straightening up, he motioned for Beauregard to follow him, and walked away from the fire, out of the hearing of all that were present. Johnston walked to the edge of the clearing and found his stump of a seat from the night before, and sat down. Beauregard followed, but remained standing, edgy and anxious as he waited for Johnston to speak.

"General Beauregard, is it possible that they are not aware of our presence?"

Beauregard let out his breath. "I don't know General." He replied. "It is scarcely possible that they are laying a trap for us."

Johnston shook his head. "No, I don't think so. Regardless, I have made up my mind."

Oh dear God, now what? Beauregard could hardly breathe.

"General Beauregard, I have decided that you will remain to the rear of the Army. This way, you will be able to more closely follow the movements of the Army and be able to coordinate its attacks better as the battle takes shape and follows its course. The corps commanders will report their progress to you. This way, you will be able to determine best as to where and when to send in reserves as needed."

My God, I don't believe what I just heard! Beauregard thought to himself, his mind numbed by the shock of Johnston's plan. Forcing himself to remain calm, he replied stiffly.

"General Johnston, where, sir will you be?"

Johnston stood up. He gestured with his now empty cup in the direction of the enemy's fog shrouded camps, off in the murky distance. "Why General, I will be at the front. Leading the attack."

Beauregard nearly dropped his cup in shock. What Johnston proposed was almost unheard of. He was, in effect, reversing positions with his second-in-command.

Sidney can't be serious! I must not have heard him correctly. And if I did, I have got to make him change his mind. Beauregard took a deep breath, then plunged in, amazement evident in his voice.

"General Johnston, *you* are the commander of this army. Your place is *not* at the front of your troops. You have field commanders for *that*!"

Johnston stiffened, an angry reaction beginning to build up. Beauregard, who knew Johnston's temperament well, did not give him a chance to respond, but raced on, his words pouring out.

"Sir, no one doubts your personal bravery. However, you are taking a risk that is totally unacceptable, even in the eyes of this army."

"Nonsense." Johnston snorted. "The men *need* me to lead them, to show them what they are truly capable of. How can they know unless we show them? It is my quest to lead them on this great *patriotic* endeavor. I must be at the front as we destroy the enemy. That is, as you say, where my place *is*!"

As he finished his impassioned speech, Johnston's face seemed to glow, aflame with a fighting spirit. His whole being appeared to vibrate with that berserk passion for combat that always seemed to manifest itself in those warriors who were only at their best when the stakes were at their highest.

Beauregard stared at the transfixed Johnston. My God. He will lead us to victory, or he will die in the attempt. Beauregard thought, his mind aghast at what he saw. I don't know what will change his mind, but still, I must try. He must listen to reason. Perhaps he will listen to someone else. Here comes Bragg. We don't see eye-to-eye on much, but I know he has concerns, too. Perhaps he might get Sidney to listen to reason.

The small group clustered around the fire were now joined by the newly arrived Bragg. Bragg dismounted from his horse and called out to Johnston and Beauregard.

"General Johnston, sir, good morning." Bragg's crisp salute was returned quickly by Johnston. "Good morning to you also, General Beauregard." Both men nodded their acknowledgments of the greeting. Bragg continued to speak. His words sent Beauregard's heart leaping.

"Gentlemen, I have received a report from my scouts that they have encountered enemy patrols in the fields toward the river. There have also been contacts with enemy skirmishers by General Hardee's advance skirmishers. Shots have been fired, gentlemen. General Johnston, they *know* we are here."

Johnston stiffened, but said nothing, waiting for Bragg to continue. "They cannot possibly be surprised by us. They must be ready for us, behind their defenses. We no longer have the element of surprise as an advantage. This should be considered, sir." Bragg abruptly stopped, his report finished.

I sense a chance. Beauregard thought to himself. *I will try one more time. One last chance to stop this.* He turned to face Johnston. His eyes bore into Johnston's, a powerful gaze that locked onto the other man's face, a desperate attempt to change Johnston's mind. Beauregard began to speak, slowly, powerfully, his words being marshaled by the strength of his conviction.

"General Johnston, sir, please listen to me. You have just heard General Bragg's report. In addition, there has been music, battle music, emanating all night from the federal camps. In addition, you must add to those facts that there has been almost constant cheering coming from the direction of Pittsburg Landing, all night! That can only mean one thing. Buell has arrived, and with him his men. That means Grant has been alerted. We have to believe that we are now facing not forty, or fifty thousand, but now seventy thousand plus troops. Seventy thousand entrenched and expectant federal troops, many of them veteran soldiers, just waiting for us to venture into their trap! We do not have the advantage anymore. It is a trap; one we cannot possibly take the chance and allow ourselves to be ensnared in!" Beauregard shook his fist emphatically.

Beauregard paused for breath, his eyes never leaving Johnston's face. Johnston looked away, no longer able to look at Beauregard's intense stare. Beauregard sensed a wavering in Johnston's resolve, and bored back in, not wanting Johnston's attention to get away, and resumed his arguments.

"General, this army must be given a chance. A real chance to win. In order to do that we must re-deploy, fall back, and return to Corinth. There we can prepare a trap for the enemy to step into. There lies our only chance to destroy Grant's and Buell's troops. There, he will come at us, and there, we can smash him!" Beauregard smacked his palms together.

"You forget, General, Grant came to Forts Henry and Donelson, and we all know the result of those visits." Johnson replied.

'General, I still say our opportunity lies at Corinth, not . . ."

Musket fire exploded in the nearby woods, the sound like the tearing of canvas. The sound was coming from up the Pittsburg-Corinth Road. The road was Hardee's front. Beauregard looked in the direction of the fired shots.

"There!" Munson cried. "The first gun of the battle!" Beauregard looked at him, then turned back to Johnston. Johnston was handing the empty cup to an orderly. Johnston looked around at the assembled group, then calmly spoke.

"The battle has opened, gentlemen. It is too late to change our dispositions."

Beauregard turned away, his face suddenly black and somber. He mounted his horse and turned away to ride to the new command post. Bragg and the others quickly mounted up to rejoin their respective commands. Johnston turned to Munson and Preston.

"Note the time, gentlemen." Johnston asked, Munson quickly looking at his watch. 5:14.

"Bring me my horse." Johnston ordered, Fire-eater quickly being brought to him. He mounted the magnificent steed, and sat there for a long moment, his face quiet and thoughtful. Then, as if waking from a dream, his face took on a rapid transformation. Now, Albert Sidney Johnston looked every inch the warrior-king. An Arthur prepared to do battle with the invaders from the North, the Yankees the Viking-like enemy. His face rivaled the sun in its brightness. He fingered his Excalibur-like sword, then shouted, his voice bright and hopeful.

"Tonight, we will water our horses in the Tennessee River!"

Munford looked up at the sun, now shining in the early morn, brilliant in the now cloudless sky. The young man, perhaps overcome by Johnston's god-like image, and feeling the effect of Beauregard's Napoleonic orders, exclaimed; "Perhaps this is another sun of Austerlitz!"

Johnston smiled, remembering his lessons on Napoleon's great victory. He turned to the others, a soldier ready to lead them to victory, or come back on his shield, and thundered.

"Today . . . today we must win a victory! Today, we must!"

"Today!"

SHERMAN

Shiloh Church
Sunday, April 6,1862 7:00 a.m.

Morning. It was dawning, clean and bright. The trees and surroundings gleamed soft and green after the cleansing bath the land had been given the day before. It seemed like any Sunday should feel.

Quiet. Peaceful. The blue sky reminded Sherman of the vaulted ceiling of a great cathedral. The new leaves on the trees were the church-goers in their pews, and the birds singing in the trees the many choir members in their lofty choir lofts. A beautiful Sunday morning, and yet there were those gunshots.

Gunshots. Like the sound of a schoolboy's firecracker, the distant popping so soft, yet distinct, except the sound of these firecrackers were getting louder, and more often.

Having risen early as was his habit, Sherman was now fully awake and attuned to the sounds of the morning. His warrior's instincts were calm, yet aware, refusing to give in to old fears. Calmly he listened to the distant crackling.

The camp was filled with breakfast smells. Coffee was boiling on the campfire, the kettle hung over the hot coals, and the bacon was sizzling in its pan as Sherman's aides prepared breakfast.

All around the division similar operations were taking place as the men rose to greet a new day. For many, it would be the last they ever smelled or saw.

"Morning, General. Coffee?" Sherman muttered his thanks as Taylor handed him an old, dented tin cup, its contents steaming with heat. Sherman gingerly sipped it, noting that young Taylor had managed to get some sugar somewhere, judging by the sweetness of his cup's contents. His orderly, Private Tom Holliday was busy preparing the rest of Sherman's breakfast.

"Good morning, General. A fine morning isn't it, Sir?" Holliday spoke, his hands covered with bacon grease and flour.

"So far." Sherman's voice was quiet.

Taylor's ears perked up. He sensed Sherman's uneasy mood.

"Something wrong, General?"

Shots rang out again, still distant, yet closer still.

"Hear that?" Sherman said.

"Yes sir. That's been going on for some time now." Taylor stopped to listen. A new sound had entered the scene, and Taylor peered in the direction of the new noise. "General, do you hear that? That sounds like . . ."

"Long roll." Sherman answered. The regimental drums were calling troops to battle formation. Sherman put down his cup and faced toward the direction of the sounds.

"Wonder who it is?"

"Well, it looks like we're about to find out." Sherman pointed toward the woods. A young officer was just now emerging from them and was running directly in the direction of Sherman's camp.

The heated soldier was the same excitable young lieutenant from the day before incident. He ran up to the small group, and stumbled to a stop, saluting Sherman as he did. His breaths came in deep gasps, a mixture of excitement and stress as he tried to speak. Sherman stopped him, unable to understand the man's incoherent speech.

"Calm down, Lieutenant, and catch your breath. Then tell me what it is you came to tell me."

"Thank you, General." The young man gasped out. He paused long enough to catch his breath. Sherman waited, his eyes on the officer, but his attention listening to the far-off sounds of strife.

"General Sherman, begging the general's pardon, sir, I present Colonel Appler's compliments, sir. He requests to inform you that there is a great body, a great many enemy troops in his front, sir."

Damn him. Sherman said nothing, his mind hard at work. *How does a person like Appler get a command? He's cried 'wolf' so often I don't know whether to believe him or not?* Taking out another cigar, Sherman replied to the youngster, the sarcastic note evident in his voice.

"You must be badly scared over there."

The young lieutenant stared at Sherman; a quizzical look evident on his face. "Sir?" The young man stammered out a reply. "I don't understand, General Sherman, sir."

Sherman shook his head angrily. "Never mind. You just run back to your *colonel* and tell him what I just said. You can also tell him, we'll be along, shortly."

"Yes sir, General. Immediately, General. Thank you, at once, General. Sir." The boy saluted and took to his heels, running back toward Appler's lines.

Sherman watched him run back into the trees, toward the fire cracker-like sounds deep in the distance depths of the dark and murky woods. He continued to stare into the depths of the woods, listening, listening.

"Well, General, what do you think? What do we do, sir?" Johnny Taylor was also peering hard into the dark mass of woody growth.

"Don't know, Lieutenant." Sherman grumbled around his cigar. "But I suppose we better find out. Holliday!"

The young orderly, his hands still busy with fixing breakfast, straightened to attention. "Yes sir, General?"

"Sorry, son, you better hold off on that breakfast. Get our horses. We need to take a ride. Breakfast will just have to wait."

"Yes sir, General Sherman. Right away, sir!" Holliday quickly wiped his hands off on his apron, ripped off the apron, and ran toward where the camp's horses were picketed, hollering for the animals to be saddled. He soon returned; the horses ready to go. Anticipation was evident on Holliday's flour-streaked face. Sherman noted the look of excitement evident on both Holliday's and Taylor's faces. Sherman took the reins of his horse from Holliday and swung up into the saddle on the animal's back, then spoke to Taylor.

"Johnny, I want you to alert the other regiments on our line to be prepared. Tell their commanders to be ready, just in case. After that, you come find me, I'll be up with Appler. Oh, and Johnny, one more thing."

"Yes sir?" Lieutenant Taylor was mounted, anxious to go.

Easy Lieutenant, easy. Sherman thought. "Be careful son. Keep your head down, Lieutenant."

Taylor smiled boyishly. "Yes sir, General. Thank you, General." Flinging a salute, Taylor rode off on his mission.

Sherman watched Taylor leave, then turned to the now mounted Holliday, who also had Sherman's headquarters flag gripped in his hand. "Tom, you're with me. Let's go see what's happening up there."

Suddenly, more shots rang out, their thunder much louder and closer this time. Sherman ripped a glance at the still, dark woods, then sang out. "Let's go, Private, right now!" Sherman spurred his horse, and took off, Holliday following. He rode down the lane, toward a gate that opened into the meadow, then raced onto a path that went into the woods, riding toward the sound of the guns, all the time nervously chewing on his cigar. His thoughts jumbled together, wondering what might be "up there." The crackling sounds emitting from the woods continued to increase in volume as he rode closer to Appler's position.

"Look there, General!" Holliday yelled, pointing ahead down the path. "Something's sure enough going on out there!"

"I see them." Sherman excitedly replied.

A group of soldiers had gathered around a bedraggled soldier. The soldier was leaning against a tree and was holding on to a blood-soaked shoulder. The wounded man was speaking, gesturing excitedly to the others gathered around him as Sherman rode up. Sherman reined up, and leaned down from his horse, peering closely at the exhausted man's shoulder.

"Well son, I see someone took a lick at you. What's going on up there? What can you tell me, soldier?"

The bloodied man pointed past the group. "General, sir, you better get these boys in line! There's rebs out there and they's a-coming, a-coming hard! Hundreds of them!" The man's unkempt head bobbed as he spoke. He was paying no attention to the blood dripping on his brogans, but his eyes fixed on Sherman's. Suddenly he flopped down, and sat in the grass, his eyes going glassy as he flopped onto his side in the path.

"You there, get this man some help!" Sherman roared an order at one of the onlookers. He snapped a look around at the rest of goggle-eyed soldiers, dumbly standing around staring at the crumbled heap lying on the ground. "The rest of you men, get back to your units! Now!"

Spotting an officer standing on the edge of the crowd, Sherman snapped an order at him.

"Captain, see to it that man receives medical attention! Then find out what is happening and find me and report!" The officer quickly ran off to get help. Sherman turned in the saddle, looking around to see the soldiers, some with shocked looks on their young faces, still standing there watching the young man bleed.

"I told you boys to *move*! What are you waiting for?" Sherman hollered again. Suddenly his attention was grabbed by the sudden reappearance of the captain Sherman sent for help, the officer bursting out of the woods. He spotted Sherman and ran up to him, exclaiming as he did; "General, the rebels are out there, thicker than fleas on a dog's back!"

Sherman stared at the man, stunned. *My God, have they really done it?* He thought to himself. *Are they really here? Is Beauregard really making this gamble?* He grabbed for his binoculars, better to see into the now-lighting woods with.

"General!" Sherman swung his horse around, looking at the grouped Ohio soldiers. One of the soldiers pointed toward the woods on Sherman's right. "General, look to your right!" Sherman turned and froze in shock.

A large group of gray-clad soldiers had just emerged from the woods on Sherman's right and were headed straight for Sherman. They stopped, assembling into a semi-file, their muskets quickly raised, pointed, aiming directly at Sherman and the others. Sherman saw the gray-coated officer in the lead raise his sword and then cleaved the air with its blade, screaming for his men to fire.

"My God, we are attacked!" Sherman cried as the muskets crashed in a thunderous cloud of black smoke. He dropped the glasses, flinging up his hand as if this would ward off the in-coming missiles that were headed his way. The angry rounds, sounding so much like a swarm of mad hornets, whipped around him. He felt a sharp stinging pain, as one of the lead hornets found his out-stretched hand, striking him in its lethal flight. He heard a thumping sound to his side, and swung around, only to see young Holliday, a surprised look on his face, the blood exploding from the hole in his forehead, crumple off of his horse, and to the ground, Sherman's flag still clutched in Holliday's lifeless fingers.

"My God, they got poor Tommy!" Sherman exclaimed, looking around, amazed that he was still on his horse. He stared at his now dead orderly. Holliday's lifeless form laying in the blood-stained grass where the swarm of bullets had left him. Others were screaming, clutching at wounds, or lying in the grass of the now bullet-swept meadow. They, like Holliday, had their first view of the elephant, and it had been their last, their lives swept away by the beast's insatiable lust for blood. There would be many more whose first look at the beast would be their last of their lives on that day.

"General, you've got to get out of here!" Lieutenant Taylor suddenly materialized at Sherman's side. He began to grab at the reins of Sherman's horse. Sherman continued to mutely stare at Holliday's lifeless body.

"General!' Taylor screamed again, continuing to pull at Sherman's horse. Sherman shook him off.

"All right John, I hear you. Let go of my horse!" Taylor dropped the reins, Sherman pulling on them, and snapping the head of the frightened horse around. "All right let's get out of here, out of the range of those guns. C'mon, up the hill." Sherman slapped the reins against the side of the horse's head, his mount responding in a fast trot.

They must be sending one hell of a probe out, looking to test our lines. Sherman thought, gritting his teeth against the pain in his wounded hand. Well, I think that's what they're doing. Better be sure. Find a good spot and take a better look. Damn, wish I hadn't dropped those glasses.

Sherman reined up. "Let me have your glasses, Lieutenant." Sherman held out his bloody hand.

"General, you're bleeding! You have been hit, sir." Taylor pulled out a handkerchief, his eyes on the blood dripping from Sherman's out-stretched hand.

"I'm fine. Just give me the damned glasses!" Sherman snapped, peering at the trees lining the distant creek. He grasped the binoculars, wincing at the pain in his hand, and lifted the glasses to his eyes, peering to see through the still mist-filled oaks and pines. His view was not helped by the clouds of gun smoke now filling the meadow.

Then, as if a ghostly wind had caught its breath, the shady mists suddenly disappeared, and out of the depths of dawn's gray steel, there appeared before Sherman's awe-struck eyes, that which the mists had been hiding in the forest's dark and murky depths.

Bayonets. Hundreds of them. Like a river, the gray shiny current just poured out of the woods, hundreds of them.

Hundreds of them, for wherever Sherman looked, all he could see were the gray steel man-openers marching toward him.

Good Lord! This is no probe.

"Lieutenant, let's get out of here!" Sherman hollered, then snapped the reins, the horse taking off in a gallop. Sherman headed back toward the Fifty-Third Ohio's camp, and its hapless colonel. Sherman looked back over his shoulder, only to see more gray-clad troops filing out of the woods, the foggy meadow filling up, like some apparition in a bad dream. Sherman could not see the remainder of Polk's and Hardee's troops still hidden in the dark depths, but he could sense the power building up among the scrub oaks and pines.

Sherman soon spotted Appler, standing in the near distance of the Ohio troop's camp. The man was surrounded by his staff, all of them staring toward the sound of the gunfire. Sherman galloped up to the white-faced, transfixed Appler and shouted; "Colonel, snap to it! The enemy is coming! Form a line, *right here*, and stand your ground! You must defend it at *all costs!*" Sherman looked around and spotted an artillery battery off to the right. Sherman noted that its men were busy around the guns, preparing for action. "There is a battery of artillery to your right to help you. I will see to it. I will send reserves. Hold your position. I *will* support you! Now move man, quickly now, get to it!" Without waiting for a reply, Sherman galloped off, headed for the nearby artillery battery, Taylor hot on his heels. Appler just stood there, watching Sherman ride away. He then turned, white-faced and trembling, back to face toward the direction of the on-coming gray ghosts.

Brigadier General Patrick Cleburne was an Irish-born Southerner. He had arrived in America thirteen years earlier, running from his self-perceived failure. Unable to please his father, who had wished him to enter the apothecary trade, Cleburne had joined the British Army, and had learned well the many gory lessons of war. He had immigrated to the United States, and had drifted around, eventually ending up in Helena, Arkansas. In Helena, Cleburne had purchased a part-ownership in a drug store, perhaps as a subconscious move to please his Irish family. He would eventually take up the study of the law and would become a prominent Helena attorney in the process.

Cleburne, while admittedly shy around the ladies, feared no man, and had a bit of a reputation as a vicious street fighter. He and another Helena attorney, Thomas Hindman, had fought off a murderous street attack by political foes of Hindman. Although both men were seriously injured in the brawl, Cleburne had killed one of the street thugs, and chased off the other three would-be assassins. When war came, he had quickly joined the Confederate cause, and shown his natural leadership abilities, rising quickly to become a brigade commander under Bragg. Now the fiery Irishman's men were about to face their first test that being the troops of the Fifty-Third Ohio.

Cleburne's men were advancing to the left and front, moving toward the Union lines when they encountered the swampy thickets of Shiloh Branch, the creek that bordered the Fifty-Third Ohio's encampment. The brigade was forced to split into two segments to swing around the swamp, the Sixth Mississippi and the Twenty-Third Tennessee swinging to their left, and the Fifth Tennessee and following regiments slogging through the muddy right of the morass. Cleburne had already been thrown off his horse once, the usually nimble mount having lost its footing in the mire of the rain sodden fields, and Cleburne ending up in the mud. Now, covered in mud, and mad as hell to boot, the Irishman directed his troops into and around the muck-filled swamp, and into the assault. On came a thousand men their shoulders hunched against the maelstrom ahead, their fiery leader in front, his muddy sword pointing the way. With a roar they stormed into and through the tents of the Yankee camp, a tidal wave of gray, only to reel back in agony, their ranks blasted by the firestorm of shot and shell emitting from the camp's defenders. The hail of bullets and fire stunned the onrushing gray wave, stopping it in its tracks, and causing it to stream back into the muddy ravine, a trail of mud and blood-soaked bodies left in their wake.

Appler could see the gray-coated officer screaming at his men to try again. Appler watched in horrified awe as the Confederate officer, who miraculously had survived the Yankees' defensive volleys, his uniform covered in mud, pointed his sword directly at *him*, and shouted for his men to follow. With a roar the retreating rebels stopped and reversed their retreat. Now the mud smeared graybacks, their high-pitched screams reverberating in the air, charged along with their maddened leader. The blue clad defenders continued in their disciplined fire, Sherman's insistence on the continual drills paying huge dividends, their deadly accurate volleys carving huge swaths through the gray ranks. The backwoodsmen and farmboys from Tennessee and Mississippi fell back again, only to be reinspired to follow Cleburne a third time, the charismatic leader inspiring all by his personal bravery. Cleburne screamed a horrible oath, and charged up the muddy slope again, his boys following yet again.

Appler looked around. His men were holding their own, pouring fire into the gray ranks, mowing men down left and right. Yet still the enemy came on, inspired by the bearded, gray coated maniac that led them. Their high-pitched banshee-like screeches were terrifying, both in pitch and volume, the combination sending waves of terror up and down the dismayed colonel's spine. They were *still* coming, *right at him*! It was too much for the high-strung Appler.

"This is no place for us!" Appler screamed, dropping his sword. He turned and ran to a fallen tree, and fell to the ground behind it, placing its trunk between himself and the on-rushing gray hordes. His staff stared at him in horror, torn between continuing the fight and running, as they continued to exhort their men to continue the fight against the rebels. They watched as the enemy suddenly stopped their mad dash toward the Yankee defenders, only to form up into firing lines. Too late the Ohioans realized what was coming next.

The rebels had stopped, and for a long split second it was dead silent. Then the command *"Fire!"* rang out. A sheet of flame exploded from the rows of rebel muskets, the missiles screaming toward the terrified Fifty-Third's line, knocking down men like ten-pins. The screams of the wounded and the dying snapped what was left of Appler's already frazzled nerves.

"Retreat!" Appler jumped up and screamed. "Save yourselves!" He took to his heels, running from the scene of carnage. His panic-stricken men began to mill about, some throwing down their weapons and running after their commander, fleeing the fight. Others grimly took back up

their muskets, and prepared to stand their ground, come what may. They returned the enemy fire, raggedly at first, then more determinedly as more blue-coated troops joined the fight. The air became filled with projectiles, whizzing back and forth through the smoked-filled air, the missiles searching for victims on either side, neither side willing to give ground.

Sherman watched from a short distance away. He had noted the cowardice of the Fifty-Third's commander, but also the coolness of the remaining soldiers. It was also clear to Sherman that the remaining men were in serious need of help.

Sherman charged up to a row of cannons lined up near the crest of a hill, the battery's members immediately snapping to attention as Sherman drew near. The battery's officers were grimly watching the fighting, talking among themselves. Sherman immediately noted that the battery's guns were situated so as to have a clear field of fire on the advancing Confederate forces.

"Whose battery is this?" Sherman shouting, looking around at the assembled men. A young lieutenant stepped forward, a grim look on his face.

"General sir, it's mine, sir. Lieutenant Waterhouse, sir. I command it."

"Well Lieutenant, the enemy is attacking! This is no probe. They're a'coming! Set your guns to work. Give them as much shell as necessary, but if they come up close, hit them with your canister, and plenty of it!" (This last acted as a giant shotgun shell, spraying its targets with thousands of murderous chunks of metal, shredding whomever it hit into bloody pieces.)

"Yes sir, immediately, sir!" The cannon crews were already in motion. Within seconds the throaty roar of the assembled field pieces entered the fray, the blasts, great gouts of flame and smoke jumping from the mouths of the guns as their projectiles smashed into and knocked down the assembled Confederate troops as fast as the guns could fire. The Union artillery was a surprise, and had caught the rebel attack in their flank, and was smashing them up. Sherman noted the results with a grim smile.

"Hit them hard, boys! Don't let them regroup!" Sherman shouted, waving his cigar, and wincing in pain from the damaged fingers, the wound still bloody. "Damn that hurts!" Sherman looked at the damaged hand, flexing the fingers, relieved everything still worked. "At least their all still there." He muttered ruefully.

No time to worry about this now. Got to stop those boys down there. Got to get our boys some more help. Can't let them down, no sir, not like that fool colonel. I hope Grant's been notified that something's up. Damnation, I still don't believe this! "Johnny!"

"Yes sir, General. I'm right here." Somehow Taylor had managed to stay with Sherman during the mad dash up the hillside.

"Johnny, you make sure those guns keep firing. That is a direct order. Keep your eyes open and watch out for more troops coming out of those woods. If I don't get those boys some help, this will get really messy, real fast. I'll send someone to replace you, but for now, I need you to be my eyes and ears right here! When your replacement gets here you find me real quick . . . it may not be easy. I may be moving fast. You understand me, son?"

"Yes, General. I understand my orders." Taylor looked scared, but his voice was calm.

"Oh, one more thing, Lieutenant."

"Sir?"

Sherman stared straight into Taylor's dirty and sweaty face. "Watch out that damned elephant doesn't trample you like it did poor Tom."

Taylor smiled, his grin sending streaks through the grime on his face, and saluted Sherman. "Yes sir. Thank you, sir. It won't sir, but don't let it get you, either."

Sherman grinned and spurred his horse back down the hill in the direction of the Fifty-Third Ohio. The angry bees continued their mad voyages through the thickening air, their flight only stopping when they struck a tree, or a man's body. Screams filled the air, they being the abrupt exclamation points to the bullets' main sentences. Sherman reached the front line, only to see that the veterans of the Seventeenth Illinois, whose camp bordered the Ohio boys' camp, were now supplementing the shaken survivors of the Fifty-Third Ohio. At some places, no more than thirty feet separated the combatants, both sides exchanging verbal barbs along with the gunfire. Sherman could hear the Southerners hollering *"Bull Run,"* the Union boys shouting *"Donelson"* in return.

Got to get something on this hand. Sherman pulled on his cigar. More bullets whizzed by Sherman ducking in response. He heard more than felt one rip into his uniform, the missile tearing the shoulder strap in half, and scratching his shoulder. The piece of cloth flapped around on his shoulder.

Damn, that one was close! I better get off this horse for a minute. Sherman jumped down and leaned back against a tree. He heard his name being shouted, and looked up to see Captain William Reuben Rowley, one of Grant's aide-de-camps, riding up. Sherman pointed at the officer.

"Captain, you tell Grant if he has any men to spare, I can sure use them; if not, well, I'll do the best I can. We are holding them pretty well just now, pretty well, but it's hot as hell. You tell him that, Captain!"

"Yes sir, General. He wants to know. That's why I'm here. He's back at the landing. I'll get right back and tell him, immediately, sir!" Rowley spurred his horse, turning and riding hard back toward the river landing and Grant.

Well, that's good to know. Trust Sam to get right onto something. He must have heard the fire at his camp. Must be louder than I thought.

The once green meadow was now stained red with the blood of both sides. *Those boys got guts.* Sherman thought as he got back on his horse. He watched the gray ranks continue to lose men. He watched a gray whiskered officer scream orders as the remaining rebels began to pull back toward the imagined safety of the trees. Some men were trying to help their wounded comrades reach the imagined sanctuary of the woods. He noted with a professional detachment that those that reached the trees would continue to scream their defiance, even as their comrades fell to the ground, their wounds quickly staining the ground and the bark of the trees, crimson. He peered hard at the smoke, trying to separate the gray uniforms from the dirty smoke-filled air. He noted the flash from the guns' muzzles, their deadly lighting reaching out to smite the unfortunate victims.

"Shoot at the flashes, boys!" Sherman hollered. "That's where they're at!" His reasoning was that gave the green men a better point of reference to pick targets with.

The few remaining rebels still continued their fire from the edge of the creek, and from along the tree line. Suddenly Sherman felt his horse jerk, then stiffen, and then begin to fall. Realizing that the horse had been shot, Sherman kicked free and dropped from the stricken animal before it fell on him.

"General, you all right?" a young captain, his face a mask of sooty black gunpowder, grabbed onto Sherman's shoulder.

"Yes, but the horse ain't!' Sherman snapped, watching the mare kick in its death throes. "What's your regiment, Captain?"

"Seventeenth Illinois, sir. We're lined up just up that there hill, in support, sir." The officer pointed up the hill, toward the spot John Taylor and Waterhouse's battery continued to make it hot for the remaining attackers.

"Your name, Captain?"

"Jones, General, sir. Captain, Seventeenth Illinois."

"Well Captain, here's an order for you. You run up to those guns there on that ridge. You find Lieutenant Taylor. You tell Lieutenant Taylor where to find me and send him down here. I will be right here or about here anyway. Then you take your boys, and you provide infantry support for those guns up there, you back them up. Understand what I'm telling you?"

"Yes sir!"

"Captain, one more thing." Sherman paused for a moment, then continued, trying to make himself heard over the sound of the guns. "You tell those boys to shoot straight. You tell them I have confidence in their ability to knock those rebels back into those swamps. You give them hell, son. Last of all, you take care now, you hear me, Captain Jones?"

The last made the officer grin. He snapped off a salute. "Yes sir. Don't you worry now, General. We'll take care of things for you. You just watch!" Jones then took off, hollering for his men to follow. Sherman watched the Illinoisans charge up the hill, their banner fluttering as they surged up to the top and assumed their positions. It took but a few minutes before their muskets joined the fray, sending the crackling crescendo to new heights of fury. Sherman smiled as he watched the untried troops swing into action, their training taking over.

Sherman turned back to survey the field, his gaze sweeping over the gleaming wet grass of the meadow. The enemy's fire from the woods appeared to be slackening off. *Perhaps they're running out of ammunition over there*, he thought. His eyes continued their inspection of the field, and then stopped, his view arrested by the appearance of a new body of troops entering the swampy meadows.

Well, where the hell did, they come from? Well, there's no question now. They're serious about this. This is certainly no probe. He grinned, noting the difficulties the newcomers were having to cross the morass of the swampy meadows.

We can nail these boys too. His cigar bobbed up and down in his teeth. His ears detected the sound of approaching hoof beats. Johnny Taylor, relieved from his artillery duties, had arrived. Sherman wasting no time with pleasantries, began to speak.

"Lieutenant, I want you to ride to the opposite flank, to the other end of this line, and warn all the brigades in line to prepare for a general assault on their lines. They are to hold, *repeat, hold* their ground. Then you are to see to it that word is sent to Generals Prentiss and McClernand, advising them of the situation. Then I want you to go and advise General Grant of the present situation. I have been informed that he is at Pittsburg Landing. I have already sent one message, but you have been in the fighting yourself and you can give a more detailed explanation to this point. Oh, and one more thing, John?"

"Yes sir, General?" Taylor had been furiously scribbling down all the messages Sherman wanted sent.

"Find me another horse. Quickly."

Taylor looked up from his notes, his eyes glowing with a light and determination Sherman had not seen before in the young man. No longer a boy, Lieutenant Johnny Taylor was now a man, the transition having taken place in that iron forge known as combat. He had faced his first bullets, had tasted the acrid taste of gunpowder, had seen violent death first hand, and he had not run. He was a warrior.

"Take mine, General. I'll grab another. Don't worry, sir, I'll take care of all of this. I won't let you down!"

Sherman met Taylor's look, seeing the steel in the younger man's eyes. *I can only hope I don't get him killed*, he thought.

"Well, my boy." Sherman chuckled, a light note in his voice, "didn't I promise you all the fighting you could handle?"

Taylor grinned. "Yes, sir, you did!"

Sherman grinned back. "All right, get going! Find me when you're done."

Taylor saluted. "Yes sir!" He ran over to a rail fence where some horses, their backs saddled but empty of riders, were tethered, the nervous animals prancing in place. Taylor grabbed the reins of one, swung up, and galloped off.

Sherman watched for a moment, then swung up on Taylor's horse, wincing in pain from the injured hand. His eyes searched the enemy lines, probing, looking for weaknesses. He began to ride down the line of shooting men, his calmness evident to all, no evidence of the "old crazy Sherman" for anyone to see. He spoke calmly to all. His instructions clear, and concise. He carefully instructed the blue-coated soldiers to shoot low and watch for gun flashes in the smoky mist. He rode to the right, to where Buckland's brigade was situated. Buckland's men were sheltered by heavy timber, the natural cover preventing the now massed rebels, who were attempting to rush the federal lines, from seeing their true strength. Sherman spotted Buckland, busy positioning his men, and rode to his side.

"Well, Colonel, what have we heard?"

Buckland was surveying the field with his binoculars, pointing his men to their positions in order to meet the oncoming gray onslaught. "Good morning, General. Sir, I estimate that we're facing about four to five regiments at strength out there. It certainly looks like the enemy has decided to make a serious attempt to take this position. They want this camp."

Yes, they're serious all right. Sherman thought. *Well, so are we.* He grinned around his cigar at Buckland, then spoke. "Well Colonel, what do you think we should do about those five *determined* regiments?"

Buckland smiled back. He looked back at the Confederate battle lines, their flags, explosions of red and blue, mixing with the glistening shine of the bayonets in the bright morning sunshine. Their high-pitched yells echoed off the trees buttressing the Yankees' defense line. It was an inspiring and unnerving spectacle all at once.

Buckland looked back at Sherman. He noted the calmness in Sherman's face, the almost gentle look of joy, the steadiness in his hands. Sherman was now busy with the process of bandaging his wounded hand, his concentration focused on the wrapping of a cloth around the bloody hand. Buckland marveled at how the bullets zipping around Sherman's head were not distracting him at all. There was no fear evident at all, only that look of quiet determination. Sherman now looked at Buckland. He was waiting for an answer.

"Well, General, we'll let them know that they're in for a hell of a fight! Let them come. We'll take care of them. My boys are ready, primed, and waiting to give them hell! We have good ground here, good cover, and they have to come up that damned bloody slope to get at us. They will find that a very tall order, General."

Sherman nodded, pleased with Buckland's reply. A good answer, Colonel, good answer. Still, I need to get up some more artillery support for you. He continued to peruse the situation, his head on a swivel. I have to make sure that Hildebrand and McDowell aren't all smashed up. Got to check with Prentiss. McClernand possibly, too. They might have smashed right through to him. We never should have had all those green boys out in front like that! I'll bet when the rebs came storming through camp it couldn't have been pretty. Can't let these boys down. It's going to get really hot, really hot and heavy today, yes sir it is. Well, we have been pushing and pushing those boys, right down the river. I guess it was time for them to push back.

Sherman snorted, his cigar continuing to wiggle around in his clenched teeth, and the thought processes continuing. We got this hill. It's pretty good ground. They will have to come through those creeks and swamps, and then up that hill at us. We have got a good line of defense here on this ridge, and good natural cover. It helps. Those rebs sure are firing a lot of ammunition. It's like trying to walk through a hailstorm of bullets out here.

Buckland seems all right. Sherman watched his subordinate direct his men. His orders were clear, and crisp. Sherman noted with approval how quickly the men had followed Buckland's orders, throwing up additional defenses, hay bales and fallen trees, to supplement the natural ones. *His boys are doing well, the brigade seems to have handled this assault, but I'll bet there's more coming. We've got to hold, give those other boys, the other divisions, time to come up. Got to give Sam time to get those other boys in place, get them here. Buckland's smart to throw up that breast work of logs and hay bales. This way he is keeping those other boys out there occupied. They can't get any closer, at least not yet.*

No, so far they can't get any closer. They keep trying to get up, run through the camps, but that swamp out there is holding them up, thank God. They all have to split up to get around it. Thank God for this hill! Sherman lifted his binoculars to his eyes, scanning the Confederate ranks with an experienced eye. He stole another look at Buckland. The other man was busy with his responsibilities.

He's fine. I'm getting out of here. There's more work to do elsewhere. I'm sure. I think he can handle this. It looks like those are Tennessee boys out there coming at us. They got some artillery up, at least it sounds like it. They're doing some shooting, but it's too long. They're missing the front of the lines, but they must be tearing up the back of that hill some. I think they're just as confused as we are. Good, that will help some.

Sherman headed back toward Shiloh Church and Waterhouse's Battery. He felt he needed to check, to reassure himself that the Yankee batteries would keep up their fire. Suddenly something in the distance caught his eye. He lifted his glasses to his eyes and stared through them, his eyes trying to pierce the smoke, his eyes straining to hear through the noise of the battle. Another movement caught his eye and he strained to see through the grayness of the smoky air, trying to see what it was that had caught his attention. Another movement in the smoke, and Sherman could see what it was; more gray and butternut clad troops emerging from the smoke and mist.

Damn, here they come again! Now they're coming on the double-quick! God, look at all that infantry! There're thousands of them! What's going on behind me, damnation?! No wait, here's Hicks!

Colonel Stephen Hicks commanded the Fortieth Illinois Volunteers. The regiment was attempting to set itself up in a battle line on the edge of the embattled Union encampments. Its commander was busy exhorting his men, desperately attempting to put his men in place to stop the approaching enemy. Sherman rode over to Hicks, and leaned over to shout into Hicks ear, the noise of battle nearly drowning out Sherman's words.

"Colonel Hicks, I need you and your regiment to hold and check the enemy; I need you to *hold* them with your regiment until I can bring up the rest of the division. Can you do that for me, Colonel? We will need your help, I need you to do this, if we are to slow down this enemy attack. Can you help me?"

Hick was known to be a resolute soul. He eyed Sherman, and noted the cigar, so often seen bobbing around like a cork in water, now was parked tightly in the side of Sherman's mouth, not moving a whit. He looked over the smoke-grimed uniform, the half-torn off epaulet on Sherman's shoulder, the bloodstained bandaged hand, and saw that none of it was disturbing Sherman's concentration. Hicks noted the clearness of his commander's eyes, no fear evident there, just sheer determination blazing from the dark eyes. There was no trace of fear in Sherman's voice, no shakiness in his voice, nothing but calm resoluteness ringing through. Sherman was angry, but not spooked. Hicks replied in the same vein.

"I reckon we can, General. You just tell me what you want, and me and my boys will take care of it, right off."

"I want you to charge them, charge them and slow them down. Stop them if you can. Now."

Hicks saluted. "Yes sir. I will take the necessary steps *immediately*, sir. By your leave, General?" Sherman nodded. Turning to his men, Hicks raised his sword, and shouted.

"Come on my Suckers, let's go! Fix bayonets! Glory to the great state of Illinois! Charge!"

Hicks ran out to a position in front of his men, and began to run down the slope, his screaming men following, their regimental flags streaming straight behind them, the banners' colors bright, as they rumbled down the rocky slope at the advancing Confederate line. As Sherman watched, the Federals slammed into the approaching gray ghosts, a melee quickly ensuing as the rival forces rammed at each other, bayonet, sword, and rifle butt mixing with equal passion amongst the passing bullets. It was a sight to see.

My God, those are brave boys! Brave, but not enough. I've got to get them more help. My God, what a fire the enemy is laying down. They sure don't seem to be concerned about conserving ammunition, by thunder!

Sherman spotted Major Samuel M. Bowman, commanding the Fourth Illinois Cavalry, and accompanied by his staff, riding toward where Sherman was seated astride his horse. Bowman reined up, saluting Sherman as he did. Bowman noted Sherman's blood stained and bandaged hand, and the bullet-ripped epaulet.

"General, you all right?"

"No damn it Major, I'm not!"

Easy! No, I didn't mean it way. Careful, they'll get upset and scared if you do.

Sherman collected himself. "Sorry Major, no I'm all right, but I need you to give me some extra men for messengers and orderlies. One of mine has already been shot, and I sent Lieutenant Taylor off on a mission for me. Can you help me with this? Two, three, should be enough."

Bowman smiled, and nodded, relief evident on his face. "Certainly General. Sir, you take what you need. Are there any other orders?"

"Take your boys up that there road, (Pittsburg-Corinth) and cover the infantry's flank. Help hold those people off. Do your best, give 'em hell, but if you see any additional heavy troop concentrations coming down that road, you send a rider back quick as you can and let me know! The devil's to pay, sure enough! Any questions, Major?"

"No sir, But General, I beg to report sir. It's a real mess down there, down along those creeks on our right, sir. They, the rebs I mean, have broken through into Hildebrand's rear. Their, us I mean, got so scared they were just running off, and the rebs were on us so fast some of the boys barely had time to grab their horses, saddles, and arms, and clear out. Hell, General, some of the team drivers was so scared they just cut the traces off the wagons, jumped on, and runned off."

Damn, I knew we were in trouble out there. So Hildebrand got smashed up. Hope he's all right. Sherman took a deep breath, then spoke.

"Thank you, Major. I know you will do your best. Anything else?"

"No sir, General. I will send some men to you, directly, sir."

"Thank you, Major. Now, move."

Bowman saluted, turned to the captain riding beside him, and quickly issued instructions. The junior officer then turned his horse, and dashed back to the waiting column of horsemen, and returned with several mounted troopers. Bowman, with a quick nod to Sherman, spurred his horse away, the rest of his staff following. Bowman bellowed out an order, and the remaining column of troopers quickly fell in behind him, the whole group moving at a quick trot down the road toward the flank and the enemy.

The captain saluted Sherman and spoke. "General, these men will serve as your couriers."

Sherman nodded his assent. "Good. Thank you, Captain. Rejoin your command. I'm sure the major will have need of you."

The young officer saluted. "Thank you, sir!" He quickly rode off in pursuit of the Illinois cavalry.

Sherman glanced at the young would be messengers. They returned his glance with nervous ones of their own, uncomfortable in his presence, and in their new roles. "Don't worry boys. I don't bite." He grinned wolfishly at them. "Stay close. I'm going to need you." He headed back toward the hill occupied by Waterhouse's battery.

The Illinois men had been joined by another artillery unit, Battery B, of the First Illinois Light Artillery. The First Illinois boys set themselves up across the road, just down the road from the Shiloh Church, and across the road from Waterhouse's battery. Together, the two units bracketed the road, and commanded the area in front of the log church, facing south down the Pittsburg-Corinth Road, toward Rhea's Field. The two Chicago-based artillery units were doing their level best to raise havoc with the Confederate attempts to rush their lines. The Confederate forces had brought up a Confederate battery in support, and the rebel gunners had taken up the duel, fire and smoke filling the air between the opposing guns. The air was heavy with a strange mix of shrapnel, one that was a mix of lead and wood, the wood coming from the tree limbs being blasted into long toothpicks by the singing cannons. A Confederate shell arched high over the field and dived straight down into a waiting Union caisson. The resulting explosion blazed high with a frightful blast of wind, knocking flat those within close range, and causing others at the Yankee guns to duck momentarily. Those who had ducked quickly sprang back to their guns, resuming the deadly dance, Waterhouse's men adding their voices to their cannons' screaming defiance of the enemy artillery.

Sherman grinned at the Yankee gunners show of defiance. It was good to see that even though some of the infantry units had fallen apart and had run at the first shock of battle, other units, with the help of artillery support, were holding their own and not allowing the rebel units to advance any further into the Yankee lines.

122 | DANIEL F. KORN

Keep it up, boys, keep it up. Sherman thought to himself. Now if we can just hold them there until we can get up some more support. Those Chicago boys and their guns are doing a good job of putting up a good scrape. Sherman saw the gun crews pointing at something that had caught their attention, something in the south end of the field. What do they see? Better take a closer look.

Sherman lifted his glasses to his eyes and peered through them, again trying to see through the smoky rays of sunlight toward the south end of Rhea's Field. He soon spotted the large mass of troops moving slowly through the wet fields, but with purpose, northward across the field toward the woods bordering the field.

They're trying to flank us. They might be in for a surprise. Peabody's boys should be over there. They may give those rebels a rude awakening. Now if we can just hold them here, and Buckland's brigade does their job, we should be all right. All right, just keep up that fire, boys, and keep your heads down too.

Sherman turned and looked back in the direction of the creek known as Shiloh Branch. I need to check on Hildebrand. I'm worried about that brigade. They're still out there in front a piece, and it's a mess out there, it truly is. I should have known better then to expect them to hold. Got to get more help out there.

That creek (Shiloh Branch) will slow them down. Hell, it already has, but it's not enough. I'm glad those two batteries are there. Those boys are keeping it good and hot for the rebs.

Right now, they are saving us, but for how long? How long before the enemy brings up more men? He's got artillery too. I wonder what's taking Beauregard so long to get more of his own up? I don't think he planned for all this wet ground. Sherman grinned and continued to sweep the ground with his glasses.

Buckland's all right, out on the right. He seems to be able. He's got good boys, Ohio boys. Still, I need to get more strength out there, out to the right.

By thunder, our boys are putting up a hell of a fight! Trouble is, so is the enemy! Well, I should know, Southern boys don't lack for courage.

Got to keep cool, steady, buy time for Grant. We'll win this, but I've got to buy time for Sam. I'm sure he's on his way. We can fix this. Damn it, I wish I had gone ahead and made more defensive provisions instead of listening to Smith!

Sam will send everyone he's got. We just have to hold on until then and continue to make it hot for them. We can do that. We have to. Got no choice.

"Damn this hand hurts."

GRANT

Savannah Landing
April 6, 1862 7:00 A.M.

Major General Ulysses S. Grant was in a poor mood. His leg was paining him greatly, and thus it was difficult for him to get around. A superb horseman, he had suffered an ignominious fall when his horse had slipped and fallen on wet ground, trapping Grant as it fell, and pinning his leg under the poor beast. His ankle had swollen so much that the surgeon had to cut away the boot, (a not-so-trivial thing to Grant, known as he was for his frugal ways). Now, Grant was forced to hobble about with the aid of a makeshift crutch, something that Grant found both annoying and embarrassing.

Grant's previous military experience had been a series of ups and downs. A graduate of West Point, he had become good friends with now Confederate commanders, James Longstreet, George Pickett, and Simon Buckner. While an average student in the classroom, his true skills showed on horseback and in the field. He had served with distinction in the Mexican War, fighting at El Molino del Ray, (the King's Mill), and had taken a large part in the storming of Chapultepec Castle at Mexico City, where his reconnaissance work, initiative, and management of an artillery unit had won him laurels. Yet, like so many others, it was in the peacetime Army while holding a series of less than distinguished positions that Grant began to slide down a hill, finally ending up in California as an army paymaster. There his loneliness and forced separation from his beloved wife, Julia, would eventually drive him to the bottle, incurring for him a reputation as a drunk that would follow him, somewhat unfairly, for the rest of his life. He left the military in a manner of some disgrace, and worked at a series of civilian jobs, with varying degrees of success. When the war broke out, he was working as a leather goods clerk in a family owned operation. He decided to attempt a return to the military, reasoning that experienced officers may have good opportunities to succeed. Rejoining the Army as a captain, Grant soon received a promotion to colonel. He began to rise rather rapidly through the ranks, becoming a brigadier general in May of 1861. A quiet unassuming individual, his carelessness about his appearance and dress led some to believe that he was somewhat slow witted. They were wrong, for that oft shabby appearance concealed a razor-sharp mind.

Grant was not a charismatic leader like Johnston, not at all. He believed in systematic training, good communications with his men, and a moderate approach to discipline. While not someone to boast of tales of glory, he was a born leader who understood that everyone yearns for a chance to succeed. So far, his farm boys-turned-soldiers had been willing to follow him anywhere.

Even Grant would have to admit that his recent successes at Forts Henry and Donelson had gone a little to his head. He knew that his new nickname that of "Unconditional Surrender Grant," had been splashed all over the Northern newspapers, and that his picture had even made the cover of Harper's magazine. Not bad for a former leather goods clerk.

He had made some changes to his appearance and habits. His characteristically long beard was gone, replaced by a well-groomed shorter version. His uniforms were better, tailored for him, and he made more of an effort to keep them cleaner, though not much. His newfound fame had even changed his smoking habits. A pipe smoker, he began to appear everywhere with a cheroot stuck in his mouth. In this, he was much like Sherman, his subordinate. The cigars were gifts, many boxes bestowed upon Grant by the admirers of his newly won fame and victories.

A prodigious whittler, he had developed the habit of when a march or a battle was in progress, sitting by the roadside, chewing and smoking his cigars, carving on a decreasing pile of sticks, even as the piles of shavings grew around him. His troops did not like to see him engaged in such activities, knowing that it always meant hard fighting.

He was not a friend of fixed, defensive fortifications, a leftover from his Mexican War days. He had made little effort to encourage his six division commanders to build defensive positions around their encampments. Those encampments occupied the woods and meadows between the two creeks near Pittsburg Landing. In fact, Grant had been somewhat complacent about the whole situation, having set his headquarters a good nine miles up the river at Savannah, occupying the beautiful Cherry mansion while he awaited Major General Don Carlos Buell to arrive with his men. The plan was to then take their combined forces and then move on to take Corinth, Mississippi, their armies holding a true superiority in numbers over the local Confederate forces.

There had been reports of enemy cavalry in the area, and Sherman had sent him reports concerning enemy activity, but nothing seemed to be too alarming. Sherman had even sent ten prisoners that his patrols had captured, but Grant had not even bothered interrogating the prisoners. He didn't think that there was anything they could tell him that he didn't already know about the enemy forces. He was not aware of Johnston's presence, nor that of Johnston's troops in the area. He did not believe that Beauregard was crazy enough to force battle with them but would instead try to assume a defensive posture. Grant had already wired Henry Halleck, his superior, and the department commander, that there was nothing to worry about, that he felt that there was not the slightest chance of being attacked in his camps. All was quiet, on this western front.

Grant sat at the breakfast table, reading the morning reports, chewing on his breakfast of dry toast. Not much of an eater, he was attempting to ignore the pain in his leg by concentrating on the reports and the food. Suddenly his quiet

Sunday morning was interrupted by the sound of suspicious sounding thunder in the direction of Pittsburg Landing, freezing him as he lifted his coffee cup to his lips.

I thought all the storms were finished. Grant thought. He turned in his chair to look out the dining room's big bay window. *No, no clouds out there.* He stopped chewing and began to concentrate on the distant rumble.

No, no that's not thunder after all. It sounds like . . .?

The door of the dining room slammed open. Grant's chief of staff, Colonel Webster, stepped quickly into the room.

"General, do you hear that? It sounds like . . ."

"Artillery." Grant finished the sentence for him. *But where?* He thought to himself. *Crump's or Pittsburg Landing?* He put down the coffee cup. "Colonel, go get the rest of the staff together. We better get going. Tell the captain of the *Tigress* (Grant's command vessel) to fire up the boilers. We need to take a ride. Captain Rowley!" Another of Grant's aides, Captain William Rowley, stuck his head into the room. "We need to get a move on. Help me out of this chair! We've got to do something about that!" He jerked his head in the direction of the distant thunder. Rowley sprang to help pull the chair back, Grant pulling himself to his feet and reaching for the crutch. "Hurry gentlemen, I believe the ball may be in motion and we need to make haste. Colonel, help me get this sword and sash on." Webster jumped to Grant's side, helping him to buckle on the cumbersome sword.

Grant stumbled out to the mansion's veranda, silently cursing both his leg, and the horse that had fallen on him. The rest of the staff was frantically stuffing maps and equipment into cases and running back and forth to the boat landing. As they quickly loaded up the riverboat, the ship's boilers were already beginning to fire up, her smokestacks steaming in the early mist of the cool morning.

Grant stumped down the steps off the veranda, hurrying as fast as his crutch would let him down the slope toward the dock and the waiting vessel. *What a time to have a bum leg,* he fumed. *It's going to be a deuce of a time getting on and off a horse. I have to do something with this infernal crutch. Got to take it, I'm sure I will need it. Tarnation, what a time to get caught with our pants down!*

We've no time to waste. Thank God Sherman is down there. I never thought old Beauregard would ever try us here. I thought for sure he would wait for us to come to him. To come get him. It made sense for him to fight a defensive war. Well, he sure fooled us, fooled me! We can't make this mistake again. God, I hope Sherman's all right. His boys are right out front.

The crew of the waiting steamboat was busy, quickly clearing the decks, and throwing the mooring lines off the boat as Grant stumped up the gangplank. The ship's boilers were now fully fired up, rich black smoke now pouring from her twin stacks. The last of his staff was clambering aboard, the clerks' and orderlies' arms filled with last minute items. Grant pointed to the river, in the direction of the now louder gunfire.

"I believe we are ready, Captain?" Grant waved to the river boat's pilothouse, her master already at the wheel. "I believe we may be needed at Pittsburg Landing. Let us make haste to get there. Quickly, Captain." Immediately the last of the lines were cast off and the boat pushed out from the dock. She slipped quickly into the rushing current, her huge paddle wheels beginning to turn, faster and faster, driving her toward the waiting conflict.

Grant turned to a waiting aide. "Major, just as soon as we land, I want you to get on the telegraph and send two messages. One is to go to General Buell. Tell him our Savannah meeting is canceled. Instead, he is to bring the rest of his troops up to Pittsburg Landing, post haste. The second is to go to (Brigadier) General (William) Nelson, (a former naval officer and physically a mountain of a man, who now commanded Buell's lead brigade.) He is to march his brigade from their camp, (at Savannah), to a point opposite Pittsburg Landing, across the river, and to be ready to cross as soon as possible. We might need him before this day is done."

"Yes sir, General. I will take care of it just as soon as we land, sir."

"The moment we land, Major. The very moment we land." Grant's voice was hard. The aide looked up, a little disturbed by the uncharacteristically hard edge to Grant's voice. It was not characteristic of him to be that way.

"Yes sir, General. I will take care of it immediately upon our arrival, sir."

It's not his fault. Grant suddenly smiled. "Sorry Major, I know you will. Captain Rowley?"

"Sir?"

"I want you off this boat as soon as we reach Pittsburg Landing. Ride and find Sherman and get his report on what is going on up front."

Grant thought to himself; Cump will be on top of it. He will have the picture, knowing him.

"Yes sir, General.' Rowley replied. "The instant we land, sir."

"General Grant?"

Grant turned to see the river boat captain standing, hatless, in front of him. The red-faced old river-man quickly saluted. The old man shook with barely concealed excitement, and Grant smiled at the sight.

"Captain, how much longer to Crump's Landing?" Crump's was on the way to Pittsburg Landing, about halfway between Savannah and Pittsburg Landing. The captain wiped his hot, red, perspiring face, the perspiration caused by the man's excited state and the effort to rapidly start up the ship's boilers and get her ready for the necessarily quick departure. "Just a few minutes, General, just a few minutes more. It be just around the big bend in the river ahead, just ahead of us now. We'll be there in a short while, just a short while . . ."

Grant suddenly grimaced, the injured ankle flaring in pain. He looked around, spotted a bench, and clumped over to it, sitting heavily down on the plank bench. "Good. Swing up close, close as you can, but don't stop, just slow down for a minute. I need to get a message to General (Lew) Wallace to be ready for what may happen." Wallace's division was camped at Crump's Landing.

"Yes sir, General. Don't stop, just slow a bit. As you wish, General Grant."

Grant looked up. The sounds emitting in the distance were increasing in intensity, the boom of artillery clearly heard over the rumble of the steam boat's engines.

"Faster, Captain. Faster."

The old river-man snapped off a salute, immediately spun around screaming orders for the boiler men to pour on the wood. The old river steamer's smokestacks erupted with a new intensity as she took the bone in her teeth, fairly flying now, her paddle wheels churning the brown water into a brown froth as she surged ahead. Those standing on deck grabbed for something to hold on to, the officers and soldiers grabbing on with one hand to the ship rails, the other busy holding onto their hats. They roared through the muddy Tennessee waters, the wake from the ship's rapid passage slamming into the banks lining the river's edge. Grant mentally noted the new leaves and blooms blossoming on the trees and bushes lining the river, their trailing vines being swept onto the shore as the fast-moving vessel left them in her wake.

We make a great target. Grant thought to himself, gritting as a new bolt of pain ripped through leg. Hope there's no stray Confederate horse batteries sitting around near the shore line. One shot through the boilers at the rate we are going, and we'll all be swimming for it, those of us who don't blow up with the ship or sink with what's left of her. That would be a problem. Never was much of a swimmer. Don't suppose it would matter much. I'd probably just sink away.

God, I hope Sherman's all right. I think that's Crump's up ahead. It looks like Wallace is out there waiting for me. Good.

Grant was right. General Lew Wallace was standing on the hurricane deck of the *Jesse K. Bell*, his own command vessel, awaiting Grant. He too, had heard the distant thunder, deduced what it probably was, and realized that Grant would also hear it, and make haste to reach the fight. Grant looked up to the pilothouse, waved his arm, and shouted.

"Captain, please forgive me, but I do want you to stop. Just pull right beside the other boat. I do need to talk to General Wallace for a moment. Be ready to go the instant we are done." Grant pulled himself to his feet and clumped over to the *Tigress's* rail as the captain expertly slowed his vessel down and swung it alongside the other waiting steam boat. Lines were quickly tossed across to hold the two vessels together as Grant looked up at Wallace and waved.

"Good morning, General Wallace. Fine morning, is it not?"

Lew Wallace looked down from his perch high on the other vessel, smiled, and saluted Grant. "Good morning, General Grant, sir. Yes, a fine morning, a fine morning indeed. Sounds like something's happening down the river. Your orders, sir?"

"I want you to put your men on alert. Be ready for a possible attack on your lines. The enemy may be coming at you. They may not be also. Be ready to move and move fast when I need you. Understand?"

Wallace gestured behind him toward the shoreline. Grant looked over to see the hustle and bustle of troops preparing to move. "Sir, my brigades are already being concentrated again, ready to go. We just need orders, sir."

Grant waved, a deprecatory gesture. "Just wait here for further orders, General, they'll be coming. I'll let you know, just as soon as I know something." He looked again at the *Tigress's* captain. "All right Captain let's get this boat going again. Fast."

Grant sat back down, this time in a deck chair that had suddenly appeared. The mooring lines were quickly pulled in and the *Tigress* continued down the river on her mission, Grant studying the shore line, looking for signs of the enemy.

It's almost 8:30. That firing has been going on for some time, Grant thought to himself. Well, we should be there soon. Damn, I wish we were there now, blast that infernal Beauregard!

"General, here comes a messenger boat." Rowley pointed down the river. A steamer was racing toward them, her whistle wailing away. It was obvious that she was coming toward them, and soon the *John Warner* pulled up beside the *Tigress*, a plank quickly run out, and a boyish lieutenant scrambled aboard the *Tigress*.

"I'm looking for General Grant!" The young officer stammered.

"Right here son." Grant lifted a hand. "What have you got for me?"

The officer saluted. "Lieutenant Brown, sir. General (W. H. L.) Wallace's compliments. The Army's camps are under a general attack. General Wallace wishes for me to tell you that the right and center are being driven back, and that the enemy is in great force, sir."

"Anything else."

"No, sir. I am sorry, General Grant, that's all I can tell you, sir."

Grant did not move. He sat quietly, digesting the news. Then he settled back in the chair, his face calm and placid in repose. He then looked up at the sky, the thick black smoke from the steamboat's twin smoke stacks passing through it in big clumps of dark clouds.

"Oh, that's all-right Lieutenant. When we get there, why, we'll just surround the enemy, lad."

Everyone's face broke out in a collective grin at Grant's supposed joke. They quickly sobered up when they realized he wasn't smiling. The two boats quickly separated, the *Tigress* continuing her race against time. Grant resumed his observation of the shore line passing by, watching, looking, thinking.

Hold on, Cump. We're coming.

BRAGG

Rhea Field
April 6, 1862 7:00 A.M.

Braxton Bragg was absolutely furious. His three divisions, ten thousand men spread over five brigades, had become totally fouled up. Bragg had attempted to implement Beauregard's complicated battle plan, only to find as Bragg had feared, it was just too complicated for his boys to follow. It was far more suited for trained, professional troops, not for Bragg's rough farm boys and backwoodsmen who were supposed to follow it. It was just as Bragg had feared it would be.

Bragg's men had started off following Beauregard's directive to the letter. Bragg had started his advance one-half hour after Hardee's men had moved out. Bragg's was the second wave, a thousand yards behind Hardee's second wave. At first things went fine, the men moving smartly, but now with the swampy, broken terrain, the noise of combat rolling over them in waves, the smoky gunfire mixing with the April morning mists, Hardee's boys were having enormous difficulty in maintaining their front, Ruggle's lead division having to tramp through and fight their way through the dense thickets west of the Pittsburg-Corinth Road. As a result, Bragg's men were forced to slow down, and as a result, Bragg watched as Hardee's attack, so carefully designed to be a right-wing wheel upon the Yankee flank, began to disintegrate into a frontal assault on the Yankee lines. Bragg watched helplessly as Cleburne's proud brigade was systematically being destroyed in a series of useless attacks upon the right flank. Bragg could see the gap that was developing between Cleburne's right flank, and the rest of Hardee's corps.

Beauregard's grandiose plan had called for the Confederate Army to make a magnificent charge in three waves, each corps advancing over the front in one great line, first Hardee's, then Bragg's, then Polk's with Breckinridge's in support to go in where needed. Now because of all the delays, Bragg's was not ready to do their job.

"Damnation, if the Yankees spot that gap and stick a division in there, we could lose everything before we've barely gotten started." Bragg fumed as he watched, his famous temper on the verge of an explosion. His corps, so systematically trained by Bragg, was not ready to move when needed. His brigades were all out of line. On the far left, (Colonel Preston) Pond's Brigade was lagging far behind, caught in all the swampy brush of Shiloh Branch. (Colonel Randal) Gibson's Brigade was also late, although Bragg knew that at least in part, he was responsible for the delay, having ordered changes in the position of the hapless brigade not once, but *twice*. Now, only one brigade, (Brigadier General) Patton Anderson's was in place, ready to support Cleburne's attack. Bragg looked at his watch. 8:00.

"Damn, this is not supposed to be like this!" Bragg stormed. "I don't have the men here to properly send in this attack! Here we stand, within sight of the fighting, the enemy right *there* in front of us, and all I have is *one* brigade, just *one* to meet the enemy! I need men! *Where* are my brigades? *What* is taking so long?"

"General, it's a pretty bad mess out there, sir." Patton Anderson was standing by Bragg's side. "The Yankees have got some good artillery in place and are using it well. Hell General, my Florida and Louisiana boys had a hell of a time getting through that swampy ground and those thickets. When that Yankee artillery started dropping those shells in on my simple Florida boys, why, they just panicked a bit, and started running for the rear. I had a deuce of a time getting them regrouped, but we did." The former United States Marshall and congressman chuckled at the memory.

"General Anderson, it's a mess for everyone!" Bragg retorted. "Hardee's boys are taking a horrific pounding up there, just horrific. My God man, they're getting cut to pieces! We need to get up there and support them!"

"Yes sir. Sorry, I didn't mean to imply . . ."

"Yes General, I know that." Bragg cut him off, continuing to alternate looks through his field glasses at the carnage on the field with looks behind him to see if more of his troops were coming up behind him. His anger continued to grow as he watched Cleburne's men steadily being ripped apart.

"My God, General Anderson, just look at those brave boys!" Bragg hollered." Go, boys, go!" The Arkansas, Mississippi, and Tennessee regiments were continuing in their futile efforts to advance. Bragg pointed as one gray-coated officer, a major in the Fifteenth Arkansas, boldly advanced in front of his men in a desperate effort to lead them on. He was blazing at the Union line with his revolver, screaming for his men to come on. Bragg and Anderson watched in horrified awe, as a Yankee volley targeted and blasted the brave officer into bloody shreds, his bravery rewarded by death.

Buckland was charged with defending this sector, and his Yankee troops were contesting the enraged Southerners with all they had, firing from behind every tree, rock, and log, using the gullies and ravines for what protection they could, and contesting every inch of that deadly space. There was nothing being held back, and both sides were scratching and clawing with everything they had.

"General, look behind you!" Anderson shouted. "Down the Corinth Road!"

Bragg turned around. Troops, gray troops, were marching down the main Corinth Road.

"Those are Polk's men, not ours! Russell's Brigade!" Anderson exclaimed, seeing the proudly displayed flags of the Eleventh Louisiana.

"Polk's? He's the *third* wave!" Bragg replied. "They're not even supposed to be here yet! They must have passed our boys on the way. My God, we are all fouled up! Well, no matter, he's going in *now!*" Bragg made his decision, tired of all the delays.

Colonel R. M. Russell rode proudly in front of his men, his Louisiana troops striding with purpose up the wooded road. Russell rode up to Bragg, saluting Bragg with a flourish of his broad brimmed hat.

"General Bragg, my compliments, sir. We appear to be early. May we be of service?"

Bragg snorted. "We've waited long enough!' Bragg rode out into the Pittsburg Road in front of Russell's column, forcing them to stop. "Colonel, get your men in position. You're not waiting, you're going in now, with Anderson's brigade. Cleburne's boys are being destroyed! We must give them some support. Damn, we have to do something about that blasted Yankee battery! Let's go get them. Get them lined up and step off. No, go man, go!"

Russell saluted. "Yes sir, General Bragg, immediately, sir." Russell turned to face his men, and shouted, "All right boys, you heard the General!" Quickly, his men began to stream into line off the road, the lieutenants and sergeants busy with placement, the men marching into place to the right of Anderson's waiting men.

Now we might be able to do something! Bragg thought to himself. Now instead of one brigade there will be two brigades coming to support Cleburne. We'll see how well those Yankee lines surrounding that damned (Shiloh) church handle fresh troops. They got to be exhausted up there, and this might just be enough. Now, by thunder, we'll show them what our boys can do!

"Go boys, go!" Bragg thundered, sensing that the Union defenses on Shiloh Church knoll were about to deal with a new savagery as the battle for Rhea's Field was about to enter a whole new phase.

Two thousand rebel voices screamed their high-pitched defiance of the Yankee shot and shell. The well-ordered lines began their advance, ignoring the desperate fire being thrown at them.

"Look at them!" Bragg exclaimed, his face red with emotion. "Brave boys! Follow them! Push them up boys, push them up! Send in the remaining brigades as soon as they arrive. I'm following the attack!"

"General Bragg, good news, sir. We have finally gotten up more artillery support."

"Where?" Bragg shouted, barely able to keep his emotions under control.

"East of this (Pittsburg-Corinth) road. In the trees, Hodgson's Battery. Louisiana artillery. They're lined up with Shoup's Arkansas boys and their guns. They're just waiting for the word."

"Well, what are they waiting for? Turn them loose, by God, and tell them to shoot the hell out of those Yankee guns. Shoot up that line and blow them to hell!" Bragg sputtered, turning to ride off and follow the attack, hoping for good results.

Unfortunately, as he watched, Bragg saw that Anderson's and Russell's brigades were finding out what Cleburne had already learned. Buckland had chosen a good defensive position. The swampy ravines and heavy foliage of the dense thickets and underbrush were forcing the well-ordered Confederate lines to break up in order to pass through the dense growth and swampy ground. As a result, the Confederate troops were having a hard time bringing concentrated force against the beleaguered Yankee positions, who were keeping up a very concentrated fire up against the attack.

"General, your too close to the front." One of his aides was attempting to pull on Bragg's reins, trying to get Bragg to stop.

"Damnit Lieutenant, let go of the horse!" Bragg snarled. "Just attack, and that front will move ahead, and I won't be too close!" Bragg raised up on his horse and pointed with his sword at the enemy-occupied ridge. "C'mon boys, move forward! Attack! *Attack, men, attack!*" It was becoming a case of Southern dash and desire against Northern pluck and endurance.

Russell's lead regiment, the Eleventh Louisiana, stumbled toward the Federal lines. The slippery slopes leading out of the ravines were making it harder for Russell's and Anderson's other regiments to keep up. The Eleventh was getting too far ahead, and her companies were losing touch in the nearly impenetrable thickets. The wings of the attack were becoming disjointed. As the first gray troops broke through the underbrush, they suddenly saw the camps of the Fifty-third Ohio standing in front of them. The mixed bag of Louisiana and a few Tennessee boys stormed by the bullet riddled remains of the old Rhea cabin, running over the multi-colored carpet of dead and wounded comrades left by Cleburne's earlier attacks.

Suddenly the air was torn apart by a massive musket volley from the Yankee lines hidden on the other side of the ravaged camp. In a flash, the Eleventh Louisiana disintegrated, the horrified survivors screaming and fleeing back toward the rear, running into and through the following regiments, tearing great gaps in Anderson's following regiments that not even the Yankee guns had been able to do.

Oh, my God, they'll panic the entire line! Bragg spurred his horse forward. The entire remaining line was thrown into confusion by the panicked Eleventh. The other units began to falter, beginning to turn and follow the Eleventh backwards. The entire attack was in danger of stopping and being thrown back. Bragg rode right into the middle of the mess of panicked soldiers, men bouncing off the sides of his horse in their frenzied attempts to flee the carnage.

"Stop men, stop! Don't show your backs to the enemy! This is not our way, go back go back!" Bragg flailed desperately about with the flat of his sword, raining blows on the cowering troops, trying to stem the flood of gray. The Yankee fire continued to pour down on the frenzied masses of troops, not slackening in the least.

Soldiers were scrambling back, left and right. Bragg cursed as he recognized the flags of the Eleventh Louisiana.

"Damn them!" He thundered, his face a glowing red sea of rage "I should have known better then to trust Polk's men! They're just a mob! Damn them! Stop you cowards, turn around and face the enemy!" He continued to rain blows down with the flat of his sword, the blows striking the backs of the fleeing men, without any good.

"General, look out!"

Bragg's horse suddenly stumbled, and then quickly fell, pinning Bragg under it. A Yankee sharpshooter's bullet, intended for Bragg, had instead struck the horse in the forehead, killing the poor animal instantly. Bragg swore as he tried to pull free, his body slipping on the muddy ground, his face grimacing in pain.

"General, are you hurt?" It was Russell.

"Hell, yes damnit! Get me out from under this poor beast!" Soldiers quickly pulled Bragg free, all ducking as the Yankee bullets whizzed all around. Bragg gingerly stood up, feeling his leg.

"Can you stand sir? Can you walk?" Russell watched as Bragg took a few tentative steps.

"Just get me another damned horse!" Bragg winced in pain. The leg was badly bruised.

Another aide quickly dismounted, handing Bragg the reins to his animal. Bragg nodded his thanks, and slowly swung up on the horse, the others helping him to mount up. He looked at the assembled officers and men, then back out across the bullet torn field at the smoke wreathed ridge. The Yankee line was continuing its fire, the Confederate attack continuing to fall back in disarray. Bragg looked at Russell.

"Get this line stabilized!" Bragg stormed; his eyes boring into Russell's. "Keep going, *forward!*" He turned, as did the others, the sound of cheering coming from his right. "What's that?" Bragg pointed as hollered. A courier, his face covered with sweat and blood, rode up and dropped from his horse, next to Bragg. His breaths came in great sucking gasps for air. Bragg bent over, impatient for the man's report.

"Well man, what is it? Tell me, boy!" Bragg shouted in the courier's red-streaked face.

"General Bragg, sir.' The man's lungs were heaving as he spoke. "I beg to report, sir. Thirteenth Tennessee, sir! We are driving the Yankees back on the right, sir. They are giving ground over there, retreating from their positions."

"Somebody tell me what time it is!' Bragg roared.

"Just about 9:00, General." The fight for Rhea's field was now into its second hour.

"Good. Continue with your report, soldier."

"Yes sir. Johnston's brigade has arrived and gone directly into the fight on the left, supporting our attack. The Yankee infantry is giving way, and the Yankee batteries in support of them are being forced to move or be destroyed."

"*About damn time.* Bragg fumed. He looked down over his side, at his injured leg. It was beginning to swell up, and throb with pain. He took out his own watch, verifying the time.

We've thrown a good portion of four brigades at them. That's 5,000 or so men. Inexperienced men. Well, not anymore. Against that blue belly infantry and their artillery. Seven times we've stormed that ridge. Seven frontal assaults. Seven times they've beaten us back and beaten us bloody as they did it. Now we got hundreds of dead and dying boys laying up there in that muck. God, just listen to those wounded.

From the field, ravines, and creek bed could clearly be heard the cries of the wounded. Their piteous moans mixed with the screams of the artillery, and the ripping thunder of the musket fire. The dead men merely watched, their voices stilled forever, their glassy eyes locked into a gaze no living man wished to see.

Bragg shook his head, his brain digesting the courier's report. He lifted his glasses to look once more at the Yankee lines, stopping once to quickly wipe them on his uniform coat, the glasses having gotten muddy when Bragg was on the ground after having the horse fall on him. His eyes widened as he gazed upon the remains of men, animals, smashed guns and caissons strewed about the torn-up hillside. It was the area defended by the Fiftieth Ohio and Waterhouse's Battery, but not anymore. Bragg looked with delight through the glasses, realizing that the Yankee artillery was attempting to hitch up and pull back, but also seemed unsure of what to do. He could see two officers, clearly arguing about something.

One, hatless and to Bragg's experienced eye, obviously injured on his leg, was arguing with the other officer, this one mounted on horseback and obviously senior in rank to the other man. Suddenly the mounted officer pointed at the ground behind where they were standing, leaned down to the other, and said something. The other officer, obviously distraught, and limping on the wounded leg, merely saluted and began to issue commands to the remaining cannoneers. Bragg watched as the officers moved back but a few hundred yards from their original positions, the remaining artillerymen struggling with their field-pieces. The guns were stuck in the mud, and without the trace horses, difficult to move.

They're having trouble moving those guns. They don't have enough horses left. Bragg quickly turned around, and seeing General Anderson, quickly waved him over.

"General Anderson, take your brigade, along with Russell's for support. Go help those boys out. Take what's left of Cleburne's boys with you."

"General Bragg, those boys of Cleburne's are pretty fought out." Anderson replied, looking around at what was left of the Confederate regiments around them.

"It doesn't matter!" Bragg retorted. "You can see what I can see. We need those guns. Take them. Now, go, General, do it now."

Anderson saluted. He knew better then to argue since he could see how Bragg's state of mind was. He could also see the struggle the Union artillerymen were experiencing and recognized the opportunity. Quickly the orders were issued, and the attack renewed, the gray troops scrambling up the ridge once more. Trying to catch the Yankee defenders by surprise, General Johnston had sent two regiments, Blythe's Mississippi boys and the Fifteenth Tennessee in on the Yankee left flank to assist in the attack. Bragg watched with joy as the gray troops swarmed up the hill, Johnston's men unseen by the Union defenders until it was too late. The Mississippi and Tennessee boys swung in and around the flank of the confused defenders, and smashed into what was left of their defenses, swarming over the makeshift fortifications, and streaming toward the remaining guns. Bragg watched as what was left of the Seventy-Seventh and Fifty-Seventh Ohio infantry regiments tried to stop the Confederate gray tide, only to be broken, and swept away, collapsing under this final rebel onslaught. Bragg watched with glee, the last remnants of Yankee infantry fleeing, the southern boys screaming like banshees in pursuit. The rebels jumped over the logs and hay bales, stormed into the new gun emplacements, shooting and bayoneting the few remaining Yankee cannoneers who attempted to stop the rebel capture of their guns.

No human can continue to withstand such an onslaught. Bragg watched with joy as the Confederate flag was raised triumphantly over the captured Yankee guns. He noted with a grim smile the few remaining live Federal troops, their brave commander one of them, now Confederate prisoners-of-war.

What a joy to see that flag waving over those guns. Suddenly his smile turned to a frown, as the rebel flag bearer, so triumphant in victory a moment before, abruptly pitched forward onto the ground, the flag spilling onto the ground with him, a Yankee musket ball having found its mark. The flag was quickly picked back up, with curses and shaken fists being flung at the retreating blue bellies.

I hope that's not an omen, Bragg thought. He rode forward, up toward the captured Yankee position. His borrowed horse gingerly picked its way across the body strewn ground, the animal nervously working its way around the human wreckage. Bragg looked at the (Shiloh) church building less than a hundred yards distant, the wreckage of war surrounding it, the remaining Yankee camps off in the distance.

It's 10:00. Bragg fingered his pocket watch. His staff was overjoyed, cheering right along with the jubilant soldiers, looks of relief and sheer joy evident on all their hot, dirty faces. Bragg smiled at their joy.

Hell, I feel a little like whooping and throwing my hat in the air myself. It's good. Besides, we've got plenty of daylight left. We've taken out the enemy's left flank, or at least a big part of it, but at what cost? Bragg's face sobered at the thought. Then he shook his head, the smile returning. Doesn't matter, the boys did it. Look at them now, jumping and chattering like a bunch of schoolboys, chasing the damned Yankees out of their camps, right to the river. I can't believe that we surprised them so completely, not like this.

They weren't prepared, not really. No defense lines, hardly any pickets. Did they really think it would be this easy for them that we'd just roll over? Hard to believe, but damn, they sure put up one hell of a scrape. They hurt us.

No time to stop now, can't let them catch their breath. If we do, they may be able to regroup. No sir, got to keep going, keep pushing the boys forward. Got to take this road and keep driving, keep driving in on their left, north, back where they came from. Glad we finally took those guns; thank God we finally did. Keep driving them in, collapse that line, push them toward the center, like rats, right into that river. Thank the Almighty. We finally did it. Got to send a messenger back to tell Beauregard and Johnston.

Oh Sidney, you will be pleased, but at what a cost. Bragg closed his eyes for a moment. The sounds of the wounded men had taken over from the cheers of just a few minutes before. Everywhere Bragg looked there was blue and gray bodies spread all over, some sprawled on the ground, others draped over the remains of trees, fences, and broken elements of war. It was a horrible sight.

Yes Sidney, the cost is high. There's many a good boy out there who will never see his mother again. Both sides, doesn't matter what color they wore. Damn, did they put up a fight! Got to be proud of them.

Can't let the boys stop now, got to keep them moving. If they get bogged down in looting those Yankee camps, we'll lose all the advantage we've earned. I imagine there's plenty in those tents the boys would just love to grab. Wonder if there's any good coffee there? I'll just have to see to it that we keep them moving, keep pushing forward. Damn, what a morning, I sure am proud of them, even Polk's ruffians.

But what a cost.

GRANT

Pittsburg Landing
April 6, 1862 9:00 A.M.

The sound of the battle was simply stupendous. To the men on the decks of the *Tigress* it seemed as if the battle was raging just over the tops of the bluffs overlooking the landing.

Where did they all come from? Grant stared through shocked eyes at the tangled confusion that had overtaken the wharves of Pittsburg Landing. Swarms of wild-eyed wounded men, teamsters, their throats raw from swearing at the top of their lungs, and crazed stragglers running from the fight, all jammed into a massive pile huddled below the river bluffs. To Grant it appeared to be nothing less than a herd of sheep thrown into a panic by the approach of a pack of hungry wolves.

I've got to get some order here, Grant thought. The steamboat had bumped up against the landing, the crew quickly tying her up to the dockside. No sooner had the

Tigress been safely docked, than a great clamor arose, the men aboard trying to get off, only to have to fight their way through the frenzied crowds at dockside. Frantic men tried to clamber aboard by grabbing onto ropes or running up the planks and keeping the ship's guards and crew members busy trying to stop them. They cursed the crazed men for cowards and threw them into the brown waters of the river, or shoved them back onto the landing at gunpoint. Grant turned to Rowley and shouted, trying to make himself heard over the din.

"Captain, off with you. Find Sherman. Find him fast and report back to me. Be quick about it."

"Yes sir, General. Right away." Rowley jumped down to the landing, pulling his horse by the reins down with him. He quickly mounted the animal and began to shove his way through the mass of frenzied men, heading up the road leading to the top of the bluffs. Within minutes he was lost to Grant's sight. He turned to see Colonel Webster standing by him.

"Colonel Webster, judging by that noise up there." Grant pointed to the top of the bluffs. "I believe we need to get an ammunition train set up and headed to the front. I believe those boys up there are going to need some more cartridges and shells, lots of them."

"Yes sir. I will see to it."

"Immediately, Colonel. There is no time to waste."

"Yes sir, General Grant." Webster pointed at Grant's leg. "Sir, we need to get you on your horse."

"Don't forget the crutch. I will probably need it."

Webster and the others quickly pushed Grant up into his saddle. Webster quickly secured the crutch to the saddle's facings. With a muttered thanks Grant began to ride down onto the landing and began to push his way through the crowd.

"Captain Rawlins!" Grant hollered. A pallid, dark bearded officer pushed his way through the crowd, shoving his way to the side of Grant's horse.

"Good morning, General." Rawlins saluted. "What can I do for you?"

"I want these people moved."

The thirty-one-year-old Rawlins smiled. Ever since the days in Galena, Illinois before the war, Rawlins, a former attorney, and a man who was slowly dying of consumption, had been with Grant. Now Grant's friend and aide, Rawlins had taken on the watchdog duty of helping Grant stay sober, and free of melancholy.

"Yes sir, the Twenty-Third and Missouri and Fifteen Iowa just got here from St. Louis. We could use them to do it."

Grant nodded. "Good, I'll want the Sixteenth Iowa also. Where are the Fifteenth Iowa boys? Still here?"

"Yes sir, camp's off to the left, right over there." Rawlins pointed.

"Good. Find me their commanding officer."

"Well General, I do believe that's him, right over there." Rawlins pointed at a small group of officers standing off to one side of the docks, obviously not part of the mess around the wharf.

Grant pushed his way over to the small group. He quickly scanned the group, spotted the eagles on one man's shoulderboards, and turned his gaze on him.

"Colonel, you are to take your men up to the top of that bluff." Grant pointed to the spot he wanted occupied. "Set up a defense line. Tell your men to fix their bayonets. Stop all stragglers who cannot show blood and turn them around. I will send more troops to assist you."

The officer merely stared blankly at Grant, then dumbly asked a question.

"Excuse me sir, but *who* are you?"

Grant frowned. *Well, so much for being on the cover of Harper's or being the commander of this army,* he thought. "I'm *General* Grant, *Colonel.* Now get your men moving. Captain Rawlins here will show you the way. He will give you your orders. Now, get going. Captain?"

"Yes sir." Rawlins now sat on horseback next to Grant.

"Escort the Fifteenth up to on top of the bluff to deal with stragglers. Put the Sixteenth in line next to them and extend that line. My authority. Any artillery available?"

Rawlins smiled. "Yes sir. Bouton's Battery. Second Illinois Light."

"Good. Put them up with the two infantry regiments. Stop everyone who tries to come through. They had better be able to show blood. Then get those stragglers rounded up and sent back in. Nobody quits. Everybody fights. Colonel Reed?" Grant called to a disheveled officer standing on the wharf, gesturing to him to come to Grant.

"General Grant, sir." The rumbled officer saluted. "What can I do for you, sir?"

"We seem to have a problem here, Colonel." Grant waved his hand around in an arc. "Can we do something about this mob?"

"General, we've tried everything, including threats to shoot them, if necessary, if they don't go back." Reed looked around. "Most of them seem to have the "Bull Run" syndrome. The, you know, "my regiment was cut to pieces and I'm the only survivor!' This has made the situation . . . difficult."

Grant's face darkened, and he began to frown. He leaned down from the horse until his face was mere inches from Reed's. "I don't care *what* they say. You are to do *whatever* is necessary in order to assist Captain Rawlins here, and the provost marshals to get these *people* rounded up and sent back to where they belong. Everyone fights. We are *not* going to quit and run, Colonel. Not this army. Any questions?"

"No sir!' Reed stepped back and saluted. "I understand. Everybody fights. We'll do our best, General, sir."

Good, Grant thought. "Dismissed, Colonel." Grant turned to Rawlins. "You too, Captain, get those boys up there on top of the bluff. Dismissed."

"Yes sir." Rawlins was gone.

"All right. Colonel Webster? Let us go and find General Sherman."

"Yes sir. Corinth Road, General."

Grant rode up to the top of the bluff and headed down the road. His horse was kept busy, dodging around the debris on the road, canteens, backpacks, and weapons strewn *everywhere.* There were shirkers running and attempting to hide, using the rider-less horses, broken wagons, and caissons to attempt to hide from the provost guard. Grant focused on the road in front of him, deliberately not looking to either side as he rode, his heart racing faster then he could ride.

My God, what am I going to find up at the front? Thank God. I've already started Nelson's boys here. Buell should be on his way by now. I'm glad I've got those two regiments in reserve up on the bluffs. I hope Buell's here before nightfall. We might need them sooner. Could probably use those two gunboats as well. (The Tyler and Lexington, both of which were heavily armed riverboat-type gunboats.) We'll probably need them before all this is done.

We never should have put those inexperienced boys out front! Trouble is, wasn't much we could do about it, most of the army is the same way. Well, after this day, they won't be inexperienced anymore. Those that live, that is.

"General?" It was Webster. "Here comes Captain Rowley."

Well, that didn't take very long. Grant thought, riding ahead to meet Rowley. The aide was tearing up the road as fast as he could, dodging the flotsam of war that was strewn all over the road.

"Well, Captain, what have you got? What news of Sherman, and the other divisions?" Grant waited for Rowley to catch his breath; the young officer exhausted by the hard gallop.

Rowley saluted. It was obvious that the young man had been in the thick of the fighting. His uniform was smoke and blood-stained, and torn in several places, whether by brambles or bullets Grant could not tell. His face was stained by gunpowder and smelled strongly of smoke. Grant could not help but mentally compare the image in front of him to the clean, freshly shaved Rowley he had sent off to find Sherman. Rowley took a quick swig from his canteen, and then began his report.

"General Grant, General Sherman wishes me to tell you that if you have any men to spare, he can sure use them. If you don't, he says that he will do the best that he can. He says to tell you that he thinks that they are holding on pretty well, but that it is hot as hell, sir!"

Grant sat quietly, his mind digesting the report.

Thank the Almighty that Cump's all right so far. Sounds like he's got a good handle on things, maybe he's found his place. Hell of a way to do it. It's got to be bad, judging by Rowley's appearance. Keeping his voice calm and even, Grant asked. "Anything else, Captain?"

Rowley nodded and continued his report. "Yes sir, it appears that while General Sherman is holding on the left flank, but the center and the right flank are definitely being pushed back. Our defenses are being helped by the heavy brush and swampy conditions of the terrain, but the rebels just keep sending in assault after assault. They just won't quit. They have pushed up this road, (The Pittsburg-Corinth), and have just about reached the (Purdy-Hamburg) crossroads. They are in a line, spread out about a mile on either side, and just keep coming. The area around that (Shiloh) church that was Sherman's camp is now *within* the enemy lines. The enemy is trying to extend their left flank to get past our right. This is where they have had most success. Their losses appear to be quite severe, but . . .?" Rowley hesitated.

"Finish, Captain. Tell me what you know."

Rowley shook his head. "General, it's a real bloodbath out there."

Remain calm, Captain. Grant thought. You have seen some bad stuff. You will probably see more before this day is through. Grant pointed at the blood on Rowley's uniform.

"Are you hurt, Captain?"

"No sir, it's not mine." Rowley blurted out, still a bit shaky after his hell-bent-for-leather ride through the lines.

"Good. All right son, how much of the field does Sherman hold."

"General, he still controls the field west of the Purdy-Hamburg and Pittsburg-Corinth intersection. The Thirteenth Missouri, their (W. H. L.) Wallace's men, is guarding the intersection. The remnants of Hildebrand's Brigade have formed up on the left of the Thirteenth. There are only parts of the Seventy-Seventh, Fifty-Third, and Fifty-Seventh Ohio regiments left. The brigade was so smashed up that they say that Colonel Hildebrand just broke down and cried like a baby. He's attached himself to General McClernand's staff for now.

"Hildebrand? Is he all right now?"

Rowley shook his head. "Don't know, sir. They say he was pretty upset at his losses. They say he tried to keep his men from running, but that they just threw down their weapons and ran for it. Not all of them, but a good part. I guess some of the regimental commanders did to."

I guess we'll need some new brigade commanders after this. Grant thought, keeping his face impassive, but the cigar in his mouth getting a good work out. Regimental commanders too. I know Cump had expressed reservations about some of them. Well, combat does have a way of sorting those things out. Too bad about Hildebrand. At least he's still alive.

"Anything else, Captain?"

"Sir, Buckland has extended what's left of his brigade along the Purdy Road toward the field to his right, (Ben Howell Field)."

"What kind of shape does Buckland look to be in?" Grant asked.

"General Grant, it appears that Colonel Buckland has done a fine job. His men have used their ground well, and the rebels are finding it hard going with him. His men are fighting hard."

That doesn't surprise me. Cump likes him. "Good. What about McClernand?"

"He still has control along his sector, but with the collapse of our forces to his right, it appears that he may have to pull back."

"What about McDowell's Division? Any news?"

"I don't know, sir. I could not see them. I thought I needed to get back to report to you."

Grant sighed. The noise of the fight was getting louder. It's getting closer to us. They are pushing us back. We have to make some dispositions to deal with this.

"Is that all, Captain? Anything else to report?"

"No sir, that's everything."

Grant didn't say anything, just puffed on the cigar. The others looked down the road, the noise of the fight getting closer to them. Grant finally spoke.

"Good report, Captain. Well done, son. Stay close. I will probably need you soon."

"Yes sir. Thank you, sir."

Well, it's a mess all right. There's no sense getting upset about all of it. Grant continued to pull at the cigar, the puffs rapidly filling the air around him with a cloud of smoke. Time for that later, right now I've got more pressing matters to deal with. I hate to admit it, but we're going to have to pull the men back, bring them closer to the (Pittsburg) landing. I'll have to use the cavalry to stop the stragglers, cavalry's no good in a fight like this. Can't use horsemen in those ravines and creeks anyway. I hope Wallace and Nelson get up here soon. Buell better hurry. We'll just do the best we can with what we got, but it's going to be rough. We'll manage, though. We have to.

He looked around at the rest of the little group, noting their expectant looks, their expressions telling Grant that it was up to him. He spurred his horse, headed toward the front.

"Gentlemen, let's find Sherman."

SHERMAN

James and Sowell Fields
April 6, 1862 10:00 A.M.

Sherman had been a very busy fellow. Throughout the unceasing din of the morning's turmoil, he had been constantly on the move. His men had watched their commander dash up and down the battle line on horseback, reforming regiments as they crumbled, slamming troops in to plug the holes in the human dike as fast as the holes opened, and ducking bullets left and right.

He never seemed to waver, nor to be bothered by the incredible chaos around him, even as he continued his unceasing management of the Federal defenses. He kept drawing his men back, inch by bloody inch, consumed by the deadly chess game he had become a part of, trading his pawns, but never giving the pursuing Confederates a fair shot at a checkmate move, and forcing the enemy to commit more and more of his own pieces to the attack, even as the maelstrom of shot and shell, buckshot and musket ball, swept back and forth over the blood-soaked chessboard.

Four horses had died between Sherman's knees since the morning's carnage had started. His reddened eyes now stared out of a face dark from smoke, his red beard and hair stained black by the clinging clouds of sooty gunpowder. All around him, both man and animal screamed in fear, excitement, or agony. His wounded hand and shoulder ached with pain, yet on his face there was a look of almost serene joy. Battle, it seemed, was a tonic for Sherman's usually hot and jumpy nerves.

He saw and understood *everything.* Suddenly the same man who had worried himself to the point of lunacy back in Louisville, now could sit his horse motionless, watching, listening, *studying,* the enemy, while all around him the dead and wounded piled up in gory heaps. His nerves, so easily pricked in the past, now suddenly had turned to veins of ice. Here at last, in the midst of the gore, lightning, and thunder of a great battle, Sherman had found his true calling. The artist had finally found his true art, his canvas on which to paint, and on it he would paint with broad strokes the colors of war.

Grant had finally found Sherman. The Army's commander had ridden up to join his subordinate, only to sit quietly at his side, watching the fight, as the intense fury of Southern determination continued to fall on the just as determined Yankee defenses. After all the initial shocks of the early morning surprises, the Northern troops had begun to steady, and Sherman was ordering counterattacks.

The fighting raged, back and forth through the destroyed Union camps. Tents, knapsacks, utensils, and foodstuffs were strewn about everywhere. The regiments were mixing, a soup of gray and blue mixing in the cauldron of the insanity known as hand-to-hand combat. The two Federal commanders continued to sit their horses, Sherman watching the fight, Grant watching the fight and Sherman. At last Grant finally spoke.

"General Sherman, I see you have your hands full." Grant shouted.

Sherman grinned, his red lips glistening in his dirty face. "Yes sir." He shouted back. "You might say we have been a bit busy, especially now. They're trying to make it mighty hot for us. Glad you're here. How's the leg?"

Grant grimaced. "Oh, it will be all right. Don't like the crutch much."

Sherman grinned at the response, his eyes never leaving the field before him. Grant continued to speak.

"General, I've already given the necessary orders in order to get you more ammunition, more cartridges and shells. An ammunition train is on its way to being sent up, directly."

"Thank you, sir. I believe we will need them very, very soon." Sherman continued to give orders, the former cavalry-men-turned messengers riding back and forth with his directions. Grant smiled, pleased at what he was seeing in Sherman's performance, the coolness under fire, the quick decisions Sherman made as he continued to reevaluate the situation, the clear-headed directives Sherman issued as the fluid situation ebbed and flowed. It was a beautiful performance, and Grant was very impressed.

"General, I didn't expect them to attack us here." Grant dourly admitted.

Sherman grinned, again the wolf-like smile. "Well General, I believe that we were *all* surprised." Sherman replied, his eyes never leaving the fight. "But don't you worry none, we'll handle them. Just send me what reinforcements you can. We've had a bit of trouble. Hildebrande's (Third) Brigade has been pretty much destroyed. I don't know if Jesse (Hildebrand) will ever be any good as a brigade commander, again. They tell me he's pretty much a basket case right about now. Buckland's (Fourth) is pretty much torn up to, but *those* Ohio boys are holding up, and on hand. McDowell's all right. We need to move him, set up a new line, buy more time for you to get up more reserves. Major Sanger?"

"Yes General?" Sanger appeared somewhat shamed face. It was he who was at least partly to blame for the debacle with Waterhouse's Battery attempted withdrawal, after the artillerymen had given such a gallant effort.

"Take word from me to General McDowell to move his men out. He is to send them to the rear of this line, into that next field, (Sowell's), and they are to be faced *south*. Tell him to put that house, the one on the edge of the field, (The George Sowell residence) on their *left*. You see the one I mean, Major?" Sanger nodded his understanding, busy scribbling down Sherman's directions. "We'll bring up the rest of the boys just as soon as we can. Understand? Got it all? Move them fast, Major!"

"Yes sir, I understand." Sanger saluted. "Immediately, General." Sanger hurried off.

Grant nodded; his pleasure evident with Sherman's plans. The two men continued to watch wordlessly the endless *zip-zip* of the musket balls, the unending explosions of canister, the grapeshot mowing down rows of men at a time. All around them men were busy, tearing open the paper cartridges, pouring the paper, gunpowder, and ball down the hot barrels of their muskets and ramming it home with their weapons' ramrods, capping their guns, and finishing the act with the discharging of their weapons, then repeating the whole process over and over again, three or four times a minute. They were no longer men. They had become machines.

They're not even conscious of their actions. Sherman realized, the knowledge an enlightenment to him. *They've lost all sense of awareness.* He watched as the grim soldiers barely blinked when dirt, gravel, pieces of bark and twigs slapped at their faces. Both he and Grant watched with a detachment as one soldier, firing hard and fast, forgot to remove the ramrod from his weapon's barrel before he fired it, not realizing his error until he saw the errant tool quivering in the throat of an enemy soldier not fifty feet away. The crazed soldier swore in anger and pulled another ramrod from a pair of lifeless hands at his feet and continued his mad shooting, only to pitch forward the next moment, the blossoming hole in his head, his life's hot wet blood spraying from his wound, and soaking the already wet ground beneath him. No man knew if now-this very moment- would be his last on this earth. Grant finally turned to Sherman and spoke.

"General, I believe you will do your best, and will continue to hold the enemy. I believe I am needed more elsewhere, down the line. You have your orders. I'll do my best to send you reinforcements."

"Yes sir, General Grant." Sherman reached out with a dirty paw. His hand touched Grant's sleeve. "We will talk more later, sir. Good luck. Be careful, General." Sherman saluted.

Grant smiled, touched by Sherman's concern, and returned the salute. "You too, General. You too." Then Grant was gone, swallowed up by the smoky sunshine, the bullets zipping around him, as he rode off to find McClernand.

Well, there he goes. Sherman watched Grant disappear in the smoke. I hope he makes it through this all right. We need him. We need them all.

Be careful, Sam.

BEAUREGARD

Fraley Field
April 6, 1862 Mid-Morning

The day was growing crazier by the minute. Throughout the morning, Johnston had flitted about from one situation to another, never staying long in one place. He spent his time moving troops around, all along the front, doing it in such a way as to drive the already exasperated Beauregard to the point of almost complete frustration. Johnston's actions were having the effect of forcing Beauregard to guess as to what to do, even as the Creole-born general was attempting to keep control of the situation.

"I wish he would just make up his mind!" Beauregard had snorted, referring to Johnston. He was referring to a move Johnston had made earlier in the day, when Johnston had sent orders to Breckinridge to send three brigades from Breckinridge's Reserve Corps, with instructions to send the troops in on the Confederate left, which had the effect of tying up precious men in the attacks on the stubborn Yankee right. Beauregard would not have minded quite so much, except for the fact that within an hour's time, Johnston's ill-advised moves had caused a gap of nearly a mile wide to open in the Confederate lines near Lick Creek. This had forced the main Confederate battle line to be greatly extended to cover the gap, or the entire line could have been flanked, with possibly disastrous results for the Confederate army.

"Thank God the Yankees didn't see that before we did!" The horrified Beauregard had exclaimed, and he had quickly countermanded the order. He had come to the realization that Johnston, by being so close to the front, had no true understanding of the scope of the fighting, and thus, could not see the whole picture.

My God, does Sidney truly know what he is doing? Of course not, he's too close to the front. He knows better than to do this. Beauregard's thoughts were angry. He had decided to leave one of the reserve brigades on the left, as requested, but had recalled the other two back, and sent them to the right instead. It had been just about an hour later that a message had arrived from an obviously excited Johnston countermanding Johnston's original order regarding the three brigades and telling Beauregard to do precisely what Beauregard had already done with the three brigades. However, it was the second part of the message which was extremely agitating to the already disturbed Creole, and did nothing to soothe his aching head. Beauregard handed the message to an aide, who quickly scanned it.

"General, my God, this message from General Johnston says that you are to rely on your own information to make tactical decisions! According to this, you are no longer to wait for General Johnston's input or directions before making a command decision! Does General Johnston truly realize what he is doing? He's taken himself out of the command of this Army and put you in charge!"

Beauregard sat on a campstool, one hand rubbing his furrowed forehead. He looked up at the astonished soldier and then spoke, a deep anger evident in his voice.

"Yes, Major that is effectively just what General Johnston has done. What a way to run an army! Well, we will just have to make do and try to win this thing!"

Beauregard stood up, wincing from the pain slicing through his head. He looked around at the new headquarters location. Although the Confederate command location had been at the Y formed by the intersection of the Pittsburg-Corinth and Bark roads, as the day had advanced and the battle raged on, Beauregard had decided to move the command post to the northern end of Fraley Field, in order to be closer to the action himself, and to Johnston. Beauregard had hoped that this move would have the effect of possibly keeping closer contact to Johnston and thus keep foul ups from happening. However, Johnston had refused to stay in one place. He continued to move all over the battlefield and had continued to keep indirectly meddling with the moves of the Army, making both the decision process and Beauregard's migraine, worse.

"Damn it! All these orders and counterorders are only just slowing us down even more! I have got to get all these boys into proper positions. I have got to get more of them to the center! Major, did you send that message to General Stephens to take his brigade and move them to the center of the line?"

"Yes sir, General. I saw to it, personally, sir. But General, sir, it appears that with all the delays caused by all the changes and with the problems of moving all the troops over that uneven terrain, well sir, even if all of General Breckinridge's brigades move quickly, the very best we can do is to have them all in position no sooner than about 11:00 A.M."

"I know that!" Beauregard snapped, the effect of his retort being that the other officer backed away. It was quite obvious how upset Beauregard was. Beauregard just stared off in the direction of the fighting. He shook his head in consternation. "The plan looked so good." He fumed, the headache waving through his head. "We had a good plan, an efficient way to launch an attack and sweep those people into a trap."

The reality of it all was now quite evident to the beleaguered commander. What had started out as a possibly smooth, efficient, and a neat plan of action to destroy the Yankee Army had disintegrated in the rugged Tennessee swamps. The geography of the region was the *real* enemy, its topography so full of little plateaus, gullies, and ravines, all of which were with covered with thick, briar-filled, twisted brush. They had all combined to thwart the Confederate formations as they had tried to move through the area. In addition, the Yankee defenders were effectively utilizing the natural surroundings for cover, each bush-filled ravine and gully filled with knots and clusters of determined blue-belly defenders. The effect was that all coordination was being lost between the attacking formations.

Now, instead of Beauregard's plan of three Confederate corps moving in a line that stretched from creek to creek, each corps' brigades moving in unison, and attacking in waves, each one crashing in one behind the other in hammer-like blows against the opposition, the whole thing had disintegrated into each line feeling its way along and feeding its units piecemeal into the line ahead.

The result of all of this chaos was that brigades, regiments, right down to companies, had become so intermingled that unit commanders were losing touch with the men of their own commands. Confederate troops were being commanded by officers that were complete strangers to them. Noon was fast approaching, the final reserves had been committed, and that precious combination of time and coordination so necessary to the success of any attack was rapidly, irrevocably, slipping away from the Confederate high command. That which had been a structured aggregation of corps, divisions, and brigades, had crumbled into a frantic mass of adrenalin-fueled and angry men, crammed into what approximated a battle formation, trying to fight a hundred ferocious skirmishes, strung out along a crooked mile-and-a-half long front.

The Yankee high command had reacted far faster than the Confederates had thought they could, bringing up their own artillery to add to the fray, and now between the two sides two hundred cannons were adding their booming accompaniment to the confusion.

What could the private soldier think? As confusing as the loss of any disciplined structure had to be to the soldiers in the ranks, it was even more so to the officers, so used to being part of that structure. How could they not be? How could any of them understand that the battle they had all entered so gaily, many looking on it as some kind of a lark, had plunged them into a maelstrom of hellish proportions?

For all that even the "veteran" soldiers amongst them, those who had survived the confusion of Wilson's Creek, Donelson, or even Manassas, had ever encountered, this was far worse than anything any of them had ever endured. To the backwoods boys not so long removed from the loving care of their mothers' arms, or the safety of their little farms, it was as if the war-God Mars had reached down with his great hands, and shaped all those past struggles into one gigantic ball, then breathed fire into it, expanding the ball, three, no, four times in size, then compressed it between his mighty palms with one gigantic clap of his hands into an area smaller than any of those events. To those poor inexperienced, wet-behind-the-ears amateurs, it truly had to be the day of Armageddon. For many it was the final clarion call, the gods of war demanding their lust be satisfied, and only vast sacrificial quantities of the innocents' flesh and blood would suffice.

"Major, we need to do something different before we completely lose control of this fight." Beauregard was not about to give up. Headaches be damned! "I want orders issued to each of the corps commanders to each take a sector of the battlefield to command and control." He paused, waiting for the wave of head pain and nausea to pass, his brain fighting to keep control over his pain and the situation. He looked around at the trees surrounding the field, listening to the sounds of the fighting, trying to gauge the direction of the battle by the level of the din rising above the trees. He started to shake his head, then stopped, the pain continuing to exercise its control over him.

"Send orders to Generals Hardee and Polk to take control of the left quadrants of our line, and Bragg and Breckinridge to do the same with the right quadrants. That should help get things under control, eh Major?"

"Yes sir." The younger officer was busy scribbling down Beauregard's directions. "I am sure that it will help, General Beauregard."

"Yes, Major, it *might. If* everyone follows their directions, we still may have a chance to carry out the plan and achieve General Johnston's original goal. *If* they do what they are supposed to do, we could still turn the Yankee left flank, cut off their line of retreat to the (Tennessee) river, and still drive them into the (Snake) creek swamps. Then we can force those blasted blue-bellies to surrender or to be cut to pieces! *But that is one mighty big if!*"

"Well sir, let us hope for divine Providence to intercede on our side."

Beauregard scowled. "One can only hope, Major, one can only hope." He sat back down on the stool. "We'll just have to put our faith in Providence, as "Bishop" Polk would say. Perhaps the Almighty will yet smile upon us today. Still, I can't help but think that there are still some new *twists* coming up today, and real soon like, real soon."

He was right.

PRENTISS

The Sunken Road
April 6, 1862 Mid-Morning

Union General Benjamin Prentiss had already had a very rough day. The crusty old Mexican War veteran had seen his division get itself badly roughed up, and it was only the middle of the morning. The Sixth Division had been in the process of making breakfast when the gray and butternut Confederate tide had rolled into his camp, stunning the surprised Union forces with the ferocity of the rebel attack. The screaming Confederate regiments had swept through, driving the bewildered Yankees away from their cooking fires, the rebels stopping for but a moment to grab some Yankee hot food, then continuing the chase. Prentiss and his men, a trail of dead and wounded bodies marking their retreat, dashed across the open fields away from their camp for almost a mile, the Confederates in a slower pursuit, what with stopping to eat the Yankee breakfasts. This gradually caused a gap to open up between the Sixth and the pursuing rebel forces, the lure of hot food overcoming the ardor of the Confederate pursuit. Prentiss and his men crossed up and over a slight ridge, only to come down off the ridge into an old, eroded wagon road, that which had wound its generations-worn path along the edge of a patch of scrub and tall oaks.

Prentiss stopped, and looked around, his breaths coming in hard gasps. The sides of the shallow natural trench-like passageway were lined with brush and formed a natural defense position, a bastion, a natural fortress.

"Major, get the boys lined up in here, now!" Prentiss exclaimed, his eyes searching up and down the wooded road, looking for any would-be ambushes. He noted how the dense thickets lined the top of the side of the road that faced back toward the meadow the federal forces had just finished stumbling across. The road sat in just the perfect position, just beyond the crest of the low hill in front of them. It offered superb protection for any would-be defenders who sought its sanctuary.

"Do you see what I see?" Prentiss continued, his eyes continuing to dart from side to side. "They have to come across that same meadow to get at us, right up this hill, and right at this ridge. It's the *only* way to approach this road. They *have* to come across that field!"

"You are right, sir!" Prentiss's aide, a Major McBentley, nodded his head, his florid face still red from their run across the field. "We can see them every step of the way across! They'll have no shelter from our fire! It's perfect!"

Prentiss nodded. "Get 'em lined up. I want the best shots up front. The others can load for them. We ought to be able to make it pretty damn hot for the rebs, blast them! Let's see if we can't get some artillery in here as well. Think you can do something about getting some, Major?"

"Yes sir! Right away, General!" McBentley scurried off.

This is a good spot. Prentiss looked around again, contemplating the possibilities. All right, here is where we make our stand. This division is not retreating back one more step. We took the rebs first blows and we are still standing. Now's it's our turn and we're going to do our damn best to return the compliment and give them hell! I owe it to those boys lying out there in that field, bless their souls!"

He looked down the path, at his officers hard at work, busy lining the troops up on the side of the sunken road, best shots to the front, the men lining up their rifle sights, looking for targets on the opposite side of the field. Prentiss pulled his pocket watch out of his pocket and checked the time. 9:30. *Good. We still have most of the morning. All right then, let's do some damage here.*

The troops were lined up, the muskets now resting on the lip of the trench-like road. Per Prentiss's orders the best shots were in the front, the other men lined up behind them, rifles already loaded, and ready to be handed up to the men on the wall. They would be able to lay down an almost continuous rate of fire.

Those on the line looked over the top of their rifles, their sights lined up on the trees on the other side of the meadow.

They waited with deadly purpose, their eyes never leaving their sights, waiting for the inevitable targets to show themselves.

"Here they come!" The cry echoed up and down the wooded path. The first enemy troops had appeared on the other side of the meadow, the wave of attackers pouring out of the dark woods. All along the line there was the audible *click* of hammers being drawn back on triggers, and an almost unanimous hush as hundreds of men collectively held their breath, almost like a giant sigh. They waited for the order, the order that would turn loose their weapons on an unsuspecting enemy.

"Wait until you can't miss boys!" Prentiss sang out. "Make every shot count and *aim low!*" His words were repeated up and down the sunken road, the row of muskets primed and ready, the shine of the metal gun barrels obscured by the bushes lining the trench. The Confederate forces were continuing their march, advancing boldly across the field, their stomachs now full of the purloined Yankee breakfasts, their confidence high. They marched straight across the grassy meadow, straight toward the waiting guns, straight toward the waiting maw of death and destruction.

They don't see us. Prentiss thought to himself. *They don't see us! Well, give them ten more seconds and they're going to get a hell of a surprise.* He waited until the enemy had reached the halfway point across the meadow. He lifted his arm, sword in hand, then brought it down, hard, and roared.

"Fire!"

With a roar the entire Union line exploded in a thunderous crash, the line of muskets firing as one. A huge cloud of filthy black smoke billowed out in front of the federal line, a wave of murderous lead missiles screaming across the field and smashed into the unsuspecting rebel formation.

In a flash the entire Confederate line disintegrated, the wave of Yankee metal tearing it to shreds. Shocked screams of anger, pain, and fear filled the air. The twisted and torn remains of the Confederate soldiers lay almost in a solid line across the meadow. It looked like an entire of row of fence posts had suddenly, and bloodily, been uprooted and toppled onto the ground. The survivors streamed back toward the woods on the far side of the meadow, their numbers far less, their new confidence shattered. The Yankee line erupted in cheers, the Union defenders throwing their kepis into the air. Prentiss grinned at the sight, then erupted.

"You think they're *done*?" He walked down the line, the men quieting as he walked by. "They *will* be *back*! Get *ready*! The day has barely begun. It's going to get real hot before we're through here. Give them nothing! *Nothing!* This time they *won't* be surprised."

He was right. Those were Bragg's boys out there, and they did come back. The attacks continued, and Bragg did not stop. Hour after hour they kept *coming*. Prentiss got up artillery to back his boys up. Extra ammunition arrived, the cannons kept firing, the rifles kept shooting, the bodies continued to stack up in small mountains, and still they kept *coming!* It was a hellish sight to see.

The assault had now gone on for hours. Wave after wave of fresh Confederate troops had stormed the Yankee stronghold, only to be ripped apart and beaten back every time. The Yankee defenders were doing a fine job of dispensing incredible damage to the Confederates, dropping them in bunches as the gray and butternut clad men, their flags flying with pride, their voices raised in raucous shouts, continued their stubborn assaults on the Yankee position. Piles of wounded and dead men now littered both the blood soaked, bullet and shell-torn meadow and sunken road with their forlorn presence, a testimony to the Yankees' valiant defense, and the Confederates' determined desire to drive the Federals out of their bastion.

It was now late morning, and Grant had arrived just in time to witness one of the attacks being repulsed. The large meadow, so thick and tall with fresh April grass earlier that morning, now looked like a giant scythe had gone through it, so effectively had the Yankee fire mowed it down.

Hundreds of decimated Confederate troops lay everywhere in the field, their torn bodies cooking under the murky April sun's unwavering gaze, a testimony to Bragg's determination to overcome the Yankee defenses. The sun was hot for all, pouring down as it did on defender and attacker alike, but it was especially hard on the wounded, and their piteous cries for water went unheard in the incredible din of the fight.

Grant sat silently, watching as Prentiss moved his men around. He was aware that Prentiss had left the front at least once already, a quick break, a luxury that Grant did not think well of. Many of Prentiss's men had run away, but not all of them. Those regiments that had stayed were being stubborn, using their artillery bravely, defying the odds, their effectiveness evident by the carnage in the field.

Grant noted with silent admiration the bravery of the attackers, his smile a grim one as he watched the Confederates storm across the killing fields. He watched with Prentiss as the rebels charged into the teeth of the Yankee defenses once more, running, scrambling, *crawling*, to get at the men in the sunken road, only to have their formations blown apart, the survivors sent reeling back across the field, a mass execution if there ever was one.

Grant nodded his silent approval of the defensive work. He watched the remains of this latest attack stream back across the ruined meadow back into the far woods. He shook his head, admiring but wondering also at the foolhardy bravery he was witnessing.

They're crazy. Grant thought to himself. Crazy. But if they want to keep wasting themselves this way, and ignoring other options, well . . .?

"General Prentiss." Grant turned to Prentiss. "General, you must maintain this position at all costs. Hold them off."

Prentiss looked into the expressionless eyes. He saw no compassion, only a deadly purpose. My God, what is he (Grant) thinking? Can't he see that they're just going to keep coming? It's going to be a contest to see who runs out of men first, us or them. Prentiss pulled his eyes away, no longer willing to make eye contact with Grant's. Is it possible that this is what he is trying to do, make them waste their men in these attacks? Well, I believe that they are going to make him quite happy that way. They sure don't show any indication to stop. Grant may be on to something. Prentiss swallowed and lifted his hand in a salute.

"Yes General, I have my orders, sir." The two men locked eyes once more, Grant holding Prentiss's gaze.

"At *all* costs, General." Grant spoke softly, but there was no mistaking the steel in his voice. Prentiss finally looked away, back at the line, his remaining men busy reloading their weapons. In the distance they could hear the rebel yells again growing in volume, a prelude to another attack. Prentiss turned away, and rode away from Grant, his mind now busy with keeping faith with his men to do their bloody jobs, and somehow, keep as many alive as long as he could, and hold off the enemy as long as possible. He rode down the line, shouting encouragement to his boys. Grant watched him go.

It's a rotten job I've given him. Rotten, but necessary. We are sacrificing his boys, but if they want to keep wasting time, men, and ammunition here, then we'll let them. They're giving us an opportunity. We may be able to do something here, trap them, but I need time, time to bring up Buell and Wallace. We've got a chance here, a golden chance to bag their whole army. They think they have got us, but we'll see, we'll see. I think we may have them. Just give me some time.

Grant looked once more at the fighting. He heard the screams, the roar of the cannons, the crackle of the musket fire. He turned his horse and headed back toward the river, his staff closing in around him protectively, trying to shield him from the fire, the rebel attack coming on, once again.

Just give me the time.

JOHNSTON

The Peach Orchard
April 6, 1862 Late Morning

It was almost noon, and again Beauregard had moved the command post. Now he was occupying the old log church called Shiloh, in the midst of what had been Sherman's headquarters camp. Now the camp was occupied by the southern forces, and it was here that Beauregard was resting his aching head.

The illness had returned, the symptoms reminiscent of the earlier malady. The day's trials had done nothing to soothe him, the pressures of the day's decisions only making his head ache more. On top of all the confusion was the knowledge that the Yankees were finding places to fight back and were keeping their lines together. The Confederate's grandiose plan had come completely apart, the army becoming more and more frustrated by the lack of success against the Yankees' defenses. The Confederate high command, while happy with the initial successes were becoming increasingly agitated by the failure of the soldiers to break through the enemy lines and finish the job.

"That damned sunken road they found! Those Yankees have got themselves a real "hornet's nest" there for themselves." Beauregard muttered; his eyes closed against the pain in his head. Earlier, he had heard some rebel soldiers complaining about the federal defense position, the angry men, survivors of the earlier assaults on the deadly tree-lined lane on the ridge. The "hornet's nest" the men had called it, and it was proving to be an apt name. The Yankee's almost fanatical defense of the cattle road had stopped the Confederate troops dead in their tracks, and now the advance had stalled. The commanders on the scene were compounding the problem by refusing to just "go around" the federal stronghold, insisting that southern pride demanded that it be taken, and slowing things down to the point that the entire advance on the right was now totally stalled. On top of this was the word, despite Johnston's harsh directive of the night before, that straggling, and looting was becoming a major issue. Beauregard had just received word that Johnston himself was on the way to try and fix the problem with the stalled advance.

Good, let him go and do something. Beauregard thought to himself, the headache angrily throbbing in his temples. That's what he wants to do anyway, be out in front and leading the charge. He wants to be out front, right in the enemy faces. I swear he thinks he's back in Mexico, leading a cavalry attack on some Mexican position. Still, if I had been treated like he was by the Yankee government just before the war, I guess I'd want to do whatever I could to get back at them. Just let him go. Hopefully this will make him happy. He sat up, wincing from the pain in his head, and fighting the nausea. He looked around at his staff, all who were studiously pretending not to notice his pain, knowing it only made him feel worse. His thoughts were still on Johnston.

I hope he knows enough to duck out there. That's all we need is for Sidney to get himself shot.

Some problems, mishaps, or even outright mistakes could be overlooked by the Confederate high command, but straggling was not one of them. It could only make all the other problems only worse. Johnston knew this well. He also knew that whether due to hunger, needs, or just plain curiosity, when the average, hungry, ill-equipped southern soldier was presented with a golden opportunity, it was often more than his hungry, ill-equipped, self could stand. Many a young soldier in the midst of a charge through the Yankee camps, would simply stop to gorge himself on Yankee white bread, and drink his fill of hot, sweet, coffee. Others would rip through the fabric of the departed soldiers' tents, and forage through their belongings. They would loot the supplies, take personal items, and even read the letters that the Yankees got from home. These last items they would devour with a certain relish, especially the ones from wives or sweethearts, as if to find out what northern girls were, "really like."

Johnston arrived upon the scene of one such expedition, the remains of a camp experiencing the "foraging" that was taking place. In a clearing where once had been a camp, gray-clad men were now interspersed among the remains of what had been federal tents. Johnston spotted an officer, a young lieutenant, as he suddenly appeared at the tent flap of one of the remaining intact tents, his arms loaded with plunder. Johnston, his face flush with anger, quickly rode up to the officer, stopping the man's flight with an angry bellow.

"Lieutenant, just what in hell do you think you are doing?" Johnston roared, his face black with anger and gunpowder.

The young officer looked up at Johnston astride his horse. The youngster's astonished eyes opened wide with sudden fear. He had just remembered Johnston's orders about what to do with looters. He started to stammer, fear evident in his high-pitched voice.

"General Johnston! Sir, I, uh, that is . . . um . . .?"

Johnston angrily cut him off. "Lieutenant!" He snarled. "You are an *officer!* Is *this* the kind of example you are supposed to set for the men under your command? We will have *none* of *that, sir!* We are not here for mere plunder!"

The young man, shame written all over his face, stared at Johnston. His eyes filled with tears. With a crestfallen look, he dropped his gaze, his prizes falling from his arms to the ground as he did. Shoulders heaving, he silently sobbed, all elation gone from his being, his humiliation evident at being scolded so harshly by his leader in front of his men.

Johnston watched silently, the harsh look on his face gradually replaced by one of sympathy. After all, he thought, they are so young, even their commanders. I should be commending this young man and his men. They have shown great gallantry in capturing this camp, after all. Still, I must show them some example . . .

He looked around and spotted a tin cup sitting alone on a camp table. He rode over to it, leaned down from Fire-Eater, and without dismounting, plucked the battered cup up from the table.

"Let this be my share of the spoils today!" He shouted, holding the cup high for all to see, and smiling at the now grinning youngster. The other men watching roared their approval of his actions. He turned Fire-Eater back toward the road. The soldiers followed him, shouting their approval of Johnston as they headed back toward the fighting, the adoring young lieutenant in the lead. Johnston galloped ahead, his grinning staff trailing at his heels.

Johnston continued his ride toward the far right of the line, pushing the men along as he did, always moving in the direction of the right flank, toward where the advance had stalled. He rode toward that tree and brush infested sunken road, where some determined Yankees had decided to make a stand and continued to defy the Confederate attempts to dislodge them from their holes.

His prize, the captured cup, Johnston held in his hand, the index finger hooked loosely through the loop in the cup handle. He pointed ahead with it now, the cup the pointer, his *sword*, toward that far right flank of the Confederate attack, the end of the line.

At the extreme end of the sunken road lay a peach orchard, its ten acres in full flowered bloom, their blossoms pretty in their April finery. Here the Yankees had massed a heavy line of infantry, and supported it with artillery, mixed in amongst the fruit-blossomed trees. As Johnston approached, he observed the smoke from the cannons blowing in large swirls up and through the tree branches of those same trees. He watched as the trees' flowered limbs, emblazoned as they were with their lovely pink and white blossoms, exploded into a brightly colored rain, dropping the petals in massive colored showers to the ground. There they were whipped up again, into miniature funnel-shaped pink and white clouds, the April sun-blessed blossoms, fluttering like a flock of pink and white butterflies, fluttering as the bullets zipped through their billowing formations.

Here Breckinridge was in charge. The handsome Kentuckian had ordered charge after charge to attempt to dislodge the stubborn defenders from their holes and breastworks in the fruit field. The Yankee defenses were strong, determined, and refused to break, the Confederate assaults being fierce, but spasmodic and uncoordinated. It seemed a strange sight, the men of both sides screaming, in attack or defense, the cannons roaring in anger, the fruit trees whipping in the malevolent wind, their branches ripped and torn bare by the winds of war, their blossoms settling down as if a frothy blanket upon the ground's red sheets. The Confederate leaders seemed bent on winning by bayonet charge a place that the defenders were determined to force the most expensive of prices for. So far neither Bragg in his assaults on the now aptly named "hornet's nest," nor

Breckinridge in the peach orchard had been able to get in, nor were they willing to break off and stop the attacks.

Johnston and an aide, Isham G. Harris, the exiled pro-Confederacy governor of Tennessee, rode up just as the fruit field fight was entering a crucial phase.

"By God, General, I've never seen such heavy fire!" Harris exclaimed. The former two-term Democratic United States congressman had joined Johnston's staff after being forced to flee the governor's mansion, and the state, when the Yankees had captured Forts Henry and Donelson. Now the balding, mustachioed, bellicose secessionist rode with Johnston, hoping that Johnston would be able to drive the hated blue invaders from Harris's beloved Tennessee, and restore Harris to the governorship. He was willing to follow Johnston to the gates of Hell to win back Tennessee.

The two men watched as Breckinridge gave the orders to mount another charge. Johnston noted with professional casualness how severely beaten up the called upon brigades looked, the men having already participated in some of the previous attacks on the Yankee stronghold. He observed the surliness, the angry looks with which the bloody and exhausted men met their sergeants' attempts to get them back in line to attack again. Johnston grabbed his field glasses, and looked at the Yankee position, festooned as it was with flags and angry blue-bellies screaming their defiance, their muskets and cannons at the ready. The ground in front of their positions proved how effective their defensive abilities were, the ground covered with the debris of the previous attacks; the wrecked peach trees, the dead and wounded

196 | DANIEL F. KORN

laying in droves, the whole thing covered in a coverlet of floating pink and white blossoms. A coverlet that moved as the fallen men crawled, writhed, or wiggled in agony, begging for help, all of them caught in the middle of the no-man's land they had spilled their blood trying to cross.

Johnston looked back at the surly Confederate troops, then once more at the field before him. His warrior's blood began to boil as he gazed upon the wreckage of the previous attacks.

"I must handle this!" Johnston exclaimed, riding forward and leaving the bewildered Harris behind. He rode into the clustered troops, giving the angry men no choice but to move or be trampled. They looked up, angered in their faces, only to have it replaced by awe and reverence when they recognized their leader. Johnston's reputation was preceding him, and his efforts that day had done nothing but enhanced that reputation in the eyes of the common soldiers in the ranks. They crowded around him, touching him with reverence, listening to his mesmerizing words.

"Men! They are stubborn!" He pointed at the Yankee lines, still awash in swirling smoke, the Union artillery continuing to sing its song of death and destruction. "We must use the *bayonet*!" He rapped the captured tin up against the tips of the rebel weapons to make his point, then continued his plea.

"These must do the work!"

Harris looked on, seeing that Johnston, if nothing else, at least had their attention.

"General!" Harris cried, his own blood up. "I think these boys are looking for some direction, for some help, for some *leadership*!"

Johnston looked around. He saw the tiredness, the powdered blackened faces, the torn and bloody rags they wore for uniforms. He saw anger, sullen, but ready to strike, and he saw no fear. He looked deep into their eyes, searching their souls for what he thought was there to find. He was not disappointed. Every man looked back at him, waiting for that *something*, a signal, *anything*, a someone to take charge, to take command of them, and *lead*!

Johnston pulled on Fire-Eater's reins. He rode out in front of the assembled troops, and then slowly rode down the line, until he had reached the very center of the front line of the formation. He looked up and down the entire line, along the very length of the entire formation. He looked up and down the entire line, and then he stood up in the stirrups, and removed his plumed hat, placing it over his heart. He then turned his steed to face toward the Yankee defenders. The sun blazed down, reflecting off the souvenir tin cup, and Johnston basked in the reflected glory. He replaced his hat upon his head, then lifting up his prize, the tin cup, he pointed it like a sword at the Yankee lines. Fire-Eater pranced around, the magnificent bay sensing his master's mood and feeling it as well. It was a moment frozen in time, a moment of glory, a moment to be seized forever. Johnston was ready.

He looked over his shoulder at the waiting men. They were watching him with a mixture of awe and anticipation.

198 | DANIEL F. KORN

Johnston raised himself up to his full height in Fire-Eater's stirrups and roared.

"Men of the South, *there* is the enemy! You have asked for someone to lead you in this attack. Very well, *I* will lead you! *Follow me!*" Then he touched his spurs to Fire-Eater's flanks and charged, directly toward the waiting enemy.

With a roar the waiting troops sprang into motion, surging forward, a great rushing gray wave made up of hate, anger, fear, and joy, all following Johnston as he rode toward the waiting defenders. A sheet of flame erupted from the Union lines, the bullets zinging through the air, and zipping and cutting their way through the gray ranks. The regimental colors, their colors blazing in the sun, dropped as their bearers were shot down, yet barely had their bullet-riddled cloth folds touched the ground, when eager would-be bearers quickly seized them up to carry on the attack. Even as the enemy fire reached out to touch the new bearers with the bolts of lighting, still others reached down to grasp the banners and lift them back up as the gray-clad men raced across the red dipped fields.

This is the way it should be! Johnston exulted in his mind, his thoughts racing along on the power of the assault. This is how a leader should be, riding at the head of a great army, riding on a great steed, leading a great, willing, courageous army, one willing to pay the price to achieve great glory. The flags flying as we charge, the men cheering as we attack, oh, how glorious it is!

How will the historians write of us? How will those future chroniclers tell the story? What will they say? Will they speak of tales of great bravery, of boldness, that we were truly the "knights" of our time? Will they tell of our great, golden crusade?

The vanguard of the attack had reached the Yankee defenses, the men screaming like banshees as they stormed past Johnston into the blazing guns. Johnston rode back and forth, defying the Yankee guns, defying *death*, hollering, screaming, coaxing them on, daring the Federal troops to stop them, to stop *him*.

How will they paint us? Will they say we were fools, off on some quixotic crusade, tilting at windmills, mad fools doomed to disaster? Or will they say we were simply dupes, serving an evil master, an abomination that holds men as property, just like cattle, an abomination against mankind, perhaps even God, this thing called slavery?

Johnston shook his head, angry with such defeatist thoughts. *No time for any of this!* He thought, his emotions pouring hot and heavy through his whole being. *Attack! That is all that matters now. To attack, and win!*

The mad charge swept over the field, bodies dropping like flies as the deadly federal missiles continued to find their marks. Red blossoms mushroomed on many a gray soldier's blouse as he charged, the blossoms wet, raw, and angry, the life forces suddenly spilling out from what had been a living, breathing, *feeling*, soul a moment before, and spewing forth onto the already blood-soaked ground.

Yet the mad Confederate River swept on, deadly in its newfound determination, an irresistible tide as it swept through the trees, a gray tidal wave unstoppable in its force, the high-pitched rebel yell accompanying the gray river.

Johnston found himself screaming in unison with his men. It was a joyous cry, one of elation, excitement, and sheer adrenaline, all mixed together with a touch of raucous fear, a testosterone high like no other. Johnston felt nothing else but the high of *battle*, the feeling drowning out all other perceptions of pain or fear even as the enemy's bullets ripped the air around him.

Seven times these men have charged this line. Johnston thought to himself. Six times we have failed to take it, but by God, not this time, by heaven, not this time!

He reined up Fire-Eater, watching as the hordes of battle-maddened men poured by and around him. They stormed into the Yankee defenses, screaming and flailing with their weapons as they climbed over the rocks and fence rails, those rocks and fence rails that the Federals had defended with such determination. Sword and pistol, rocks and fists, bayonet and rammer, whatever was available to be used all were brought into the fight, the final fight for what remained of the peach field. The Yankee defenders howled their defiance, but their depleted numbers could no longer stand up to the mad charges, the Arkansas Confederates terrifying in their determination to win. The defenders of the peach orchard fell back, forced to leave their wounded and dead to the tender mercies of the Confederates, who stood watching the Federal troops run, howling their joy at taking the Yankee stronghold, their mad charge over. Johnston rode into the remains of the Union defenses, viewing the carnage.

They're everywhere! He thought to himself, even his experienced eyes shocked by what he saw. As far as he could see, there were blue and gray-coated bodies lying everywhere. They were draped over rocks, tree trunks, the dead and wounded mixed together in a gruesome scene of destruction. They covered the ground like some kind of red, brown, gray, and blue hodgepodge carpet. Piteous cries filled the air, unheard before in the din of battle, but now quite audible in its aftermath. The air stank with an exotic blend of gunpowder, blood, and sweat, a strange perfume of whose only purposes were death and destruction. Johnston inhaled mightily of its fragrance.

My God, is this the way it was back in those ancient times? There are so many! Mexico was never like this, not this many. He carefully guided his mount through the wooded area, the horse picked its way carefully through the remains of what had been a beautiful orchard, now merely a pile of so much blood-soaked kindling. He turned his head, his thoughts disturbed by the rumble of many approaching hoof beats behind him. It was Harris, Doctor Yandell, and some of the other staff. He smiled and waved at their approach.

"General Johnston, are you all right, sir?" Yandell shouted, his concern very evident by the tone of his voice. His surgeon's eye swept the field and was horrified by what it beheld. Never in his experience had he ever seen such a scale of bloodshed. The others just stared, struck dumb by the

202 | DANIEL F. KORN

scene, the wasted lives and devastation a monument to the hours of hard fighting this place had seen.

"I'm *fine*, Doctor." Johnston waved the tin cup still clutched in his hand. "However, I believe these brave men could use some assistance from you." He motioned to the gory scene surrounding them. "Please see what you can do. Both sides." This last comment he finished with a gallant flourish, touching the tin cup to his hat in a salute to the fallen of both sides.

Yandell blinked, then smiled. He was obviously happy to see Johnston apparently unhurt. He was not surprised by the man's act of decency. "Certainly General. As you wish, sir." Yandell replied, with a salute. He rode off, into the nightmarish scene, then dismounted. He walked further into the smoke-filled haze, and disappeared into the broken woods, the smoke quickly obscuring him from Johnston's sight. Yandell would have plenty to do, the butcher's bill being as high as it was.

Shots were still being fired, the musket balls pinging off the rocks around them. "General, we . . . I mean you . . . should move back a bit." Captain Lee Wickham ducked; a bullet having just whipped by his ear. Wickham had followed behind in the charge and had managed to make it through unscathed. He stared at the smiling Johnston, amazed that nothing had happened to Johnston during the charge, and wondering what gods had been smiling on the general that would let him make such a foolhardy ride, yet escape, seemingly miraculously untouched. Wickham too, was astounded and awed by their leader's apparent disregard for his own personal safety.

Johnston grinned. "What's the matter, Captain? Didn't you enjoy our little foray into the devil's teeth?" Another shot whizzed by the bullet nearly clipping the plume from Johnston's hat.

Wickham ducked again. This is too close for him. Too close for an army commander to be to the front. He smiled back at Johnston.

"Yes Sir." Wickham replied. "But we still need to go back, General. We are too *close.*"

Johnston shook his head. I suppose he's right. The fun is over. I suppose it isn't the smartest thing for a commanding general to lead a charge. He's right, I do need to stay back a bit, and not expose myself so recklessly. But it wasn't needless, those boys needed direction. I'll never forget the look in their eyes when I said I would lead them. What brave boys. I'll never forget them, or that look.

Never!

JOHNSTON

The Peach Orchard
April 6, 1862 1:30 P.M.

The most recent assault was over, the Yankees falling back as Johnston rode back to his waiting staff. He looked at Governor Harris, and gaily shouted; "Well Governor, they came very near putting me hors-de-combat in that charge!" Johnston pointed at his boot. A Yankee minie ball had nearly cut the heel away. Johnston cheerfully continued his personal inspection of his person, checking for damage. His once-proud uniform showed the passage of several minie balls.

Isham Harris shook his head, astounded by Johnston's gay manner and his seemingly lack of fear. He touched Johnston's shoulder, and fearfully asked; "Are you wounded, sir?" Harris pointed at the tear in Johnston's coat. The rip showed clearly where the projectile's passage had torn through the commanding general's coat, narrowly missing the shoulder blade. Johnston stuck a finger through the hole, examining the what-might-have-been.

"No, it's only a scratch. They'll have to aim better than that to get me!' Johnston waved his gloved hand, dismissing the thought. His warrior's blood was up. This was no time to be concerned with minor scratches. *I do feel strange, almost a little light headed. Probably didn't eat enough this morning. Sure, haven't had time to eat anything since then. That last charge with those Missouri and Arkansas boys was "close!" Well, they won't be growing peaches in that orchard this year, no, not for a while. It was nip-and-tuck in there for a while, damn those blue-bellies!*

He shook his head, trying to rid himself of the strange feeling. Harris watched him closely, looking Johnston over with a concerned eye.

"General, are you sure you're all right? Do you have any orders, sir?"

"Yes Governor, I'm fine." *Well, I am.* He thought to himself. *Just a little foggy, that's all. Probably the adrenaline wearing off. I'm not quite as young as I used to be.* He scribbled on a piece of paper. "Here, Governor, if you would please, sir. Take this order to Colonel Statham." Johnston handed the paper to Harris. "I want him to take his Mississippians and finish off that battery. Drive those people out of there."

Harris took the paper. "Certainly sir. At once. But sir, are you sure you're all *right*? You just seem . . . well . . . strange?"

Harris continued to watch Johnston; a look of deep concern evident on the politician-turned-soldier's mustachioed face.

Well, I do feel funny. Johnston thought. He shook his head, smiling as he did. "I am *fine,* Governor. Thank you for your concern. Let's be on with the day, shall we?" Johnston pointed toward the ridge, the fighting on the far side still going on.

Harris smiled back, partly mollified by Johnston's cheerful rejoinder. "Yes sir." Harris saluted. "Immediately, sir." Harris turned and quickly rode off to deliver Johnston's directive. Johnston turned to the officers setting their mounts behind him. Captain Lee Wickham and Major Theodore O'Hara had both faithfully followed their commander into the charge. Both men's clothing showed clear evidence of bullet holes. Fortunately, neither had suffered more than a minor scratch.

"C'mon, gentlemen, let's ride. We still have work to do." The three men quickly began to ride toward the edge of the field.

That damn Yankee position is holding up pretty tough. Those guns the Yankees put up along that line west of that (Hamburg-Savannah) road sure gave us hell. What a thing of beauty it was to watch that (Statham's) brigade leap the fence into that (Sarah Bell) field and make that charge. It gave me such a thrill to hear our boys give out that yell of theirs and go in with the bayonet. What a magnificent sight it was to see "our" flag, those stars and bars, waving over our brave boys as they made that charge. My God, how grand they looked! My God, how good it felt to lead them!

Johnston felt his chest swell with pride, and his eyes filled with tears of joy at the memory. How grand it felt to be at the head of a great charge, to lead men into the fight, not just send them in harm's way. This surely is the way to fight! I should have lived at the time of the great Crusades. That surely was a time for men of war to lead!

Johnston shook his head again. The light headiness seemed to be getting stronger. He looked at the two men beside him.

"What time is it, gentlemen?" Johnston asked, then pointed at the ridge. Statham had gotten the message, and his men were making a new assault.

"Two o'clock, General." Wickham replied.

Almost nine hours since today's events started. Johnston shook his head. We've been at this for nine hours. Lots of boys learned some valuable lessons today. They're not newcomers to this anymore. Johnston smiled, then put his field glasses up to his eyes, watching the Tennessee troops make their charge.

Look at those Tennessee boys' storm that ridge. They're full of confidence now. The Yankees keep knocking them down, trying to push them back, but by God, they just keep coming. They're not going to be stopped, no sir, not those boys!

Now here come the Mississippi boys to help. Go get them Statham . . . go get them!

The view of the crest of the hill where the latest charge had taken place was magnificent. Johnston watched with glee as banners streaming in the breeze, the gray troops renewed the attack on the ridge. Johnston tore off his hat, waving it gaily over his head, pointing and hollering along with the attacking troops who were now advancing through the stubble of what was left of the fruit orchard.

"Go boys, go!" His eyes glowed at the sight, their light reflecting the intensity of the bright firestorm erupting a gain on the ridge. Again, it had become very loud, the sound of the fight intense in pitch and volume. O'Hara and Wickham grinned, their voices joining Johnston's in encouragement of their soldier's endeavor. It was obvious that both men were enjoying Johnston's excitement. Suddenly, shots whipped around the party, causing them to duck, and Fire-Eater to rear, front hooves kicking hard into the air, the big bay whinnying in fear.

"Whoa, big fellow, easy Fire-Eater!" Johnston hauled on the reins, pulling the shaken animal under control. "We can handle this. This is nothing new to us. Easy big boy, easy now." There was a thudding sound, Fire-Eater shuddering, whinnying, and continuing to fight Johnston. Wickham turned and looked over at the agitated animal. Seeing nothing he rode closer, and then saw the blood, dripping down the side of Johnston's boot.

"General, you've been hit!" Wickham shouted; his voice barely audible over the sounds of the battle. "We had better go down under the hill, where we won't be so exposed to the enemy fire, those bullets are really flying!"

"Damn, they must have nicked me after all. Johnston thought angrily. "No." He replied. "Hardee's fire is very heavy as well. We must go where the fire is *heaviest!"*

O'Hara stared in amazement at Johnston. "But General, your horse is wounded!" O'Hara blurted out in protest, pointing at the blood on the big bay's side. The blood was obviously fresh.

"Yes, and his master, too." Johnston replied.

They must have stung me better than I thought they did, the damned blue-bellies! I still feel lightheaded, a little shaky, but I don't see anything, no wounds. It can't be serious then, just a nasty bee sting! We can't stop now for this. No sir, we're winning! He smiled again, not wanting the younger men to see his concern.

"It's all right boys. It's all right." Johnston continued to smile, and clenched his fist, a gesture of strength. "Nothing serious at all, just like a bee sting, must be a scratch, that's all. Let us keep up, we don't want to fall to far behind the advance, now do we? Ah, here comes Harris back."

Isham Harris quickly rode up. He had rushed to give Statham his orders, and had then just as quickly returned, not wanting to be far from Johnston. There was a premonition rumbling through all of Harris's being. He peered anxiously at Johnston's dark face, further blackened as it was by the day's vast expenditures of gunpowder. He closely perused Johnston's clothes, looking for any telltale signs of injury, noting as had the others, the blood dripping from Fire-Eater's side. It was dripping off the side of the animal's side, where Fire-Eater's flank and Johnston's high boot touched, the blood dripping in crimson drops from the heel of Johnston's boot.

"Your report, Governor?" Johnston spoke, sitting straight and tall in the saddle. There was no indication of injury or shakiness anywhere in his posture.

"Sorry, sir." Harris began to speak, Johnston focusing his full attention on the other man's face, his eyes peering hard at the other man's mouth.

The sounds of the battle must be louder than I thought. Johnston thought, straining to hear. Why can't I hear him? What's that roaring sound, it sounds like a train rumbling through my brain. Damn, there must be something in my eyes, the smoke maybe. I'm having trouble focusing. Why do I suddenly feel so . . . so very tired? Everything feels so weird, it's like all I want to do is to sleep . . . just go to sleep. I feel like I'm vibrating inside, can't keep my balance. I don't think I can stay on my . . .

"General, are you all right?"

Suddenly he swayed in the saddle, nearly falling from Fire-Eater's back. Harris and Wickham moved quickly to catch him. Each immediately set themselves to either side of Fire-Eater, each reaching out an arm to catch and hold Johnston upright on his mount. Harris leaned in close, frantically sliding an arm around Johnston, and leaning in close to speak directly into Johnston's ear.

"General, are you wounded? Where are you hit, sir? Talk to me, General, please, talk to me!"

I can barely hear him. "Yes." Johnston mumbled. "And I fear seriously." Quickly the surrounding officers formed a shield around their stricken leader and led Fire-Eater down the hill and over to the shelter of a nearby ravine. Cover now was necessary, and the treed ravine provided the closest available sanctuary from the continuous gunfire.

"Where's Yandell?" Harris screamed.

"The General sent him off earlier to take care of some wounded men, including some Yankees!" Wickham bitterly replied. "He saw that there was a lack of surgeons and sent Doctor Yandell to help . . . even with the damned Yankees! I'll try and find some help! Find that wound, damn it!" Wickham turned on his horse and headed out across the field, galloping off in the direction of Beauregard's latest headquarters.

The others quickly dismounted and gently removed Johnston from Fire-Eater's back, laying him carefully down into the soft, sweet-smelling grass of the ravine, under the shade of a large leafy oak tree. Harris turned to another aide.

"Captain, please go find the general's other aides, and bring them back here, quickly!"

"Yes Governor, I'll do my best!" The younger man hurried off. Harris turned his attention back to Johnston, now lying on the ground, his plumed hat serving as a pillow. Johnston was breathing, but his open eyes showed little recognition. Harris bent over his stricken leader, searching for life in Johnston's unfocused eyes. He frantically ripped open Johnston's uniform coat and shirt, buttons flying everywhere, Harris desperately searching for a wound in Johnston's body. Other than the furrow under the armpit, a mere scratch, there was nothing quickly noticeable.

"General! General Johnston, can you hear me!" Harris shouted in Johnston's empty, filthy face. "Please sir, please speak to me! General . . . *talk to me!*" Harris's voice was choked, tears filling his eyes.

Albert Sidney Johnston, the Commander-in-Chief of the Confederate Army in the West, lay there, dying in the tall grass of the ravine. He could see and hear everyone, although to him, their voices seem strangely muted.

I hear you fine, Governor. You can stop shouting. Damn, you've gone and ripped my good shirt. It was a fine one, expensive, too. So were the buttons, the best stuff. Hard to find.

My body feels funny, almost numb. I don't seem to be able to move anything. Strange. I don't feel any pain. I just feel tired, so very . . . very . . . tired.

Now what is Bill, (Brigadier General William Preston had just arrived) doing? Bill, my hat is just fine as a pillow, you don't have to put my head in your lap. I can see fine. I can hear you, Bill. I just can't seem to answer you.

Preston had propped Johnston's head in his lap. Cradling his old friend's face, and smoothing his hair, he continued to ask Johnston if Johnston knew him. Preston's tears dropped softly on Johnston's silent face, wetting the soot, and smearing as Preston attempted to clean the soot away.

Oh Bill, of course I know you, why are you making such a fuss? This is not like you. I've never seen you cry before. It must be pretty serious. I feel cold now, especially in my arms and legs. Strange feeling.

Have you boys found something? Is that where the problem is? Is that why you're taking my boot off? Is that where the problem is? Funny, I don't remember getting hit in the leg.

My God, look at all that blood that was in my boot! Is that what happened, I got shot in the leg? That's ironic, just like Achilles, well almost. What a strange way to be put out of action, a little leg wound taking me out like this.

What's that? Oh, the bullet hit me right behind the knee and severed an artery. Nobody saw it because my high boots hid the wound. What a time to have sent Yandell away. He probably would have noticed and realized what was happening and put a tourniquet on the leg. I must have been bleeding all this time, right into the boot, that's why we didn't see it. I wonder if it's too late.

Isham, am I dying? Funny, never thought it would be like this. I always thought I'd die in bed. After all that time fighting the Comanches and such, and after that trip across to Texas, well, I guess I figured I was pretty much bulletproof.

I wonder if the other boys felt the same way. Probably not, not the way most of them got it. At least I've got all my limbs, nothing missing. I guess I'll never know.

Tarnation, I'm so damn cold! Bill, stop crying and cover me with a horse blanket or something!

Major Haydon, what are you doing? I don't think I need a drink. That's good Tennessee whiskey you're putting into my mouth. I appreciate what you're trying to do, but I do not think that it's going to do one damn bit of good, just a waste of good medicinal whiskey.

Major Dudley Haydon was attempting to pour a few tablespoons of whiskey down Johnston's throat. It just merely flowed back out, dripping on Johnston's beard. Haydon, Preston, and Harris had now been rejoined by Wickham, O'Hara, and another aide, Lieutenant George W. Baylor. All stood or knelt around their fallen leader, the battle forgotten as the tears flowed.

Major, please stop trying to get me drunk. It's not going to work. I am not thirsty, at least not yet. I might be in a little while, especially if I go to the infernal regions. I hear it gets mighty hot down there, even worse than our famed southern climate.

216 | DANIEL F. KORN

It's too late, boys. I think I have lost too much of life's precious elixir. Funny, I don't feel so cold anymore. Strange.

It's growing dark. I cannot see anymore. Hearing's going too. They all seem so far away. No more noise can't hear the fighting anymore. It's quiet, peaceful.

I hope we win. I did what I thought was necessary, what I thought was best for the Army, for the Country. I did my best, Mister President, my best.

I guess I will see plenty of the boys now. I hope they're not mad at me. The Bishop's (Polk) always talking about that better place. I hope he's right; it would have been nice if he could have been here.

Maybe I will meet some of those old knights, some of those old time Crusaders. Maybe even Washington. Won't that be something? I always wondered what they were really like.

I think someone just said it was 2:30. Can't tell, too far away. Well, that's not my problem now. Guess its Pierre's.

It's all his now. Hopefully he can finish the job and lick 'em, lick Grant. Good luck to you, you old Creole. Hope you still have some of that "Sumter" luck left. It's your problem now.

Lord. I am so tired . . . so sleepy. Guess it won't be long now, until I meet you. Think I'll rest now, yes, that's a good idea. Rest.

I am sorry, Jeff. I did my best. God bless you, Mister President. God bless our cause. Don't give up the cause!

Good-bye.

GRANT

Pittsburg Landing
April 6, 1862 5:00 P.M.

The sunken road had finally been taken, the gallant defenders having at last capitulated. It had taken the Confederate army seven hours, cost them perhaps their best combat commander in the west, and used up thousands of rebel troops in wasted assaults on the Yankee defenses. It was an extraordinary price to pay for such a small piece of real estate.

They've missed their chance. Grant was sitting on an old tree stump, whittling away with an old pocket-knife, his mind hard at work on his plan.

They've missed it. They pushed us back, bent the line back, they could have totally disrupted everything and gotten into our rear areas, and instead they missed it.

The piles of shavings were growing ever larger. It was a sure sign that his warrior mind was hard at work. The other officers were staying away from him, for Rawlins had recognized the purposeful look on Grant's face. He had shooed all the others away, telling them to leave Grant alone with his thoughts, to think, to devise, to *plan*.

Why did they do it? They just kept hammering away at Prentiss, just hammering like they were pounding shoes on an anvil. Why did they waste all that time, all those men, in such wasteful assaults? Beauregard knows better. He's got Hardee, and he certainly should know better. I guess that book of tactics he wrote didn't cover that sort of situation. Still, they should have isolated that part of the line, just penned up Prentiss and the rest of them in a pocket, and just kept going . . . gone around us. They could have pushed us into the river. Well, now they won't get the chance.

To most people a battle is a mixture of fire and smoke, terror and confusion, death and destruction that defy their abilities to comprehend what is happening. Grant was not most people. He was well on his way to becoming one of the gifted few, a different breed of warrior, one of those who could look at the smoke-filled pathos of a situation, and see the patterns form in his mind, before they could even form on a battlefield. To Grant, the parts of a battle were like pieces of a puzzle, and in his mind, he could fit them together faster than others could play them out on the battlefield. It was a gift. Alexander had it, so did Julius Caesar, perhaps even Napoleon, but now it was Grant's turn. Grant could read battles.

He had never lost track of the plot, and he had quickly perceived what the outcome would be. Earlier in the day he sensed a priceless opportunity, and even though it wasn't turning out quite the way he had envisioned it, he still saw the possibilities for victory, a Union victory, on this terrible April Sunday afternoon, and not the unmitigated disaster that others less gifted saw.

Quietly, inside his mind, the warrior in Grant was seething. It did not show to most, although the perceptive Rawlins had quickly realized that Grant was very angry. While others had spent the day bemoaning the losses the Army of the Tennessee had suffered, Grant instead had continued to look for the opportunity, *the edge,* and kept attempting to bring off a battle that would have annihilated the opposing southern force. He sat there, the knife busy with his whittling, his brain busy with his plan.

Why didn't they move the way they were supposed to? By God, if (Lew) Wallace had advanced as ordered and gotten in on the right, and Nelson had done what he was supposed to do on the left, we would have had the enemy right in a perfect spot, a vise so to speak. It would have been about the same as that Carthaginian, old Hannibal, did to those Roman legions at Cannae. Hell, the enemies are men, the rebs have got to be tired, they're certainly overextended, and they're vulnerable. I'm sure they know about Johnston too, if we know, they must. Things like that you can't keep from an army, the men always find out. That knowledge can only help us, since chances being those boys over there have got to be shook up, losing Johnston that way.

What in hell was he doing, leading a charge like that? He certainly knew better. Too bad, he was a good soldier. Too bad for them, but good for us. Now, what to do about the present situation?

"General? Are you all right?" It was Rawlins. Grant looked up from his whittling, the shavings everywhere around his seat.

"Why is it so hard to follow a simple order?" Grant muttered. Rawlins knew he was referring to Wallace and Nelson.

Unfortunately for Grant's plan, neither man's division had arrived when, nor where Grant had wanted in time to do what Grant wanted. Grant's orders to "Bull" Nelson had arrived in plenty of time for the massive ex-navy officer to have done what Grant had intended Nelson to do, but the old sailor had not moved an inch from his camps until *after* one o'clock in the afternoon, too late to do much this day. Lew Wallace, for all his bluster to Grant at their riverside conference earlier that morning, had after receiving his orders, gone off and simply gotten himself and his division *lost*. Instead of marching toward the sound of the drums, he and his desperately needed seven thousand men had wandered up and down the Tennessee country roads, lost in the Tennessee river thickets, and had missed all the fighting up to this point. Now the opportunity to go on the offensive, to *attack*, was lost for this day, and Grant hated *that*. Instead, he would have to continue the defensive struggle, that which he disliked doing the most. And, on top of it all, he would have to do it with what was left to him; that being the five infantry divisions, a hundred or so artillery pieces, and about twelve hundred or so cavalry, and himself.

It will just have to do. He thought to himself.

Up to this point, Grant had spent most of his time in the saddle, trying to stay off his aching leg. During the course of his riding back and forth from the front to Pittsburg Landing and back again, a small group of newspaper journalists had attached themselves to Grant's group, with Rawlins making sure they stayed out of Grant's way. The newspapermen scribbled furiously away, noting Grant's seemingly lack fear, the soldier who stayed calm when all the others were not, the man who appeared in some cerebral way to be thrilling to the din and danger of battle. They noted how he paid no attention to the constant whine of the bullets passing by, his ignoring of the explosion of shot and shell. Even those who had come to take him to task for seemingly to not be prepared for the Southern attack, could not help but notice his bravery, his indifference to the enemy fire, his *calmness*. They noted it, and they would write about it.

"He is amazing, isn't he?" This comment came from the *Cincinnati Gazette* correspondent, one Whitelaw Reid. Reid had arrived by steamboat merely hours before, and had already interviewed several officers and men, including Ben Prentiss. The interview had taken place during one of Prentiss's trips away from his defense of the sunken road and had been noticed by Grant. Reid found himself comparing the demeanor of Grant under pressure to that of others, including Prentiss, and had concluded that most had not measured up as well as Grant.

"I certainly cannot keep myself as calm as he (Grant) does. How does he do it?"

"That's Sam.' Rawlins replied. "He doesn't let much ruffle him."

"Pretty impressive, Captain." The speaker was another journalist, Irving Carson of the great Midwestern paper, the *Chicago Tribune.* "You think he would be ducking a lot, what with all this metal flying through the air. Yes sir, it's a real . . .!

Suddenly a solid shot screamed through the assembled group. There was a loud *thunk*, and then a shocked silence.

"*My God!*" Whitelaw Reid cried, his voice a frightened gasp. He pointed at the headless remains of what seconds before was Irving Carson. The cannon ball had passed within six feet of Grant and had decapitated the luckless Carson. Reid turned away from the gory sight of his friend and promptly threw up.

Grant looked on calmly, no look of fear on his face. Rawlins appeared less so; the others held more horrified expressions. Rowley, his face now grayish white, turned to Grant and spoke.

"General, I appreciate your courage . . . but it is *not* necessary for you to be here! We must leave this place. If we don't, we . . . you could be dead in five minutes!"

Grant looked at his frightened aide. *Settle down, Captain,* he thought, *just settle down.* He looked around at the assembled group, noting the frightened looks and the half crouches that most had dropped in to, the bullets zipping around them. He looked at Rawlins, who nodded. Reid was still being sick, as he stole glances over his shoulder at the beheaded man, a note pad still clutched in the dead man's bloody, lifeless, fingers. Grant reached a conclusion.

"I guess that's so. Let's go." He had turned his horse away, and unhurriedly ridden away, the others breathing huge sighs of relief as they followed him, out of the immediate danger area.

But that was earlier today.

Now Grant sat on his makeshift stool in his headquarters camp, his pocketknife busy in his hands carving up a twig, while his mind raced with ideas.

They have made two mistakes. Grant thought to himself. Two big blunders. First, they never concentrated a majority of their forces on or against any one point. They just kept fighting a general fight up and down the line. I can't believe that old Beauregard did not see that the terrain was way too broken up to keep trying to maintain a general attack along a line of any length. Those swamps, ravines, and such, just made it impossible to do so. He doesn't seem to have kept any kind of reserve to exploit a breakthrough. He should have. They never massed enough troops in one spot to break a line, or crush a flank, Course, our boys did have something to do with that!

Grant smiled to himself. He stopped whittling for a second, long enough to brush the wooden shavings off of his lap, then picked his knife back up, the thought process continuing.

Their second mistake they made was the way they kept going after Prentiss and some of Bill Wallace's boys in that road in the ground. They should have rolled around it, turned it into an isolated island, and kept moving on. They could have just bottled our boys up, stuck the cork in, moved on, and threatened our rear. That would have been smarter, but they let their pride get in the way. They just kept pounding that road, like some crazed blacksmith pounding out shoes on an anvil. They must have made ten, eleven assaults before they got through. Took them a bunch of guns to do it, too. Grant looked up at Rawlins and spoke.

"Captain Rawlins, how much artillery did you say Captain Rowley told you they figured the enemy brought up to finally break down General Prentiss's position?"

"About fifty, sixty, guns, General." Rawlins replied. "That's what was reported."

So, they turned all that firepower loose on that one hole in the ground. Grant thought to himself. I'll bet they wasted a lot of shells on that one. Good! What a waste of ammunition. Wonder if any of the survivors can still hear/ God bless those boys, they bought us some time, and the rebs didn't gain any tactical advantage there, capturing that spot, no sir! Just a big hole even bigger that's all. They just gave us more time, gave me more time. Good. That's their second mistake.

He continued to think. His plan beginning to take more of a defined shape. Now I've got Webster lining up all our big guns up along on those bluffs along the river. Siege guns, nice big heavy stuff. We've got Hurlbut and his men set up, and they're established in such a way as to have a nice, clear, line of fire to the south and west. He's got that ravine in front of them, helping defend his front, and that's half full of water, what with all the rain we've had here, and it's downright swampy. Hell, just to reach that ravine the damned rebs have got to cross all that lovely open ground in front of it, and we got the whole thing completely covered with musket and artillery fire. Lovely, lovely. Let's see what they can do with that!

He grinned, a sardonic smile creasing his face, then turned to Rawlins.

"I hear you threatened to have a riverboat burned and a crew shot if they didn't do what you wanted?" Grant asked, a note of humor in his voice.

"Damn cowards!' Rawlins sputtered, a cough interrupting his explanation. Two transports, the *Fort Wayne*, which carried pontoons for bridge building, and the aptly named *Rocket*, which was towing ammunition barges, had arrived at Pittsburg Landing during the fighting. Star shells exploding over the river landing had frightened the transports' crews. When they tried to leave without dropping their loads, and to also stop the frightened stragglers who were trying to get on the boats to escape the fighting, Rawlins had taken quick action. He had threatened to burn the *Fort Wayne*, and to shoot the crew of the *Rocket*, if they even attempted to cut and run away, before taking care of their loads.

"Just because the rebs got a little too close with those star shells." Rawlins grumped, the coughing bout over. "Those damned cowards were just looking for an excuse to run! Just looking! Not going to let them do it! We ain't going to retreat, no sir, just like you told General Buell. This army's going to stay right here and fight!"

Grant smiled at that. "Yes." He replied. "I don't think he (Buell) took too kindly to my reply to his question."

"That damn fool!" Rawlins snorted. "Err, begging the General's pardon, but how could he have gone and asked you such damn fool question? What kind of plans have you made for a retreat? Hell, what kind of a question was that? Seems to me that he should have known better, especially with you!" Rawlins waved his hands, his movements all nervous and jerky.

Grant chuckled at the words of his subordinate and friend. He was gratified by Rawlins's defense, and grateful for his friend's concern. "Well now, Captain, I do believe that General Buell was somewhat dismayed by what he perceived as the situation when he finally got here."

Grant was referring to the fact that when Buell and his staff finally arrived at about 1:00 P.M., there had been a huge multitude of men, all refuges from the fighting, all scrambling for space along the riverbank. Buell, horrified by the scene, when he met with Grant later on the *Tigress,* had expressed his concerns about the situation. Grant had simply replied that he had just returned from the front where he had been again riding to gauge the action. He had then shown Buell his sword scabbard, damaged and bent by the impact of a spent shell fragment. The haughty, aristocratic Buell had just looked at Grant, and ignoring the other man's comments, had sarcastically asked what preparations had been made for a retreat. Grant, noting the other man's tone, had quietly but firmly rebuked Buell, telling him they were there to fight, not retreat. Rawlins was still chuckling over the exchange.

"Yes sir, General, I did like the way you told him (Buell) that you were still going to whip them, the damned rebels!" Rawlins was getting himself worked up, a fit of coughing again suddenly erupting from Grant's fiery subordinate. He stopped talking long enough for the coughing bout to stop. He wiped his lips with a dirty bandanna, and peered hard at Grant, noting the sudden look of pain on Grant's face. "You all right, General?"

"Yep." Grant replied. "This ankle's hurting some." Grant reached over to rub the sore leg. "It will be all right. Slows me down a bit, but nothing to worry about. Don't like the crutch much, but I guess it's necessary."

Rawlins studied his friend and leader's face. He searched for signs of nervousness or fear and found none. Again, he marveled at the other's incredible coolness under all this pressure. Rawlins pulled up a stool and sat close to Grant.

"Sam." Rawlins voice was low. "Be honest with me. Does the loss of Prentiss and his boys mean the rebs have gotten the upper hand on us? Is it too late for us to do anything?"

Grant looked up from his whittling, a surprised look on his face. "Oh no John, they can't break our lines tonight. Buell's here. We've got Nelson's six thousand coming across the river now. We'll be fine, besides, do you hear that?" He motioned his head in the direction of the river, Rawlins's head swiveling to listen.

It was true. Clear as a bell, you could hear the bands, the regimental band of Nelson's division playing. Nelson's men were crossing the Tennessee, and the ex-naval officer was letting everyone within an earshot know it. Steamboat after steamboat, each loaded full to the bulwarks with combat veterans, were crossing the river to Pittsburg Landing. Nelson had ordered the regimental bands to play, and each one was trying to outdo the others, each one belting out loud and lusty patriotic songs. Their thunderous beat was echoed by the rumbling footsteps of swaggering men, men who knew they were coming to the rescue of their comrades-in-arms. As they stepped ashore off the transports, the lead regiments were forced to wade their way through the swarms of refugees all over the waterfront. The veteran troops looked at the whimpering runaways, and their faces turned ugly, their eyes cold with contempt and scorn. Pushing and shoving their way through the mass of soldierly scamps, Nelson's men made obvious their contempt for the runaways, even as the skulkers tried to dissuade the newcomers.

"We are whipped!' The runaways cried to Nelson's men. "We have been cut to pieces! You'll catch it, wait, you'll see!"

"Get out of the way, ya bums, *real* soldiers are coming through!" The newcomers shouted, their officers swinging the flat side of their swords against the backsides of the fugitives, clearing the way ahead. The high level of the newcomers' confidence was contagious. Their band led the way up the bluff, away from the landing and the chaos on the waterfront. The band began to play, striking up a tune. It was *Dixie Land*.

Suddenly a smoke-tinged voice cried out, a voice that belonged to one of those who had stayed and fought hard for that day; "That's the Thirty-Sixth Indiana! That's *Buell's* men! Those are *veterans*, boys, we're saved!"

The soldiers up on the bluff, the fighters, those that had resisted the urge to run, the exhausted troops who had fought the good fight heard the music and began to cheer. They cheered and cheered, their hoarse voices screaming with joy. They knew now that they had not bled for nothing that they weren't licked yet, and there were smiles on their soot and dirt blackened faces. Grant grinned at the sight. It was a good sign.

"No, John, it's not too late for us, but it is for *them*." He pointed in the direction of the southern lines, then continued. "Tomorrow we shall attack them with *fresh* troops." He gestured toward Nelson's men, now lining up into formations as quickly as their enthusiastic officers could get them into place. "We will have the rest of Buell's men here shortly. Lew Wallace is on his way now. We'll have those fresh troops, and we will drive them, drive them right back! They've used up their chance, and they've got nothing left! Now it's our turn."

I knew I saw something in him back in Galena! Rawlins thought to himself, almost giddy with the knowledge of what he saw. *My God, he almost looks happy at the chance. I almost feel sorry for the rebs. Still . . .?*

"General, are you sure? Are they not still pressing us?"

Grant stuck a fresh cigar in his mouth. He lighted it, his hands cupped to protect the flame from the droplets of rain that were beginning to fall. He looked back and down at the landing, looking over the puffs of smoke blowing off the glowing tip of the cigar. He watched the next group of troops parade off the boats and start their march up the bluff road to join the already assembled reinforcements who were rapidly preparing their positions for the evening. He turned and gazed down along the road, where he could see Colonel Webster hard at work massing artillery along a half-mile long line, fifty-two guns in all. There was even a battery of massive siege guns, five huge cannons designed to batter down thick defensive positions made of stone and earth, but to be used here to throw their massive missiles into the Confederate lines. They were there as much as for their psychological effect as they were for their physical ones. It was an awesome display of firepower. All of the guns were now aimed at the former Union camps, now resting in the hands of their Confederate captors, and were all just waiting for the signal that would unleash their havoc on the rebel forces. Grant smiled and turned once more to Rawlins.

"They have been *pressing* us all day, John." Grant's voice was ice cold, the voice of the executioner who knew what power he possessed, and also just how to use it."But I think we will stop them here."

Rawlins gazed upon the scene. Here, with the river at their backs, was where Grant had decided to make their stand. A mile and a half of defensive positions now ran west from the landing down and away from the bluffs west onto and along the Pittsburg-Corinth Road, past Chamber's Field, then up through the intersection of the Pittsburg-Corinth and Hamburg-Savannah roads and then north. The fifty-two guns had been placed at vital spots, their batteries primed, their crews ready. The swampy, half-filled Dill Branch creek sat in front of the defensive lines and acted as a moat. This time the Yankees were digging in and digging in hard. Grant had learned his lesson. This time there would be no surprises. Grant had also ordered the gunboats *Tyler* and *Lexington* to be placed in position on the Tennessee River so as to be able to lend the weight of their fifty-three-inch shells to the Yankee defense dispositions, their guns situated to be fired right down the Confederate flank and subject the enemy to severe enfilade fire.

Rawlins looked again at Grant. He noted the cigar was puffing away, but that was all the emotion obvious on Grant's countenance, who now stood facing toward the not-so-distant Confederate lines, where the fighting was still going on.

I can see their flags. If I can then I'm sure Sam does, too. He waited for Grant to speak. Grant crossed his arms, then spoke, still looking at the not-so-distant smoke-filled fight.

"Captain, I believe it is time we sent our response that today's festivities command. It is time we sent our reply to the Confederate high command's invitation." The cigar smoke was wreathing Grant's head and face in an almost aura-like cloud.

Rawlins grinned and shook his head. "Yes sir, I believe that Colonel Webster is just waiting for the order for that *reply.*"

Grant took a long draw on his cigar. He looked again at the river landing, then up at the sky. The rain was still misting down, the clouds darkening in the twilight sky. Out on the water he could see lanterns and torches being lighted, so that now the river boats looked like giant fireflies, bobbing along on the skin of the river. Night was on its way. To end this blood-soaked April Sunday. The shadows were growing longer, as more and more lanterns were lighted to hold off the encroachment of night. Torches were in use, their flames illuminating the endless streams of men and supplies onto the landing. Dusk was upon them.

"Well, I guess it's time to *light things up*, Captain." Grant chuckled at his pun, and turned back to Rawlins, who was grinning at his friend's joke. Grant pointed at the now darkened Confederate lines.

"Captain. The order is given. *Commence fire.*"

BEAUREGARD

Shiloh Church
April 6, 1862 Evening

Johnston was gone. Although he had tried to keep it quiet, Beauregard knew that the men of the Army of the Mississippi now knew of their loss. Yet, with the highest-ranking soldier in the western Confederacy now dead, along with thousands of casualties the Army had suffered as well, Beauregard still felt good about the day.

All day he had watched as events unfolded, waiting for word about the whereabouts of the Union forces of General Don Carlos Buell, and just waiting for the other shoe to drop. *If Buell shows up at the wrong time, it could be disastrous.* Beauregard thought to himself. *Simply disastrous.* Thus, when a courier arrived from Corinth holding an incredible message, the old Creole felt like his prayers had finally been answered. The message put a smile on his lips and brought solace to his aching head.

The message was from an old friend, Colonel Ben Helm, who had a very famous relative occupying the Yankee White House. (Helm's brother-in-law was none other than Abraham Lincoln.) Helm had sent word from northern Alabama that Buell's army had been diverted and was reported to be on the road headed for Decatur in north Alabama.

Well, so much for that concern! Beauregard smiled, his faced suffused with joy. Now with Buell gone, there's no hope for Grant to get some help, and there is nothing to stop us from finishing him off in the morning! Oh Sidney, if you only knew! Richmond should be quite happy to hear our news. Wait until President Davis gets our telegram!

Beauregard stepped out from the tent; his step lighter than it had been in days past. His head still ached, but now not as much. He hailed Colonel Jordan, whose mood was considerably more somber. Jordan's spirits were low, for he was taking Johnston's death badly.

"Colonel Jordan, were you able to get that message off to Richmond with the courier?"

Jordan, his soot-covered red face reflective of his grief, nodded a yes. "Yes General, I have informed Richmond that we attacked the enemy's position at Pittsburg Landing this morning. I have informed them that after ten hours of fighting, it is your belief that we have gained a complete victory, and have driven the enemy from every position, thanks to the Almighty."

Beauregard, his red kepi pushed back on his feverish brow, picked up on the twin notes of concern and sarcasm evident in Jordan's voice.

"Colonel, do I detect an, um, a note of *uncertainty* in your voice?"

Jordan started to speak, then stopped. His head drooped down, and then he began to speak, his voice pained and soft.

"I am sorry General, I am happy about our victory today . . . it's just . . . well . . . you know, General Johnston and I were . . ." His tear choked voice trailed off.

"I miss him too, Tom." Beauregard reached out and laid a hand upon the other man's shoulder.

"It's just that I . . . well, I never thought it would end this way for Sidney." Jordan's choked voice stopped. He looked up at the evening sky, the soft pitter-patter of raindrops beginning to fall now evident. His voice reflected the strain of the day, the sorrow evident in his voice. He continued, his voice cracking. "A simple tourniquet, that's all that it would have taken to save him, but too late, *it was just too late!*" Jordan stopped, his eyes now filling with tears.

Easy Colonel, we've lost friends before. Still, I have to remember, they were related.

"Well Tom, we all know that this can happen at any time, to any of us. It was just his time to go." Beauregard patted Jordan's shoulder, then stepped away. "I am sorry. I will miss him badly also, but the best memorial we can build to his courage, the best way we can remember General Johnston, is

236 | DANIEL F. KORN

to follow up on his victory today, and soundly *destroy the enemy*. This victory will be his, and all will remember this day!"

Jordan looked up and smiled through his tears. He wiped his eyes, then brought himself to full attention. "Yes General, I do appreciate that. Thank you. I'm all right, sir. What would the General wish me to do for him?"

Good man, good. Beauregard thought to himself. *I need him, especially now.* "Here, this message is to go to all commanders. I want you to send staff to inform the commanders, *especially* those at the very front, to suspend their attacks for the night. Make sure especially that *all* commanders get the word, *especially General Bragg.* His corps has been greatly extended today."

Beauregard looked up at the darkening sky, the sun starting to cast long shadows as it was quickly setting to the west of Shiloh Church. The trees that surrounded the little glen the church sat in, were even now slipping deeper into the shadows. Clouds were rolling in, a coverlet to bring on the black of night. The raindrops were increasing. Beauregard took a deep breath of the wet evening air.

"Yes Colonel, you may send the order for the firing to cease. The victory is *sufficiently* complete." Beauregard smiled, and then continued. "Besides, the Yankees have got those damn gunboats now, in the river to shoot at us with. There is no need to further expose the men to the fire of those infernal machines. We have been at it for thirteen hours now. Our boys are tired, hungry, and in some cases, somewhat spiritless. I have been out riding our lines and I have seen all this. Why, they're even too tired to cheer our glorious victory!"

Johnston turned and looked at Beauregard. "General Beauregard, I seem to recall that there may be some very good reasons that I can think of for those men to *not be cheering* today's events." He was referring to the loss of Johnston and the innumerable casualties the Army of Mississippi had suffered that day.

Beauregard grimaced. "We must not dwell on *that* Colonel. We have *much* to do." He gestured out into the surrounding darkness. The camps were alight with numerous fires, so much more than the night before. "Those men out there are tired, they are scattered and disorganized now, and some may be out of control. I know that our latest attacks on the enemy lines have been without strength. Some of this I know by reports, the rest I have seen with my own eyes. The men are worn out. They fall asleep on their arms, right where they stand. They plunder the enemy camps, even though we gave strict orders not to allow it." *Although, realistically, how can we expect to stop it, the poor devils.* Beauregard mused.

Beauregard stopped, and closed his eyes for a long moment, resting them against the pain in his head. He opened them, turned to face Jordan, and spoke again.

"Yes Colonel, the men need to rest, rest and provision themselves. Many, I assume, are just about out of ammunition. We must give them the time, and the means, to replenish themselves and their supplies. In order to do that,

238 | DANIEL F. KORN

we must gather them all in, and once we have done that, I do not believe that there will be time to send a general assault against the enemy before darkness is complete. It would also be suicidal to send them in *without* replenishing their supplies. Either way, we have to stop." Beauregard chuckled. "Besides, *they'll* be there in the morning." He was referring to the federal forces. "They're whipped, and we will finish them off in the morning. I have little doubt of that! Send the message, Colonel." Beauregard was expansive, happy with the moment.

Jordan saluted. "Yes sir, General Beauregard. By your leave, sir?"

Beauregard smiled, and returned the salute with a flourish, then winced at the pain in his head. Jordan turned and walked away, his head still down. It was obvious that his thoughts were still on Johnston. Beauregard watched him walk away, sighed, and then turned back to walk toward the old log church. He grimaced in pain again. The headache was getting stronger, and he was feeling cold in the chill of the early evening air. He turned back toward his tent, and walked back in it, closing the tent flap behind him. He laid down on his tent cot, and reached for a camp blanket, covering his shoulders and chest with it. With a sigh he laid back and closed his eyes.

I need to get warm. He thought. I need to warm up, and think. I need to think about what we are going to do next. This day is done, and tomorrow is another, and we need to be ready to deal with it. I probably should consult with the others, especially Braxton. I am sure I will hear from him about stopping the advance.

Yes, it would probably be a good idea to discuss things with him and Hardee. I just wish Braxton would do a better job of not getting upset, that irascible old man. "Brax" does know his job, but he just irritates me so. I appreciate his thoughts, but it's my decision to make now, thanks to Sidney, damn him for his foolhardy bullheadedness!

"General?" It was Jordan's voice, coming from the tent entrance.

Oh, damnation! Beauregard opened his eyes. "Come in Colonel. What is it?"

"I have sent the recall orders. There is some concern that we may have stopped too soon."

Beauregard sat up, wincing at the renewed thumping at his temples. He felt the anger beginning to build inside. He fought to keep his temper, trying to keep from shouting, He knew that Jordan was merely trying to keep him informed.

"Who Colonel, who has complained? *Who?*"

Jordan stepped back, hearing the anger in Beauregard's voice, started to stammer out a reply. "Well, General ... I ... ah ... I wouldn't be too concerned ..."

"*Who Colonel!*" The heat had definitely returned to the Creole's voice, if not to his body. "Who says this army has stopped too soon?" Beauregard swung his legs over the side of the cot, the blanket falling to the ground, as Beauregard stood to face Jordan.

Jordan swallowed. "General Bragg, sir. I had Captain Augustin, (Numa Augustin, a Beauregard staff officer), take your directive to General Bragg. He says that General Bragg was quite upset by your decision to cease operations. He said, according to Augustin, quote; *My God, was a victory ever complete?* Unquote. Apparently General, General Bragg considered disobeying your order, until he saw that General Polk's men were already starting to fall back. It was only then that general Bragg gave the order for his men to do the same as Polk's, or at least that is what Augustin says." Jordan stopped, waiting for the anticipated explosion.

Damn you, Brax! Red-faced, Beauregard just stood there, staring at Jordan. Damn you! You hardheaded irascible old fool! We have already won a great victory today! Why start a fight now?

Beauregard sat back down on the cot, visibly forcing himself to keep his temper in check. Jordan watching, let out a sigh in relief. He waited for a reply.

Let it go, let it go. Beauregard thought himself. Now is not the time to be starting feuds, or ruffling feathers. We need rest, food, time to plan. If Braxton wants to vent, let him. Besides, he's earned it, his boys fought hard, real hard today. Anyway, I need rest, sleep, shouldn't get so worked up. After all, fighting does raise tempers, and in old Brax's case, the two go hand in hand. I'm just going to ignore this, besides those boys out there need to be resupplied, they need provisions.

Not their leaders fighting it out over turf. At least the food is compliments of the Yankees. He took a deep breath and then looked up at Jordan. "Anything else, Colonel?"

Jordan smiled, and visibly relaxed. It was a gesture not lost on Beauregard. Jordan looked back behind him, out the tent flap into the darkness.

"There's a surprise outside for you, General." Jordan pointed out the tent flap.

Beauregard lifted his head. "A surprise?"

Jordan grinned. "Yes sir. I will send him in now, with your permission."

Him? Beauregard nodded his assent. Jordan stepped out through the tent flap. There was the sound of murmured words outside, and then the "visitor" stepped in. Union General Benjamin Prentiss stepped inside the dimly lighted tent, Jordan following him inside.

Beauregard smiled but said nothing. "Good evening, General." Ben Prentiss stood just inside the tent flap, and stiffly saluted. He was coated with soot, and there were streaks of blood on his uniform, although none of it was his own. He made no further movement into the tent but stood there waiting.

"Come in, General, come in!" The bemused Beauregard returned the salute, and waved Prentiss to a camp stool. "Sit down and join me. May I offer you some refreshments?" he pointed to the whiskey bottle on the camp table. "Compliments of your Yankee quartermasters!"

242 | DANIEL F. KORN

Prentiss frowned and shook his graying head. "Thank you, General Beauregard, none for me. Maybe some water, if you have it. I would like to clean up, if possible."

Beauregard was in an expansive mood, the headache temporarily forgotten. "Certainly General. Colonel? Could you see to our *guest's* comfort, if you would please? Oh, some food also, General?"

Prentiss sat down on the proffered stool. He waved his hand. "Thank you, gentlemen. No, just some water to drink, and to clean up with. That will be sufficient, thank you." Prentiss ran his hand through his hair, and looked at his hand, noting the ash that had come off on it. His uniform stank of gunpowder and sweat, a testimony to the hard day's fighting he and his men endured. The day had been long, and his division was *gone*, and there were those who would second guess and criticize the man's work later, but he had succeeded in his mission. He had given Grant his precious, necessary, time.

Beauregard looked on, not without sympathy. "Certainly, General. Colonel, please see to it, thank you. Oh, and please see to accommodations for General Prentiss, and, if possible, a change of clothing. Make sure his men, (Prentiss looked up at that, and then at the wall of the tent), are seen to. They fought gallantly. See to it that they are shown the proper courtesies as befits them."

"Certainly, General." Jordan smiled. "I will see to it myself. Will there be anything else?"

Beauregard smiled. "No, I don't believe so. General?" He looked at Prentiss.

Prentiss shook his head. "Thank you, no, nothing else. I appreciate your concern. Thank you."

"As you wish, sir." Jordan saluted, then left on his errand. The two men could hear him issuing instructions outside the tent. Nothing more was said between the two combatants for a few moments. Then an orderly appeared, a canteen slung over his shoulder, and a basin of water perched precariously on a small pile of clothing, both Beauregard and Prentiss noting that the clothing was blue. Prentiss accepted the proffered canteen gratefully. He drank deeply as the orderly placed the basin on the table, and the clothing he piled next to it. Then the two officers were alone again. Prentiss walked over to the basin, and dipped his hands and arms deep into it, and vigorously began to wash his face. He then began to speak, as he slipped out of his uniform coat, and unbuttoned his blouse.

"Well sir, we have felt your power today, and have had to yield to it." Prentiss took another long pull at the canteen.

Beauregard grinned. "Now, General, certainly you could not have expected otherwise!" The Creole was enjoying his moment of glory. Outside the tent there were the sounds of joy and celebration.

Prentiss put the cap on the canteen, and sat back down again, not bothering saying anything for a moment. He then shook his head again and ran his hand through his dirty hair again. Then he began to speak, a slight edge noticeable in his voice.

"General Beauregard today has been *your* day, but *tomorrow* will be different. You will see. I can promise you that!"

Beauregard laughed. My God, he (Prentiss) still believes after the day he's just had. He's a good man. Grant should be sorry to have lost him. Well, at least, he's still alive. Prentiss should be grateful for that, damn you, Sidney!

Beauregard shook his head, then grimaced, the headache still alive and kicking.

"No General, it is *you*, I believe, who will see. Tomorrow we will resume the fight. Our troops will be rested and well fed. We will attack and force the Yankee Army to surrender or be driven into the river to its destruction." Beauregard waved the Helm telegram in Prentiss's face, the Creole gleefully continuing his little speech.

"You see, General, we *know* that Buell's not coming. That means that Grant has no more reserves. Tomorrow, your leader, he who has had his name in all the papers, old "Unconditional Surrender" Grant, is going to find out what it feels like when the shoe is on the other foot! Now, it's our turn to crow, and we will see how he likes that!" Beauregard stopped abruptly, his passion spent, the telegram now crushed in his fist.

Prentiss had sat quietly through the impassioned display by Beauregard. *He doesn't know that Buell is here.* Prentiss happily thought to himself. *Should I tell you, Pierre?* Prentiss then smiled, and quietly replied. "Oh, all right, General. You and your gentlemen have had your way *today*, but it *will* be different, *tomorrow*." The old Virginia-born Yankee general stood up, and walked over to the wash basin, rolled up his sleeves, and got to work, scrubbing down his bearded face, hair, neck, and arms, the water slopping out of the basin onto the dirt floor of the tent. Beauregard watched; his passions temporarily spent. Prentiss dried his face and hair, the beard still dripping, then dried his neck and arms, grunting with relief. He then walked over to the tent flap and pointed out the opening, toward the direction of Pittsburg Landing, and then spoke again.

"You will see, General Beauregard, you will see. Buell will affect a junction with Grant *tonight*, and we will turn the tables on you in the morning. Then we will see who crows the loudest."

Beauregard shook his head, amused at Prentiss's quiet bravado, the Union general's level of confidence amusing to Beauregard. He held up the telegram in Prentiss's face. "No such thing, General, no such thing. Like I said, we know Buell's not coming."

Prentiss shook his head in response and smiled ruefully. He pointed at the telegram. "I don't know what that says, General, but I'm telling you that tomorrow will be different. You'll see."

Beauregard laughed again. "All right, General, if you insist. We will let *history* be the judge of whom will be right, and who will be wrong. However, for now I do believe that this is no longer an issue for you to be concerned about. You have done your part in this day's events, and again I must commend you and your division for its gallant and excellent work today. It was superb work, just superb! Allow me to express my compliments!" He walked over to Prentiss, Beauregard extending his hand, his gallic ancestry at work, and one warrior to another. Prentiss looked at the outstretched hand, shaking his head. He then took Beauregard's hand in his own and shook it.

Thank you, General Beauregard. We did our best." Prentiss muttered, and then sat back down, letting go, his weariness having gotten the best of his exhausted mind and body.

Beauregard said nothing in reply, instead just watching Prentiss drift off into his thoughts. *Indeed you did, General, indeed you did.* Beauregard quietly thought to himself. *You made us pay a mighty price for that damned blasted hole in the ground that damned sunken road. Was it worth it? I don't know. We lost too many, too many good men, especially Sidney. Gone, all gone too soon. That's enough for one day. Regardless of what Bragg, Polk, or any of the others think, know I made the right decision to stop. It's time to rest, time for all of us to rest. Grant will still be there in the morning, and then we'll finish him off.*

"General?" It was Prentiss.

"Yes General, what can I do for you?"

"My condolences on the loss of General Johnston. I was informed officially when I was brought into your camp. He was a good soldier."

"Thank you." Beauregard replied. "We will miss him greatly."

I bet you will. Prentiss thought. I can't remember the last time, if ever, that I had seen Johnston. Doesn't matter now, anyway. Beauregard is simply not listening. Fool. Tomorrow will be different. He doesn't think Buell is here. That telegram obviously says something about Buell's whereabouts, and it obviously says he's somewhere else other than here. That's good. It doesn't sound like Pierre knows that Lew Wallace is around either. Beauregard's scouts have let him down. Wallace should be up here by now, too. That will give Sam another twenty, twenty-five thousand men. That will give Grant plenty to work with tomorrow. He'll do it too. After what I saw in his (Grant's) eyes today, I would not want to be in Beauregard's shoes tomorrow. No sir, I can just hear Grant's reply to today's events. We did our part, gave Grant his time, now it's Grant's turn to hit them back! We're not done, not by a long shot. Beauregard is wrong, dead wrong to think tomorrow will be the same as today. No sir, the only mopping up that's going to be done tomorrow is by our boys, by God!

"What are you thinking, General . . .?" Beauregard stopped.

A thunderous roar could now be heard in the distance. Prentiss got back up off the cot and walked over to the tent flap and out through it. Outside there was a crowd of staff officers, orderlies, and soldiers all staring toward the sound. Beauregard had followed Prentiss out of the tent, the two men listening to the roar in the distance. Prentiss stepped out from under the tent awning, and out into the pale light of the campfires. The black night sky, so full of rain clouds, was being illuminated in the distance, toward the east and Pittsburg Landing. Prentiss listened to the startled buzz circulating among the assembled soldiers and smiled. He looked back at Beauregard, and grinned. The Creole was watching the fireworks with great intensity, an awed look upon his dark face.

That's a great deal of artillery there. Prentiss thought, smiling, observing the now concerned looks on the assembled faces. I guess old Sam is sending his reply right now. Well, I guess we do have something to be proud of, by God!

Prentiss turned back to Beauregard, who was standing like all the rest, caught in morbid fascination by the enemy's artillery barrage. The rain was beginning to get heavy, no longer just a few drops pitter-pattering, but becoming more of a steady fall. The fireworks in the distance were increasing in intensity along with the rain, no longer just a few guns, but obviously a concentrated barrage. Prentiss pointed in the direction of the sound, catching Beauregard's eye, and spoke, a delicious ironic humor evident in the Yankee general's voice.

"Well, General Beauregard, I do believe I *will* have that drink *now*."

GRANT

Pittsburg Landing

April 6, 1862 Late Evening

It was as if the Lord himself was crying. His day, the Sabbath, had closed upon a day which had itself no equal in the known history of the Western Hemisphere. Now it was as if the skies had opened as if his eyes could no longer hold their vast waters in reaction to what his human creations had wrought this day in the Tennessee wetlands.

The rain was falling in torrents, great huge bucketfuls, pouring down in a vain attempt to cleanse the earth's wounds, the bullet-torn battlefield's bloody stains resisting nature's bath. Soldiers from both sides, their thirst unquenched, dragged their weary and torn bodies to a small pond bordering the fields, an unofficial truce in place. Most tried to wet down their parched throats, only to find that between their sheer exhaustion and wounds, some simply could not lift their heads back out of the dark waters, and thus stained the pond with their own life forces. Their actions would give the innocent body a new name, Bloody Pond.

The night sky, by itself deep and dark, was being both naturally and artificially illuminated by the tempest's own lightning, as well as by the periodic flashes of light caused by the flight of the eight-inch artillery shells of the gun boats *Tyler* and *Lexington.* The gun boats flashing cannon muzzles sent their angels of death in high curving parabolas. The rebel troops would watch the shells sweep high into the deep mantle of the night sky, only to come plummeting down into some unlucky devils' position, and blowing them to Kingdom Come, and sending the surrounding troops a'scattering. The terror caused by the gun boats' shells' flight only added to the muddy, cold, misery the exhausted troops had to deal with. It would not be easy for any of them to rest that night, nor would the miserable night be any easier on the Yankee commander-in-chief.

Ulysses S. Grant had sought shelter under a giant oak tree, it's thick branches wide and strong, new leaves sopping wet with the cold, heavy, April rain. The rain, though good for the Tennessee flora, was making it impossible to walk anywhere without feeling as if one was living in a quagmire. Grant's quartermasters had done a good job of spreading hay to help keep the commanding general out of the mud, but it had done very little good. The ground was too wet, the rain too hard, and the hay not enough. Before long, the hay was wet, muddy, and cold, none of which did Grant's swollen ankle any good.

"Damn this leg!" He quietly muttered. He had been forced to keep his boots and spurs on, never knowing when he would be forced to ride off at a minute's notice. He really had not tried to rest anyway, what with being busy checking on the disposition of all the troops, and only now satisfied with their placements. Unfortunately, the damaged ankle, which had spent the day bouncing uncomfortably against the side of the horse, was now swollen tightly into the boot, and was giving Grant fits of extreme torture.

Nelson was now fully deployed. The bovine sized general and his men had hardly seen any work this day. *So much the better.* Grant thought to himself. *Nelson will be that much readier for mischief in the morning.*

Lew Wallace had finally made his tardy appearance. He and his unhappy division had just entered the battlefield just about three miles from where they had started their morning march. They had gotten lost, wandering down paths barely wide enough for a cow to pass through, the unlucky troops marching closer to fifteen miles in order to get to the fighting, but were finally resting in line of battle. Their mystified leader had spent the entire day trying to get to the fighting, and finally arriving, too late for Grant's attempted plan for that day, but not too late for the confused commander to suffer his senior officer's ire. There had been no mistaking Grant's displeasure, and Wallace had been glad to get away from Grant's sight.

Tomorrow will be different. Grant thought, then winced again, the angry ankle sending waves of pain rolling up his leg.

"Hurt bad?" "Cump" Sherman was sitting next to him, puffing hard to keep the stogie lighted in the moist night air. The two men, sitting side by side on the old tree stump, could have hardly appeared any more differently. Grant sat quietly, calmly, hardly moving at all. Sherman was full of nervous energy, couldn't sit still, and kept getting up, only to sit back down a few seconds later.

"Yes." Grant replied laconically, his mind trying to focus on his thinking, the *plan*. His mask-like face was barely visible, even with the illumination of the lantern next to him.

"Rough day, I hear they nearly got you, twice." Sherman growled, then spat out his cigar, disgusted with trying to keep the tobacco lighted.

"They came close, "Cump," they came real close." Grant grunted in reply, trying to get his leg comfortable, remembering how death's cold, clammy, claws had reached out for him twice this day, narrowly missing him both times. Besides just missing the unlucky journalist Carson's fate earlier that day, he had been barely missed by an erratic cannon ball as the fighting wore down near dusk. The bouncing projectile had tore off the head of a captain standing next to Grant, then ripped off part of a saddle on a horse behind him. It had then continued on its journey only to clip the legs off of one of Nelson's men, just as the unfortunate soul had cleared the crest of the river bluff.

"I know you had some close calls too." Grant continued. "I hear that it was unlucky to be your horse today. I hear that Hammond and you nearly got it around dusk, too."

"We were lucky, damn lucky!" Sherman grinned, recalling how moments before Grant's near death, Sherman had also narrowly escaped the grim reaper's foul breath when a cannon ball had ripped the air, cutting Sherman's horse's reins not two inches below the thoroughly frightened Major Hammond's hands. It proceeded to tear the crown and back brim off of Sherman's hat, Sherman having just bowed down to talk to Hammond. Miraculously, neither man was hurt. "I thought Hammond was about to pass out. He'll be all right though, just shook up."

"Lucky fellow. You all right?"

"Yep, it missed everything else." Sherman grinned again, and chuckled. "I need a new hat, though."

"I hear those Kentucky boys gave you quite a cheer?" Sherman smiled in return, trying to forget the pain in his leg, and not quite succeeding.

"Yep, they did.' Sherman smiled at the memory. When the troops of Nelson's Division had reached the top of the river bluff, some of the men were from Rousseau's brigade of hard-bitten Kentucky woodsmen. In his previous command Sherman had a hard time dealing with the Kentuckians, who had caused him some grief in the past. Yet when the battle-hardened veterans had climbed the bluff and seen Sherman on his horse, his tattered hat pushed back on his filthy forehead, the black soot of gunpowder staining his fiery red beard and his dirty bandages, the many bullet rips in his uniform, those same hard-nosed veterans had put their hats on the tips of their bayonets and cheered. They cheered, *hard*, for "Cump" Sherman. They recognized the change in him and approved. Sherman had tried not to show it, but it was obvious that he was deeply moved by the Kentuckians' demonstration. Sherman had still been wearing the blood-stained and bullet-ridden garb, when Sherman had finally met up with Buell, when the latter finally showed up on the scene. There wasn't much Sherman could do about his attire, all of his other uniforms were now in the hands of the enemy.

"So, I understand Buell did not take too kindly to your appearance when you two ran into each other?" Grant asked, his mind still chewing on his thoughts, stoically attempting to ignore the pain in his ankle.

Sherman grunted in response. He took off the tattered hat and used it to wipe his soot-stained face. He spat a speck of tobacco out of his mouth, then shoved another cigar back into his mouth, not bothering lighting it yet, then spoke. "I don't think he (Buell) liked it much when I said that I had orders from you to take Wallace's six thousand men and the eighteen thousand from the Army of the Tennessee we already had in line, and attack at daylight tomorrow. I think he resented it when I told him that I thought victory was certain, even without him!" Sherman chuckled at the memory, remembering how the haughty, aristocratic, Don Carlos Buell's eyebrows had arched at that comment. "I did tell him we were glad to see him, though."

Grant grinned at this, having had his own experience with the courtly Buell that day. "Well "Cump," I believe that the good general believes he wasn't being given his due, since he believes he *is* our savior."

Sherman groaned at this. "Oh, hell, that's his problem. Let him be that way. Who cares, as long as he's got his three divisions in place alongside our four, then it doesn't matter what General Buell thinks. We are all set for the morning, come sunup. Besides, I guess that tells me that his lordship, (Buell), didn't hear what you told McPherson."

"No, I guess not."

There had been an impromptu meeting of staff officers at about dusk in the headquarters camp near the bluff, shortly after Grant's near brush with death on that very same river bluff. A smouldering fire of hay lent some illumination to the murky atmosphere, the ground covered with mud and water. Colonel John McPherson had just ridden up from an inspection of the lines for Grant. He had found Grant, sitting on a stump, the injured leg outstretched before him, busy with whittling on a piece of wood with his jackknife. Grant had asked him for his report.

"Well Mac, how is it?"

McPherson dismounted, shaking his head. "Well general, sir, I have to report that at least one-third of the army is, in my opinion, is "hors-de-combat," and the rest are very disheartened, sir. It has been a very rough day for all, begging the general's pardon, sir."

Grant said nothing, just puffed on his cigar, and continued to scrape at the twig. McPherson, mistaking Grant's silence for something else, spoke again.

"Well sir, General? Well sir, General Grant, under this condition of affairs, what do you propose to do, sir? Shall I make preparations for a retreat?"

All conversations died at this question. The other men grouped around all stared at their leader, waiting on his answer. They did not have long to wait.

"Retreat?" Grant looked up, as if surprised by the question. "No, I propose to attack at daylight and *whip* them!"

Sherman laughed at the memory, then asked. "You going to try and fetch up all those runaways?" He was referring to all the soldiers who had run from the fight.

"No." Grant replied. "I prefer to leave them out of the equation. I would prefer that there be as little contact as possible between those who ran, and those who will stand and fight. Fear can be highly contagious, and I want the good men to be able to fight tomorrow. Those others would only run again, and would sicken the healthy with their disease." He sighed, then lifted his arm, pointing at a lonely log cabin on the bluff, lantern light glowing from its window openings. What had once been a home for a river family, was now a Union field hospital.

"Besides, it's my fault anyway." He continued to point at the cabin, from which both men could hear the occasional scream come, the army surgeons going about their bloody business. "Those runaways are my fault, my responsibility."

"*Your* fault?" Sherman, surprised by this statement, snorted. "Why?'

"I had listened to you, and not to old "Baldy" Smith, I would not have had this army sitting here, without trenches or any kind of defensive works, and with all the green troops all at the front. Those men barely knew enough as to how to load their guns, let alone fight as a trained army. I *should* have taken better precautions, "Cump." You would have thought I was drunk when I allowed you and the others to make those dispositions. I'm sure *that* thought has crossed at least a few minds." Grant was referring to Halleck.

Sherman stared hard at Grant, shocked by the statement, then decided to ask the question.

"Well, were you?"

"No."

Damnit, I knew that. Sherman reproached himself. I never should have asked that question. Still, I didn't really expect that statement, not from Sam, not him. I guess he's not so far away from his old fears, either. I forget that he's had to deal with his own personal demons as well. I guess I'm so surprised after all. Hell, I thought I was going to lose it a few times myself today.

Sherman slung his soggy cigar to the ground, and stepped on it, an action totally unnecessary in the wet night. He stood up, and waved his poncho-covered arm at the shiny darkness.

"Well then, General Grant, the hell with them! Remember, they thought I was crazy, too. But sir, we have had the devil's own day, haven't we?" In some strange way, Sherman had actually found pleasure in this horrible day.

"Yes." Grant laconically replied, puffing on the remnants of his cigar. Yet, in some ways, he did feel better for getting that off of his chest. He knew that Sherman had understood, for the other man had been there himself, and had fought his own personal demons. That dark deep place, that place that others didn't know about, who had never been to that dark place, questioned your ability to *do*. Sherman had survived it, and had grown from it. *Today* was the proof of that. Grant would grow too. Today had merely been a setback to the plan, and a bad day, but one that he, Grant, would overcome. He had come too far, worked too hard to let others, whether they wore Confederate gray or Yankee blue, stop him *now*.

It wasn't the glory he was after, nor was Sherman. It wasn't the promise of promotion that was driving either man now, either. No, it was the desire to do the job better than anyone thought Grant could. No, Grant didn't care about promotions, it was *success* he was after. Now his mind was clear, and with that clarity came the knowledge, the certainty, that he would *win* tomorrow, and would drive the enemy from the field just as surely as the sun would rise in the morning. Even his pained ankle could not stop the process. When the Confederates awoke in the morning, they would see *Grant* coming for them, by thunder.

"Yes. Lick "em tomorrow. I propose to hit them the same way we did at Donelson. The time will come, you'll see. It's like when either side was ready to give up if the other side showed a bold front. At Donelson, we showed first. Those tactics will work just fine here."

Sherman grunted and smiled a wolfish smile at this. He knew that the day had changed the man sitting in front of him, just as he knew himself to have been changed by the day's events. Both men had been thrown into the witch's fiery caldron that day, and both had emerged stronger, *tougher*, willing to roll the dice, and make the decisions that would send many a man to his untimely death but would eventually in the end win it all. War *was* hell, but Grant and Sherman were becoming the masters of the game, the art, of war.

Yet Sherman knew he had not seen it all, not everything, at least not that day. He had been concerned with his part of the battle, and had done his job, and done it well, but he still did not see the *whole* picture. He could comprehend problems in their complexity, yet confusion and chaos could still distract them. Too many possibilities only complicated things for him. Grant had been everywhere that day and had seen everything. Unlike Sherman, Grant had the ability to see things in their *simplest* form. He would zero in on the crucial factors, and just disregard the rest, not allowing them to distract him from his main objective. It was this ability to disregard confusion, never letting it bother him or distract him from his set course, that was allowing him now to make the decisions to find some way to *win*.

"All right, General Grant, we'll do it. Get some sleep, sir. I will see you in the morning. Good night, sir." Sherman stood up one last time, saluted, and stepped out from under the shelter of the big oak's branches. He mounted his horse, and left. Grant watched him ride off into the night.

Rawlins walked over and looked at Grant, a questioning look on his face. Grant shook his head, *no*, And Rawlins nodded, turned and walked away, shooing the others away. Grant wanted to be left alone now.

Grant sat there, silently, listening, watching the comings and goings around him. Couriers were constantly on the move, but Rawlins and McPherson both knew what Grant wanted done and were handling the communications. They left him alone, alone with the night sounds, alone with his thoughts, the steadily falling rain continuing its cleansing ways. The groans of the wounded, the dying, still stood out, even over the thundering chorus of the gun boats, all combining to rise in swelling waves above the sounds of the pelting storm. Grant watched as the tempest was alternatively illuminated, first by the glare of the lightning, then by the Yankee gun boats and artillery fire, then back again, the guns' crashing sounds a worthy match to nature's own noisy display of fireworks.

A night in Hell itself probably could not be much worse than this. Grant contemplated the nightmarish scene in front of him. In the distant darkness of the surrounding woods he could see the hospital details, their lanterns bobbing along like fireflies in the night. They were searching for those that showed a glimmer of life, trying to save those that they could, and bringing those poor wounded men to the waiting field hospitals near the bluffs. The others that they found were merely collected, as best as possible, and placed in piles, there to await burial in the hastily dug mass graves. The sight of all these dead and wounded men was deeply disturbing, and

Grant groaned at the sight. He had never done well with the sight of blood.

What a day this has been. At least it is over, over for today. Tomorrow whichever side takes the first initiative in the morning, will make the other side retire, and Beauregard will prove himself mighty smart if he attacks before I do.

I wish I could sleep on the 'Tigress,' but I can't do that, not tonight. But I do need to get out of this rain, get dry, get somewhere where I can stretch this leg out, and try to get comfortable. Maybe that hospital might be better than sitting under this damned tree.

He struggled awkwardly to his feet. Rawlins watched from a respectful distance, but made no move to help him, knowing Grant would resent it. Grant began to hobble forth from under the weeping boughs of the great oak, heading towards the great log cabin in the clearing, its small windows glowing with the surgeons' lamps. The rain poured down on him, running in small rivers off his soggy poncho.

The cabin had originally been selected as the forward command headquarters, but when greater needs arose, it became a field hospital. Grant knew that it had a small room in the back, with a cot in it. He stepped gingerly through the debris strewn clearing, feeling his way, and trying not to trip over anything, or anyone. He looked straight ahead, not really wanting to see what human or material wreckage lay around him. He finally reached the log building and paused on its threshold. He looked over to where he knew Rawlins was watching him and motioned for the other man to join him.

"John, I am going to try, and find some place in here to rest. I need to get out of this rain for a while, and hopefully rest this bum leg. It needs it."

Rawlins nodded his agreement to this. Good, I'm glad he's gotten out from under that tree. He thought. I was afraid that the way this day has gone his luck would run out and he would get struck by lightning sitting under that damned big oak. Hopefully he'll rest. Lord knows he needs it. That leg's got to be hurting him something awfully bad after today. Still, I'll have some fresh straw put under that tree. Sam never did do well with the sight of blood.

"Yes sir, General Grant. I remember that there was that little room in the back, also. Use it, General. If there is anything else important that happens, I will let you know, sir."

"Thank you, Captain. See you later. You need your rest, too."

"Yes sir. I will try, sir, But really I am all right, sir."

Grant frowned at that last remark. "Captain, *none* of us are *all right* after today, but we will be, tomorrow."

Rawlins smiled. "Yes sir. Good night, Sam." Rawlins saluted.

"Good night, John."

Grant opened the door to the cabin. The murky light from within spilled out through the open doorway. He looked inside, only to see an interior illuminated by lanterns, the air thick with a miasma of whiskey, smoke, sweat, and blood. The belongings of the previous occupants had been shoved up against the walls, and rough wooden tables set up, everywhere there was a space to fit one. Those spaces not occupied by the surgeons hard at work were filled with wounded men, the floors covered with discarded whiskey bottles, soiled bandages, and broken medical tools. The surgeons were busy, the butcher's bill as high as it was, and they took little notice of the figure standing hunched over in the cabin's doorway.

Grant looked around the great room, his eyes taking in the dismal scene. In the dimly lighted room bandaged and bloody men lay everywhere he could see, against walls, under tables, on chairs and tables, whatever was available. At the back of the cabin was the small room. It was too small to use as an operating room, for it had probably been a small storeroom, or a small child's room at one time, and thus was not being used, *yet*. Grant stepped clumsily into the comparative dryness of the room, letting the cabin door swing shut behind him.

He carefully picked his way through the litter of men, tables, weapons, and surgical equipment. The *smell* was sickening, a combination of blood, soiled clothing and bandages, whiskey, and God knows what else. He was careful not to step into any of the pools of blood that were accumulating on the floor of the cabin and was gradually making his way toward the door of the side room, when he put the foot of the crutch into something wet, and slipped.

He stumbled, nearly falling against a table where an exhausted surgeon, his arms bloody up past his elbows, grimly worked, trying to save another poor soul's leg.

"Be careful, you damned fool, can't you see I'm busy here!" The harried physician did not even to bother to look up, his eyes and hands busy with their gory work.

"Sorry." Grant muttered, clumping around the table, and finally reaching the small room's door. It was, surprisingly, empty, a small chair and cot occupying what little space there was in the room. With a groan he sat down on the cot and lifted the throbbing leg awkwardly up onto the chair. The pain had been terrible, the ankle swollen in its boot. Now, with the weight off of it, it hurt a bit less, but just a bit.

He looked out the doorway of the room, at all the whiskey bottles strewn around the tables and floors of the larger room, the surgeons having used massive quantities of the mind-numbing liquor to drug their victims with. There had been not enough of anything to begin with, medically speaking, and what they had was fast running out.

My God, I sure could use a drink myself, but I'm sure old John (Rawlins) is keeping a pretty close eye on me. My keeper, I'm surprised he let me come in here by myself. He probably thinks I'm too tired anyway. He's wrong. I sure could use one. Still, he's probably right. If I had one now, I'd be pretty much useless to everyone, and I'd only prove the wrong people right.

I wish Julia was here. She always seems to know what it takes to keep me out of my moods. She's good that way. There again, it may not have been the best idea for her to be here, to see all of this, like poor Bill Wallace's wife has.

Poor woman, she just gets here, and she's watching her husband die. They haven't been married all that long, either. I guess she had some kind of premonition, or something, the way she rushed down here to see him. Too bad she didn't get here a couple of days earlier. I wouldn't want Julia to see this, to see that, no, not the way Wallace is tore up, no I wouldn't

Grant groaned, and laid back down on the cot, trying to let his mind relax, feeling himself letting go, and drifting off to sleep, sleep . . .

"Excuse me, sir?"

Damn! Grant slowly forced his eyes open to see a young gap-toothed man, dressed as a hospital orderly, standing there. His once white apron was coated with blood, and his blond hair stuck out from under his forage cap in yellow stalks.

"Yes son. What can I do for you?"

The youth saluted hurriedly. "I am sorry, sir. I didn't realize that you were in here, but . . ."

"You need the room, don't you soldier?"

"Yes sir, General. If you don't mind, sir. We got an awful powerful load of wounded boys out here, and . . ."

Grant sighed and sat up. The screaming in the other room had taken on a new intensity. Grant looked out the open door at the sound, noting the fact that several large and burly men were trying to hold another man down while the surgeon attempted to cut away at the wounded man's mangled leg.

"We must be out of whiskey and chloroform." Grant observed, his tone kindly.

"Almost, sir. We have to use less, try to make it stretch further. Sometimes . . ." the younger man just shook his head and looked away.

"It's all right, soldier. Can you help me up, son?"

"Yes sir!" The youngster bent over, and took hold of Grant's outstretched hand, and pulled him to his feet. Grant balanced himself unsteadily on his crutch.

"Thank you, soldier. What's your name, lad?"

"Brown, sir. Private Tom Brown. I'm part of the Medical Corps."

Grant looked the young soldier over. "Son, how old are you?"

"Eighteen, General, a month ago this Tuesday."

"Where you from?"

"Ohio, sir, down south of Akron. We'uns farmers. Pigs, corn, and such."

"Bet you wish you were back there right about now?"

The boy's eyes filled with tears. He wiped them with his cap, then softly replied.

"Yes sir. This ain't *nothing* like I thought it would be. None of the fellers did. Most of them, from my town, they are all dead, after today. No glory in *that*, sir. None at all. Sorry sir, I didn't mean that this isn't . . . well, what I mean is . . ."

Grant smiled and patted the lad on the shoulder.

"It's all right, son. It's all right. I know *exactly* what you mean. Thank you. Go about your duties and be careful. Oh, are your folks alive?"

"Yes sir, they are."

"Make sure you write them, especially your mother. Often. It's important to them. Mothers love to hear from their boys. It's important to them."

"Yes sir, thank you, sir. Good bye, General!" The lad left.

Grant sighed. Well, at least that one made it through today. Hope he doesn't tell his mother everything he's seen. She probably has enough nightmares already, just worrying about him. He began to clump over the floor back out into the main room.

The screaming had stopped. The surgeon was backing away from the table as Grant came out of the room. He looked at Grant, and began shaking his head, while others were lifting the now dead soldier off of the operating table.

"Too late, too late." The blood and sweat-soaked doctor muttered. He looked directly at Grant, held up his bloody arms, and blurted out. "There's so many of them, and it's just too late for too many of them to save them!" The doctor dropped his head and closed his eyes. His next case was already coming into the room.

Grant frowned but kept going. *What can I say?* He thought to himself. He reached the doorway of the cabin and pushed the door open, stepping out into the rainy night once more. Rawlins was there, leaning against the outside wall of the cabin.

"I didn't think you'd be in *there* very long." Rawlins spoke. He knew well that Grant, even though a soldier, still did not do well with the sight of blood.

"Too noisy." Grant muttered.

Rawlins grinned. "Yes sir. Where to?"

"Back to that tree. It's just as good a place as anywhere else is tonight." Grant sighed, pointing to the big oak he had been sitting under earlier.

"Yes sir. I made sure that some more hay got spread. It should still be dry, General."

"Thank you, Captain." Grant smiled. He knew that Rawlins would do everything in his power in order to make Grant's life easier. Grant knew he was fortunate to have Rawlins around, if only to keep him from falling into old bad habits.

Grant clumped over to the big oak, and ducked awkwardly down, his hat barely missing the rain-soaked outside branches. He struggled to sit back down, and managed to lie back, his back against the thick, rough, bark of the massive oak. He arranged his poncho to cover himself better, then pulled his hat over his eyes, then closed them. He wasn't aware that Rawlins was standing there, just outside the tree's dripping branches, the water dripping off the sodden branches onto Rawlins' thoroughly soaked hat. Rawlins stood watching for a few minutes more, then retired to the relative safety of an open flapped tent. There he sat on a stool, positioning himself so as to have a clear view of the great tree and its dozing visitor, much like a mother hen watching over her sleeping chicks. No one was going to disturb Grant without going through Rawlins first.

Sleep. Grant thought to himself. *Yes, I think I can sleep now.* He lay there, propped up against the side of the great tree, his eyes closed, his mind gently rolling. The rain now seemed like a soft, steady, lullaby. Not even the sounds of the surgeons' bloody work, or the sound of the great guns roaring in the distance, were now registering in Grant's conscious mind. Instead, they were replaced by thoughts of Julia, of his children, of *home*. The thoughts rippled through his brain, images in the fog of his now relaxed mind's eye. Even the injured leg seemed less painful. He smiled, and then gave in, his mind and body finally giving up the fight, if not quite to slumber, at least to a state of restfulness, all under the watchful eye of the ever-vigilant Rawlins.

Tomorrow. One last conscious thought. I will lick them, and take Beauregard out.

Tomorrow.

FORREST

Behind Confederate Lines
April 6, 1862 Late Evening

Colonel Nathan Bedford Forrest was in an incredibly roaring snit. His regiment of Tennessee cavalry had been assigned during the day of April 6, to guard the Lick Creek fords. Impatiently the planter-turned-cavalryman had prowled the approaches to the battle during the early phases of the fighting, until, unable to stay patient any longer, Forrest had led his men toward the sound of the guns beyond the creeks and into the fighting, he and his men participating at the edges of the fray. The Tennessee-born cavalrymen had only stopped engaging the enemy when Beauregard's recall order had arrived, much to the chagrin of Forrest. Now it was late in the evening, nearly midnight, and something was gnawing at the former slave trader, enough so that it was prickling the hairs on the back of his neck. Forrest was determined to find out the cause of the nervous sensation.

Nathan Bedford Forrest was a remarkable individual. Tennessee born in 1816, he stood six feet, two inches tall, and was blessed with a powerful physique, especially in his muscular arms and legs. He appeared to be a shrewd, calculating man with his dark eyes, dark beard, and dark mustache, the combination giving him an almost sinister presence. This image was enhanced by his heavy, almost bear-like voice, its growl intimidating, a message to others that this was not a man to be taken lightly, but to be obeyed, and quickly.

Forrest had been backwoods born, like many of his fellow Tennessee brethren, and only possessed a mere six months of formal education. Yet, his lack of formal schooling had not hindered the young Forrest, who had gone from being a common farm laborer at age sixteen, to eventually setting up shop in Memphis, Tennessee as a dealer in livestock and slaves. A backwoods brawler of great repute, Forrest was on the edge of developing a fighting style far removed from that of his more romantic Eastern counterparts. Forrest did not see war as some great, idyllic adventure, as did others. No, this common appearing man saw it as a *test*, a bloody contest of grit and endurance. He did not care for the foppery or trappings that some cavalrymen adorned their persons with. His uniform was functional, his fighting style intensely personal, whether saber or pistol, it did not matter to Forrest. Tennessee had produced many a good fighting man. Some with names like Crockett and Andy Jackson. Now it was about to produce another.

Forrest, being a wealthy, influential member of his community, it had been only natural, that Forrest, although he had originally enlisted as a lowly private, would not remain a mere enlisted man for long. A devout believer in the Southern cause, he organized and outfitted a unit of Confederate cavalry at his own personal expense and was made a lieutenant-colonel in the Confederate army. It soon became obvious to others that although Forrest had no formal military training, he was a born soldier, with intuitive military talents. To Forrest, using practical logic when it came to being a soldier, was an easy thing to do. His incredibly intuitive mind, when mixed with his powerful temper, and an explosively overwhelming desire to fight, produced a lethal combination for those who would get in his way. Forrest wanted to *fight*. He could not understand the old school, cavalier ways of fighting that so many of the other commanders possessed. To Forrest, to win, you had to fight, and fighting meant *killing*, and there was *nothing* genteel about that.

That itch was still there, a burr that Forrest just could not get shuck of. He was not satisfied with the evening's orders to stop and regroup, no sir, he was *not*. *Something* was exciting his short hairs, and he just had to scratch it. He had decided to take a small, hand-picked squad of men, twelve in all, put them in captured Yankee bluecoats, and take them out scouting, hopefully to find out what was sending all those danger signals down Forrest's spine. They took a circuitous route, gradually working their way around the enemy flank, crawling through the mud, and using the rain to mask the sounds of their travel, until they reached the lip of the bluff just south of Pittsburg Landing. Here Forrest and a few men worked their way to the edge of the bluff, crawling along on their hands and knees to find a sight below them that proved Forrest's sober intuition to be correct.

"My Gawd, Colonel, look at all them damn bluebellies down there! They's thicker than flies on a rotting carcass!" The speaker, a young sergeant named Town, his liberated blue jacket turned gray from all the mud he had crawled through, lay next to Forrest on the bluff's lip, and gawked at the spectacle below them at the river landing. "I don't believe that they know about this back at command headquarters, no sir, Colonel!"

"Hush up, man!" Forrest snarled, his eyes and mind busy with attempting to study and assess the situation just below them. The landing was an incredible beehive of activity, as river boats, loaded to the gunwales with men and equipment, all cargo of a military nature, unloaded that cargo under the garish light of pitch torches, the flames streaming in the wind and the rain. Forrest listened to the angry shouts of the teamsters, their voices mixing with the crack of their whips, the commands of officers imploring their men to move faster, the men scrambling to get ashore and *move out,* all combining together to form one great blue snake, one made up of men, guns, and ammunition, as it writhed its way up the bluff towards the new Yankee lines. The whole thing gave Forrest the impression of massive, unstoppable power, power that would be unleashed when the rattlesnake-like reinforcements would uncoil and strike.

"Hell, there's more a'coming down there, right now, more then we got in the whole damned army!" Forrest angrily muttered. "Plus there's more on those steamers out there waiting to unload. Hell, it looks like another whole damned army is just sitting there, just waiting to unload and git at us!"

"Ain't we, ought to be telling someone about this, Colonel?" Sergeant Town whispered, his eyes glowing in the reflection of the torches glow. Forrest could clearly see the look of apprehension on the younger man's dirty face.

"Well, we're sure going to try, Sergeant, we are sure going to try." Forrest started to edge back from the edge of the bluff, his mind rapidly digesting what it was he had seen, and already preparing a report. "C'mon boys, we need to make tracks back to our lines!"

They crawled back down in the direction from which Forrest and his men had first come, retracing their steps in the mud. It took a while, what with all the rain and mud, but after about an hour of carefully circuiting around the enemy flank, Forrest and his men were back in their camp. Forrest immediately dismissed most of the men, admonishing them to get what rest they could after cleaning themselves up, and to keep what they had seen to themselves. He noted the crazed, almost party-like atmosphere of the camp. Nowhere was there any evidence of any preparations for a fight on the morrow. Shaking his head in disbelief, Forrest and Sergeant Town headed for their brigade commander's tent, Brigadier-General James Chalmes.

It was now closing in on one o'clock in the morning, and Forrest was working himself up, what with the past day's excitement and lack of sleep only fueling his intensity. Right now, Forrest looked like a man on a mission, and Lord help anyone who got in the way.

"I need to speak to General Chalmes, immediately!' Forrest growled at Chalme's aide, who had sleepily climbed from his blankets at Forrest's noisy appearance.

"Colonel, the General is asleep, and is not to be disturbed, unless . . ."

"Wake him up, *damn you!*" Forrest's face was a mask of rage. "I have *urgent* scouting information regarding the damned Yankees!"

The young officer stepped back, stunned by the anger in Forrest's voice, and the ferocity on Forrest's face, but he still continued to block the tent's entrance. "I *am* sorry, Colonel, but General Chalmes . . .?"

"Wake him up! Now!" Forrest shouted, and stepped forward, menace obvious in his every move. It was clear he meant to have his way. Other camp members, drawn to the spot by Forrest's angry bellows, closed in, sensing an angry confrontation. Town fingered his pistol, not wanting to use it, but ready to assist Forrest if needed. All were saved by the sudden appearance of Brigadier General James Chalmes sleepy-eyed face through the tent flap opening.

"What the hell is going on out here?" Chalmes spotted Forrest, who was standing there with his fists balled in anger.

"Colonel Forrest, what is your concern? Please stop scaring my aides!" Chalmes stepped out of the tent, wrapped in a robe.

"Sir, begging your pardon, General!" Forrest snapped out, not the least apologetic. He took a deep breath, and then continued, his agitated state obvious in his voice. "The Yankees are bringing up reinforcements, *serious* reinforcements! They are getting ready to attack *us*! We need to make preparations for an enemy assault, and . . .?" Forrest stopped, and motioned to the carnival-like scene of the camp. It was obvious to him that little if anything had been done to prepare the Confederates in this camp for a renewal of hostilities.

"General, it is my opinion that we had better prepare to *attack* immediately! Get the boys and get ready to go! If we don't then we'd best get the hell out of here, or we will be whipped like hell, and before ten o'clock tomorrow morning, sir!" His tirade complete, Forrest stopped and stared at Chalmes. It was obvious to all how agitated Forrest was.

Chalmes stared at the junior officer, absolutely astounded by the other man's intense audacity. He was well aware of his fellow Tennessean's propensity for violence, and also knew that there was no quit in the man. He also knew that Forrest was not prone to exaggeration.

I have to handle him, carefully. The sleepy Chalmes thought to himself. Carefully. He may be right, even though the report we got was that Buell was not here. Still, there's always a chance . . .?

"I'll tell you what to do, Colonel Forrest. You, sir, will take this report to General Hardee, and report your findings to *him*. He is the corps commander. It is his call."

"*Sir? You* can't act on this?" Forrest was dumfounded.

"Go see General Hardee." Chalmes replied.

"General, it is late. It is almost one o'clock in the morning. By the time I get this to General Hardee it may be too late! We need to act *now!*"

"Then you best not waste any more time, *Colonel* Forrest." Chalmes replied, irritation obvious in the man's sleepy voice. It was obvious to Forrest that Chalmes would do no more.

"Yes *sir!*' Forrest snarled. "As you wish, *General!*" Forrest bit off the last with contempt, snapping off a salute, and spinning around on his heels to stalk to his waiting horse. He mounted and Town quickly handed him the reins. Forrest galloped off, Town riding at his heels, the two headed for the corps command post, and Hardee. Chalmes and the rest of the assembled group watched them ride off.

"Should I make preparations for the troops, General?" The speaker was the aide that Forrest had threatened. Chalmes yawned, nodded his head no, and then replied.

"No, we'll let Hardee make that decision. I am going back to sleep. Good night, gentlemen." Chalmes ducked back into his tent, removed the robe, and slipped back down onto his cot, and his disturbed rest. The others in the tent did the same, resuming their disturbed activities.

"Damn fool." Forrest sputtered. He was having a hard time not taking his anger out on his horse. He looked at Sergeant Town, the other man now riding alongside of him. "He doesn't *care*! *Fool!* Well, let's hope General Hardee has more sense than Chalmes, eh Town?"

"Yes sir, Colonel. Sometimes I have to wonder whether or not some of our generals have a lick of common sense between any of them, no offense to anyone in particular, sir."

"Well, someone had better have some sense, and listen! Damn fools! The Yankees are coming!" Forrest continued his tirade, the other man not minding. He had seen Forrest's anger before, and was more used to it then were others. He knew there was generally a reason for it. "The *damned bluebellies! They're* sure not acting like they're licked, but we sure are! We *will* get licked for sure if we don't prepare for them a'coming at us in the morning. Hardee has to listen to me!"

"Yes sir, Colonel. I agree with you sir." Town nodded his agreement, then asked a question. "Colonel, you think this rain will let up before morning? Sure plays hell with the horses."

"Don't know." Forrest grumped. "Hope so, you're right about the horses. It will make it easier on the boys in the fight if it does. Horses don't always handle so well in the mud, you know." Forrest briefly grinned, then growled, pointing to a cluster of tents just ahead, torches and campfires illuminating the site. "There's Hardee's flag. That should be his tent up there."

Hardee's camp was relatively quiet, in comparison to the one Forrest and Town had just left. There was a small cluster of tents, fires smoking in the steady rain. There were small groups of men clustered around some of the fires, the ones farthest from the headquarters tents, Forrest noted. It was obvious to him that liquor was present, judging by the catcalls and lurching behavior of the men around those distant campfires. He ignored all of them, and rode straight for Hardee's tent, easily recognized by the headquarters' flag on its staff in front of it. Forrest rode right up to it, not bothering to stop or dismount, until he was less than ten yards or so from it. He threw the reins to Town, then strode purposely toward the entrance to the tent. The storm of rain seemed to intensify with each step Forrest took, the wind beginning to blow harder, as if to match the tall Tennessean's powerfully angry mood, as he marched on his target, that of Hardee's tent opening, the corps headquarters flag drooping wetly over the entrance.

As he marched through the clearing, Forrest again noted in astonishment the seemingly relaxed mood of the camp, the unhurried atmosphere, the abundant use of liquor, the difference between the almost lackadaisical approach to the next day by the Confederates, and the intensely bustling nature of the Federal preparations Forrest had witnessed at the enemy-controlled landing. He observed, he remembered, and he swore in sheer frustration, his foul mood only intensifying in its level of consternation.

"Colonel, how can we be of assistance to you?" One of Hardee's aides, a Captain Klem, stepped in front of Hardee's tent entrance, blocking Forrest's way in.

Forrest stopped abruptly; otherwise, he would have run right into the other man. He stood there, quivering in excited anger, and snapped out his words.

"Captain. I need to speak to General Hardee, *immediately*! It is a matter of the gravest importance. It is *very* urgent!"

Klem did not move. "May *I* ask, Colonel, what this *pertains* to? The hour is quite late, sir." Klem stood there, his arms folded across his chest. He waited for Forrest's reply.

"*Pertains to?*" Forrest spat out, the words wet with anger. He reared his head like an angry bull. His hot eyes blazed in the wet darkness. He shoved his angry face forward, stopping it mere inches from Klem's astonished face. "*Late hour? By God, Captain*, the Yankees don't care what time it is! Damn you man, get out of my way, or get General Hardee! *Now!*"

His face filled with menace, Forrest dropped his hand onto the butt of the pistol resting on his side. Klem stiffened, his face betraying his surprise at the vehemence in Forrest's voice, but he did not move. Klem was not accustomed to being treated in this manner, especially by a regimental officer. Others crowded around, attracted by the sound of Forrest's angry bellow. All waited to see what would happen next.

Klem stood his ground. He had heard of Forrest's violent temper, and had heard what the other man was capable of, but nevertheless did not move an inch from in front of the tent flap. Several seconds ticked by, neither man moving, when the situation was defused by the sound of Hardee's angry voice coming from within the tent.

"Captain Klem, *what* seems to be the disturbance out there?" Hardee stepped out of the tent, clad only in shirt, pants, and socks, his thick gray hair all mussed up. It was obvious to all that he had been sleeping.

Klem let out his breath, unaware that he had been holding it in. He stepped to one side, allowing Hardee to step further out under the tent's awning. "Sir, *Colonel* Forrest says he has *important* information for you."

"General Hardee, my respects, sir!" Forrest quickly spoke up. "Please forgive this intrusion at this late hour, but it *is* necessary!"

"*What* is necessary, Colonel?" Hardee stood there, irritably yawning, his arms folded across his chest. He had seen much blood shed that day, and had finally drifted off into a deep sleep. The events of the day had continued to play over and over in his mind, and it had been difficult for him to go to sleep. He was not happy at being awakened.

Hardee looked out from under the awning of the tent. He looked out at the rain still falling, a soft drumbeat on the canvas of the tent. It had been that soft rhythm that had finally lulled Hardee off to sleep, until Forrest's angry bull-like bellowing had abruptly awakened him. Hardee looked out into the soft darkness, noting that the Confederate stretcher-bearers were still at their work, carrying their grisly cargoes off. He shook his head, and then repeated his question.

"Tell me, Colonel. What was so *necessary* to wake me up about?"

"General, again, my apologies for this intrusion, but I was told to bring you this report *directly to you.*" Forrest began to speak. "I took a small squad of men out on a scouting mission just a short time ago. We went far out in front of our lines, out around the flank, and managed to get up on top of the bluff *overlooking* the Yankee's camp and the river landing." To this statement a look of surprise replaced the sleepy one on Hardee's bearded face, his beetle-like eyebrows rising up like crescent moon-like circles over his droopy eyes. Forrest continued with his report.

"The Yankees don't look like a beaten army, no sir, they don't. We saw many, I repeat, General Hardee, *many* Yankee reinforcements coming ashore. They are a'gitting up plenty of guns, ammunition, and more men than you can count! They have the means now, and they are getting ready for a fight! No surprising them this time, no sir, no way, General!"

Forrest stopped for air. Taking a deep breath, he was about to begin again when Hardee held up his hand for Forrest to stop. Hardee ran a hand through his hair, and then began to speak.

"You say, Colonel, that you saw the Federal forces getting up more men, more reinforcements? At Pittsburg Landing?"

"Yes sir, General. I did." Forrest replied.

Hardee looked at Forrest for a long second, then spoke. "Come in the tent, Colonel. Captain?"

Hardee spoke to Klem. "Bring a lantern in."

"Yes sir."

Hardee stepped back into the tent, both Forrest, and Klem, now holding a lighted camp lantern, following him through the tent flap opening. Hardee stepped over to a table on which there was a map laid out. He motioned for Klem to hold the lantern over the table.

"Colonel, if you would be so kind, would please show us here on this map, if you can sir, where you were?"

Forrest stomped over the table, took a long look, and then stabbed a large finger emphatically onto a spot on the map. "Here sir. Right here, General. We could not miss a thing."

Hardee stared at the spot that Forrest had so aggressively marked. It *was* right out overlooking the spot where the landing was located.

I wish I knew for sure what he saw. Hardee thought. What troops, how many, what if any more artillery? Beauregard says he's got proof that Buell's on his way to Alabama. But if Pierre's wrong, then . . .?

"Colonel Forrest." Hardee made up his mind, and spoke. "I want you to take this information directly to General Beauregard's headquarters. Give your report *directly* to General Beauregard. Tell him I sent you. He will take care of this."

Forrest stiffened in shock. He could not believe that once *again* his information was being so cavalierly dismissed. Desperately trying to hold on to his temper, and mindful of Hardee's rank, Forrest began to protest.

"But, General Hardee . . . Sir, you will just listen. Please sir, every moment counts. Sir, you can't just . . .?"

Hardee cut him off. "Take it to General Beauregard, Colonel. *He* will handle this. *It's his* decision to make."

Forrest shut his mouth, angrily aware that further protest would do no good. He saluted Hardee, and then replied.

"By your leave, General. I must do so, *immediately!*"

"Yes, go Colonel. You are dismissed." Hardee did not even bother taking note that Forrest had already turned and stomped out of the tent. He sat back down on his cot, shaking his head as he listened to Forrest's angry muttering as he mounted his horse. The two men listened as Forrest could be heard riding away, galloping off in the direction of where Beauregard's camp was supposed to be.

"I hope he finds him, and gives General Beauregard that information, Captain. I hope he knows where he is going." Hardee quietly said.

"Do you think he's right, General?" Klem carefully asked. He was still a bit shaken by his encounter with Forrest's temper.

"Don't know." Hardee admitted. "Hope not. It probably isn't quite as much as he thinks it is. I hope not anyway.

Today was bad enough, certainly bad enough. I know that General Beauregard is planning to just *mop up* tomorrow. That's the plan."

At least I think that's what he's planning to do. With Pierre, sometimes you just don't know. Lord, I wish Johnston hadn't gone off and got himself killed like that!

"Good night, Captain. Take the lantern with you."

"Yes sir. Good night, General."

"Let us hope there are no more disturbances tonight."

"Yes sir. We'll do our best to see there are none. Good night, sir."

There was no reply. Hardee was already asleep.

Far down the muddy road from Hardee's camp, Forrest was busy trying to find Beauregard's camp. He did not realize that the Army of the Mississippi's command headquarters had been moved several times during the past day's events, and was now occupying what had been Sherman's old camp, with Beauregard now the occupant of what had been Sherman's personal tent. In his anger he had forgotten to find out where the Army high command was now situated, and he had no idea where the camp was.

"Damn aristocratic, ramrods up their asses, too blind to see what's smacking them in the face, West Point educated *generals*!" Forrest thundered out as he rode. He was trying to keep his horse at an easy canter, and look around as he rode. He was trying not to communicate his anger to the animal as he rode, and was failing at that as well, the nervous horse frightened by Forrest's angry oaths. The darkness, mud, and rain were not helping matters any.

"*Damnation!*" Forrest swore another oath. "Town, just look around us." Forrest gestured at the side of the road. "We ain't ready for another fight! Just look at those boys out there!"

It was true. Everywhere the eye could see there was evidence of the destruction of the day, and the lack of preparations for the coming day. The ground was covered with the remains of the federal camps; torn canvas, broken canteens and cooking utensils, shredded blankets and smashed muskets, the remains of foodstuffs, all strewn about as if a cyclone had ripped through, and torn everything in its path to pieces. What few tents that remained upright were basically worthless, their bullet-riddled sides mute testimony to their uselessness. There were boxes of cartridges tossed about, now rain soaked and useless, mixed in with the flotsam of shredded remains of animals, wood, and men. Among all this destruction the revelry of the exhausted, and in many cases, drunken Confederate soldiers continued. Liquor appeared to be in abundant supply, and although Forrest himself was not averse to the pleasures of whiskey, he knew no good could come of this. It was obvious to him that these men were receiving little or no direction at all, and had no thought as to what the morning could bring. They were but reveling in the moment, in the sheer joy of *surviving* that hellish day, and although Forrest could forgive them *that*, he could not forgive the sheer lack of planning, or intelligence, he was seeing being manifested. It was all so wantonly, inexcusably, *stupid*.

Make no doubt. Forrest thought to himself. The bluebellies will hit us tomorrow. They are coming, and we will not be ready for them! We will not be ready, damn it! He looked up into the teeming night sky, and roared, anger and frustration heavy in his bear-like voice.

"Where the hell is that damned headquarters!"

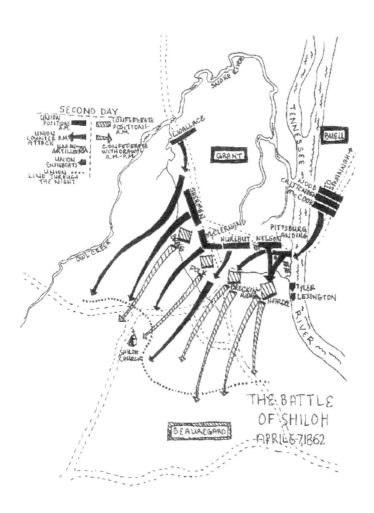

SECOND DAY

UNION POSITIONS A.M.

CONFEDERATE POSITIONS A.M.

UNION COUNTER ATTACK P.M.

CONFEDERATE WITHDRAWN A.M.-P.M.

UNION ARTILLERY

UNION GUNBOATS

LINE THROUGH THE NIGHT

SNAKE RIVER

TENNESSEE RIVER

L.WALLACE

GRANT

BUELL

SHERMAN

WOOD

TO SAVANNAH

CRITTENDEN

McCOOK

OWL CREEK

McCLERNAND

HURLBUT

NELSON

PITTSBURG LANDING

POLK

TYLER

LEXINGTON

BRECKINRIDGE

HARDEE

RIVER

SHILOH CHURCH

THE BATTLE
OF SHILOH
APRIL 7, 1862

BEAUREGARD

GRANT

Pittsburg Landing
April 7, 1862 Dawn

Grant awoke from his uneasy slumber, opened his eyes, and looked around. He saw that he was covered with a second poncho, and tried to get up. He winced, all of his joints aching from the night spent under the still-dripping massive old oak tree, his ankle worst of all. He had not slept well, but it would have to do.

He spotted Rawlins hovering close by, the able aide keeping a close eye on his master. Rawlins was standing there by a cook fire, a tin mug in his hand, and sipping on its steaming contents. Upon noticing movement from under the tree, Grant's stocky form being barely discernable against the dark wood of the oak, Rawlins stooped, picked up another mug sitting there next to the fire, and poured another cup.

"Coffee, General?" Rawlins did not wait for a reply. He carried the tin cup over to where Grant was struggling still to get out from under the extra poncho Rawlins had thrown over him during the cold wet night.

"How'd you sleep, General?' Grant accepted the proffered cup, sipping at its dark, hot contents before answering Rawlins's question.

"Fine." It was an obvious lie, but Rawlins let it pass.

"Hungry, General?"

"No, thank you." Grant's face was becoming more visible in the early light. He took another sip of coffee, then spoke again. "All right. What are our current dispositions?"

"Lew Wallace is on our extreme right flank." Rawlins replied. "Then Sherman's on his left, then McClernand, then Hurlbut on our left flank. Then you got Nelson's Division from Buell on the extreme left flank. He's anchored on the river. Next to him on his right is Crittenden's Division, then McCook's forming the right flank for Buell. So, we form the right wing, and Buell's forming the left."

"Any change in the enemy's dispositions?"

"No sir. It appears that they are still using that old church, the one that Sherman was camped around. It looks like they're using Sherman's old tents for themselves." Rawlins grinned. "Reckon old "Cump" wants back at them for that. They're on the left of him, (Sherman), and on the right of McClernand. Other than that, it doesn't look like they've done anything. No preparations."

"Cump" will get his chance." Grant replied. "All right, send word to all commanders. Prepare to advance and recapture our original camps. I want Nelson, Crittenden, and McCook's boys from Buell's army to advance *south*. I want Hurlbut, McClernand, Sherman, and Lew Wallace to advance *southwest*. I want "Cump" to take his camp back. That's all seven divisions. All together. All at once. All along the front, *everybody*. Let the artillery lead the way with a maximum effort. All the guns. Then we'll follow right behind their barrage. We don't want to give those boys over there a chance to get their heads back up before we get there."

"That's forty-five-thousand men." Rawlins responded. "Any special orders for anybody?"

"Nope. Attack. Straight ahead. Put skirmishers out front, but don't waste time. Drive them right out of those camps. We'll go right over the top of them if they don't move. They don't have enough to stop us. They lost too much yesterday." Grant stopped for a second, and then continued. "Now, it's *our* turn."

"Yes *sir*. Anything else?'

"Yes." Grant motioned in the direction of the river and the distant thunder. The gun boats *Tyler* and *Lexington* were still at work throwing their heavy metal projectiles into the Confederate camp, still dropping shells every fifteen minutes or so on the exhausted rebels.

"Send word to the gun boat commanders. Tell them to cease fire. Now. We don't want them shelling our boys as they advance."

"Yes sir. Immediately."

"That's all, John. Oh, and have someone saddle up my horse. I can't sit here anymore, and it hurts too much to stand." Grant grimaced and leaned up against the stout oak tree, trying to ease the weight on the damaged ankle, the stressed joint flaring with the morning dampness.

"General, you should have taken better shelter during the night." Rawlins quietly admonished his friend.

"The boys couldn't. Besides." Grant pointed at the log hut, the site of the surgical activities of the night before. The ground surrounding the simple cabin was still covered with litters of wounded men, some beyond caring. "You knew damn well that I wasn't going to stay in *there* all last night." Grant took off his hat, and ran his fingers through his dirty hair, the memories of the previous night's grisly scenes still in his mind's eye.

"There was the boat." Rawlins was referring to the *Tigress*.

"Couldn't do that, either." Rawlins knew that Grant was referring to the fact that Grant felt guilty about all the men out in the storm, and felt he had to at least partly share their misery.

"No sir. I guess not." Rawlins face creased with a sympathetic smile. "Anything else?" He knew Grant wasn't quite done.

"No. Just send the word. Make sure Buell knows *first*. No sense in letting him get all bent out of shape over chain of command procedures. Send McPherson and the other aides to tell Sherman and the rest of the division commanders My orders. Get in line and attack, *immediately*. I don't want any excuses. Everybody. All at once. That's all, Captain."

"Sir." Rawlins saluted, and hurried off, beckoning to the other staff members, each bleary-eyed from lack of sleep, as they emerged from cover into the morning's grayness. Grant watched as Rawlins issued Grant's directions to the now assembled staff members. The group then quickly broke up, McPherson hollering for Grant's horse to be saddled. Within seconds it seemed an orderly hurriedly brought Grant's mount for the day to him.

"General, can I assist you any further before I leave?"

"No Captain, just get going to Buell."

Rawlins saluted. "Yes sir, General. I'm on my way." Rawlins hurried off. He knew that Grant did not want anything to keep Buell from getting started, and he knew also that Grant trusted *him* to get Buell started right.

Grant looked up at the now-lighter sky. The rain had finally stopped, and the morning was dawning with the promise of better things ahead.

"Lord, let it better for us today." Grant muttered, a quick prayer between him and Providence. "I'm sorry we spilt so much of the blood of your divine creation, yesterday, on your day. *But we didn't start it*. But I am going to finish at least this part, *today*."

He pulled himself up onto the horse, and took the reins from the orderly. "Thank you, Private."

"We are going to lick 'em today, Sir." The gap-toothed youngster, his dirty face grinning at Grant, stepped back and saluted. It was a statement, not a question.

Grant smiled back, and returned the salute. "Yes, son. We will."

"You be careful, General. I heard they nearly got you yesterday, a couple of times, sir. Be careful. We need you, General."

Grant smiled at the familiar tone. It was a common thing for the Midwestern boys to do.

"Thanks, I will son. You, too."

"I'm all right, General. We is all right now. We's seen the elephant. We'll take care of business today. You watch us. You'll see."

Grant grinned. "I'm *counting* on it soldier. I'm counting on it." Grant then turned his horse, and rode away.

That's why we will win today. He thought, the pain in his ankle for the moment forgotten. All hell passed through here yesterday, and we still got boys like that one. Good boys. That's why we will win this thing. Now it's our turn. It's my turn.

Look out Beauregard. We're coming for you now.

BEAUREGARD

Army of the Mississippi Headquarters
April 7, 1862 6:00 A.M.

The dull thunder of the of Federal artillery in the echoing in the distance slowly stirred the exhausted and still headache-ridden Beauregard up from the shallow depths of his troubled slumber. The Creole pulled himself up right on his cot in the semi-darkness of the tent, and began to rub his temples hard, his fingers digging in to massage the pain, trying to push it away. He looked up as a disembodied hand suddenly pulled open the tent flap, followed by sunlight and Colonel Jordan bursting through the tent flap with equal intensity.

"Begging the General's pardon, sir, but I have received a report that the enemy's about to begin something! General, their artillery has really opened up! It's not just those dang Yankee gun boats anymore!"

Beauregard peered up at Jordan, the head pain obvious in Beauregard's bloodshot eyes. He gestured, a hand wave, in the direction of the intensifying sound of the firing, the thunderous volume increasing by the second.

"Damnation, don't those bloody people ever rest?" He slapped his hands against the sides of his head. The pain surged in rhythmic waves through his temples as if keeping the beat to the melody of the Yankee cannons' song.

"No sir, I guess not." Jordan replied. "And General Beauregard, I am sorry to tell you this, but our scouts have reported . . . that is, we have *reports* that they . . . that is the *Federals* . . . got reinforcements during the night." Jordan was holding a piece of paper with writing on it.

Beauregard looked back up, and saw the proffered note. He snatched it out of Jordan's outstretched hand, and quickly scanned its contents. He stiffened, and then jumped to his feet. He only had to see one word on the note to know that they were in trouble.

Reinforcements.

"When did *they get here?* Are they Buell's men?" Beauregard angrily spoke. "He was not even supposed to be even *near* here!"

"I am sorry, General Beauregard, but it is apparent that the Federal reinforcements arrived during the night, sir!"

"And I am just finding this out, *now*?" Beauregard snarled, his Gallic temper beginning to boil, the temperature accentuated by the rise in the tone of his voice. "Did no one deem this information *important* enough to tell me sooner?

Who *is* this Colonel Forrest, *anyway*?" Beauregard crumbled the note in his now closed fist.

"Cavalry commander.' Jordan quickly replied. "Word is he went out during the night to scout the Yankee position. They say he got right up above the Union position onto the bluffs overlooking them, and got up real close. He says he saw the Yankees coming in off the river. He says he took the information to General Hardee, but that General Hardee told him to come to you. Apparently he had a hard time finding us, what with the rain and all." Jordan finished up, lamely. He knew that it wasn't really a valid excuse.

Beauregard stared at Jordan in dismayed shock at this stunning revelation. Idiots! He thought. And nobody thought they should wake me and tell me? Hardee didn't think it worthy to send a message? Damnation, has this army fallen that much apart? Does it think that all we have to do is just show up today, and the Federals will run? What is wrong with us?

We had them last night. *We had them! Now it sounds like the tables have turned.* Beauregard felt like he had just put the last of his money into the poker pot, confident that he held a winning hand, only to see the other fellow draw aces to beat him with.

He looked out of the tent opening, the chaotic sounds coming in from outside drawing him toward the tent entrance. Beauregard swallowed hard and stepped toward the tent opening. What he saw absolutely horrified him.

Soldiers and horses were running *everywhere.* It was a scene of mass confusion, with the rosy color dawn tinted by a gray, smoking haze, one that was flavored by the chorus of man, animal, and metal screams. Trees were lending their parts to the chaotic scene, branches splintering into lethal shrapnel as the artillery bursts struck their outstretched limbs. Nowhere to Beauregard's astonishment did there appear to be *any* semblance of order or plan. The artillery bursts were beginning to strike even closer, a walking barrage, Beauregard realized, and he winced at the close by flight of a passing shell. He turned back to the dismayed looking Jordan, who waited for Beauregard to speak.

"Colonel, quickly send word to all commanders. They must prepare to repel any attack, and to hold their positions." Beauregard snapped. "They are to form defensive positions, put up defensive works, and prepare to repel all attacks. *They must not withdraw!* All troops are to make themselves useful to the fight, and prepare to engage the enemy. They *are* coming. Make sure that word gets *directly* to General Bragg and General Hardee to send whatever they have left and to fill the lines with *whatever* they have left. If a man can carry a gun he better do it now! If they disagree tell them I said we can argue later, but we must *fight* now! Order my horse saddled."

"Yes sir!" Jordan saluted. He was thankful that there was no time now for recriminations. That would have to wait until later. "I will see to it, immediately!" Jordan spun around Beauregard, hollering to the other staff who had congregated near the command tent, and telling them what to do.

Beauregard watched for a second, then turned back into the tent opening. His movement was arrested by the sound of a new voice, this one a contrast to the noise around him by its cheerful tone.

"Morning, General!"

Beauregard stiffened, and slowly turned around to see the owner of that cheery voice. It was Prentiss, a soft grin splitting his bearded features. Prentiss had spent the night sharing a tent with Jordan, right next to Beauregard's. He had undoubtedly heard almost all of the conversation between Beauregard and Jordan. The two guards assigned to him were both standing behind him, not sure of what to do.

Beauregard looked at the three men, and held out a hand, palm outstretched toward them. He stared hard at the captured Federal commander, Prentiss returning the stare. Neither man spoke for a few seconds, then Beauregard finally broke the silence.

"Well, General Prentiss, it appears that we should have perhaps, listened to you after all. But do not worry, sir, please do not worry. No sir, don't trouble yourself, our boys will soon stop whatever General Grant has planned." Beauregard spoke with a false sense of bravado, not wanting the other man to get a sense of what Beauregard was thinking. He didn't want Prentiss to think that he had gotten the upper hand in their discussion. It was too late.

Prentiss smiled, gestured with his hand at the chaotic scene around them, and then spoke.

"General Beauregard, I *tried* to tell you last night, but you, sir, you would not listen. Now, I believe you have shot your bolt, sir. I tried to tell you that you were wrong, last night. Now General Grant has got *his* dander up, and he's coming back, coming for *you*! Your boys may have spent the night, eating, drinking, and having a good time, but they definitely have *not* spent the time *preparing*. Now, it's time to pay the fiddler, because Grant *did* spend the time preparing. You're not ready for a *fight*. That much is obvious. You had your way yesterday, but today is *our* turn, its *Grant's* turn, and he's coming. Your best bet is to get your boys out of here before it's too late, *General*!"

Prentiss stopped, smug in his knowledge, and feeling good. He knew that his boys had done well, now. They had given Grant the time he needed, and by God, Grant was going to use it to his advantage, right now. Beauregard stared hotly for a moment at the amused Yankee prisoner, then quietly spoke.

"Thank you, for your considered opinion, General Prentiss. You will forgive me if I do not share it. Please excuse me, as you can see, I have a bit of work to do. These gentlemen will see to your comfort. You will please go with them now. They will see to your safety. Guards, would you please escort the General to the rear." Beauregard then saluted the other man.

Prentiss laughed, returning the salute as he turned away. "You got that right, General. We don't share the same opinion. You will forgive *me*, General, if I don't wish you good luck." Prentiss smiled again, and turned to look at his two guards. "C'mon boys, I'll protect you. We need to move away from here. It's going to get mighty hot around here."

Prentiss laughed again, and walked away, the clearly disgruntled soldiers immediately falling in on either side of him as they marched away, the smoke-filled haze swallowing them up quickly. Beauregard watched them disappear into the smoke, then turned back to watch the incredible scene displayed before him, a scene of complete and utter chaos.

Damnit, I should have known better! I should have seen to it myself that the others took the necessary precautions last night. It seems I have to do everything. I can understand Breckinridge not knowing, but Bragg and Hardee should have known better, Polk too, he went to the Point.

What did Bragg and Hardee do last night? Only a colonel had any idea that the Yankees were getting more men? What was Hardee thinking? Why didn't they tell me? Who's in charge here anyway?

We'll be playing hell to stop the Federals today. We're in trouble. We spent yesterday to get to this point and now look at us. We've lost too much.

I don't know if I can stop Grant now.

GRANT

Union Lines
April 7, 1862 Late Morning

Grant had been busy. The morning had been spent in a continuous ride back and forth along the line, visiting and checking on the attacking divisions. He spent his time spurring them on, not letting them slow down, but pushing, always pushing them to break down the Confederate resistance. Now he and Rawlins were taking a breather, and watching one of the morning's attacks take place.

Nothing fancy. Grant thought, chewing hard on his cigar. He had made sure that he had stuffed a big handful of cigars in his coat before they had set out that morning. Rawlins had made sure he had them. He knew how Grant would chew on them to help him think as the day progressed.

We've got forty-five-thousand boys. I figure they only got about twenty, twenty-five thousand, probably closer to the lower. They're exhausted, and we've got fresh troops. We should be able to run right over them, and we probably would have, if everyone had just followed orders. Now they're holding on, thanks to the delays.

Grant had watched as Nelson's command had moved out early, just as planned, the Federal left easily rolling up the small pockets of Confederate resistance they had encountered along the Dill Branch, the defenders too tired, (*or too drunk*, Grant thought to himself), to offer more than a mere token resistance, the federal forces just shoving them back. But then Nelson had gotten concerned about his flank, the bovine-sized commander rumbling that his right was exposed, and thus had *stopped* to wait for Crittenden's men to form and protect his flank. The delay had cost Nelson, possibly more than if he had just kept going, because when the former naval officer had begun to advance again along his front what *had* been mere pockets of resistance had now concentrated into a stubborn line of infantry, backed with artillery support.

"Maybe Nelson should have kept going, eh, General?" Rawlins had grumbled to Grant. "By God, it's going to cost him a damn sight more in time and men than if he had just kept going!"

However, it had soon become obvious to both Grant and Rawlins that instead of a smooth coordinated line of advance, the whole Union line had begun to sputter and move forward in spasmodic jerks, the uneven terrain, the brush, and the swampy ravines and gullies making for tough going. It was now obvious that the advance would not be easy, *regardless* of the rebel defenses. The problems the Confederates had faced the day before, were now problems for the Union attack. The Union attack had actually been forced to give up ground on one occasion, Nelson's men falling back, due to the concentrated Confederate artillery fire. The giant Nelson, raved at his men, screaming at them to *advance*, and not fall back, accentuating his concern with angry swipes of his sword through the air, nearly decapitating those that were too close to him and his lethal scythe. The attending divisions had not fared much better. They too were having their own problems advancing over the uneven terrain, tripping and falling over the briars and vines as they reached out to snare the unsuspecting soldiers.

"I hear General Sherman had to get his boys all straightened out before they could move?" Rawlins spoke again, his eyes half on the battle, half on the cigar gripped in Grant's teeth.

"Yep." Grant replied, the stogie wagging in his teeth's tight grip. "He had a brigade, (Stuart's) that needed to be moved. Sherman wanted it on his left before he moved out. It got separated from the rest of the division in the midst of the fighting yesterday. Had to get it caught up."

"Hurlbut wasn't too happy with you." Rawlins replied. "That was some excuse he had for not moving out yet."

"He won't make that mistake again." Grant shook his head in disgust. He'd had to *personally* order Hurlbut to move his division out in support of McClernand's men, who had already begun to advance per Grant's orders. It had been just about nine o'clock when Grant had ridden up to Hurlbut and asked the division commander about the hold up. Hurlbut's complaint about finding some food for his men before attacking had fallen on deaf ears, and, smarting under Grant's very terse response, Hurlbut had quickly moved his men out in support of Crittenden's advance.

"What was it he told you he was looking for?" Rawlins asked.

"A few crackers." Grant laconically replied. Rawlins grinned, but said nothing more. Both men's eyes moved back to the battlefield. Rawlins lifted his spyglass to his eyes.

"Looks like they don't plan to leave easy, General."

"Guess not. But they *will* leave."

I should have guessed that they would put up a little more resistance. Grant thought to himself. I suppose that they figured on finishing the job that they had started yesterday. They probably planned on being the ones doing the advancing, instead of us. They certainly had not adopted much of a defensive posture toward us. It doesn't look like they had any idea that we had gotten up the reserves that we did. How did Beauregard not know? He's got scouts. We know that. He had to hear them coming in, or didn't he? Did the loss of Johnston affect them that much? Did Beauregard think that we would just leave, that we would just run, jump in the river, and flee? This isn't Bull Run. I'm not McDowell. We're not running. I'm not running.

Grant frowned at the thought, and kept chewing on the cigar. He lifted his glasses to his eyes again, trying to get a better look at the rebel defense lines, looking to see if there was something he had missed, some trick waiting to be sprung. There was nothing he could see.

Why wasn't he more ready? After yesterday's fight, and the way we kept pounding away with the artillery and then the gun boats, you would have thought that he had some inkling, and would have at least had some defensive lines thrown up, some kind of breastworks or something? They had to hear them. Buell's boys made plenty of noise coming ashore. Was old Beauregard that certain of victory that he never bothered to reorganize his men, or even determine what it was we might be doing? Is he that arrogant, that pompous Creole? I'm almost insulted, except, he caught us with our pants down. The good Lord must have been watching over us this time. It would not be smart to ask Him for favors two days in a roll. We will have to do this one ourselves.

The morning progressed, the Union attack sputtering but continuing to advance. As Grant watched, Nelson and Crittenden gradually gained the upper hand in their attacks against the stubborn Confederates, the blue coated troops slowly groping their way forward, the weight of numbers making themselves felt. The brush choked ravines continued to impede their progress, destroying their alignments much as it had done the previous day to the Confederates. The Federals finally reached the wreckage-strewn remains of what had been the morning before had been a beautifully flowered peach orchard, and the neighboring sunken road. Here, where the forces of Hurlbut, W. H. L. Wallace, and

Prentiss had held out, forcing the Confederate forces into a stalemated fight, and costing them their army commander, here in the now aptly named "hornet's nest," the Confederate forces had set up artillery batteries. But now, instead of trying to destroy the Yankee defenses, these batteries were being used to try and stop the Yankee offense. One battery was raking the Union lines from the southeastern edge of the destroyed peach orchard's boundary. The other was busy commanding the field from the northwest, about a third of a mile up, at the eastern edge of the wrecked Davis wheat field. Between the two batteries, the Confederate forces were trying to maintain control of the area around the now famous sunken road, bloody pond, and ruined peach orchard.

Everywhere lay the debris of war. The two sides were preparing to contest the very same area that had seen so much blood spilled and destruction less then twenty-four hours earlier. The rain-soaked ground steamed under a blanket of dead and wounded men, dead horses, and destroyed and abandoned equipment. It all covered the remains of what had been nature's bounty. Haversacks, their sides ripped out and their contents strewn all over laid intermingled with broken muskets, and snapped wagon wheels and gun carriages, the broken, twisted, bloodied ends of wood and metal waiting to reach out and skewer the unwary soldier.

"How far have Sherman and the others advanced?" Grant asked. A courier had just arrived, delivering the message that Rawlins was now busy reading.

Rawlins looked up from his reading, a smile on his grimy face. "This says they've just about reached what was McClernand's camp before yesterday's ruckus started. "Cump" says him, Wallace, and McClernand are right on the edge of the old camp, near Jones Field. They've got Hurlbut in reserve with them, and have stretched out west to about a quarter mile or so of Owl's Creek." Rawlins stopped, laughed, and then continued. "Says they've run into some pretty artillery and are waiting for Buell to *catch up.*"

"Send them a message. Tell them don't wait. Buell's on his way." Rawlins immediately scribbled out the message and handed it to the waiting courier, with instructions to give it to Sherman. Both men watched as Federal artillery that had just arrived, now began to duel with the Confederate artillery hidden beyond the peach orchard, and interspersed among the ruins of the wheat field. As they watched it quickly became obvious to both men that the gunners on both sides were targeting each other's smoke, the blasts of flame and screams emitting from the soot-filled clouds evidence that both sides were finding and hitting their smoke-covered targets. A lull in the fire suddenly became evident as both sides tried to disperse their remaining guns to make it harder for the opposing gunners to find easy targets in the increasingly blackened air. Suddenly, just as the air had begun to clear, a roar broke out, one made by hundreds of human voices as Federal infantry surged through grayness to sweep across the field, charging into the Confederate gun emplacements, and driving the rebel gun crews from their charges.

"Those are Kentucky and Indiana boys, General. And there's more coming behind them!" Rawlins exclaimed jubilantly. "Drive "em, boys. Take those guns!"

Grant said nothing. He sat his horse, said nothing, just watching. The jubilant federal troops were able to seize one of the cannons, then were forced back as a savage counterattack struck, troops from the Louisiana bayous screeching their high-pitched yell swarming to meet the Midwestern blue coated farmboys. More Confederates poured in, two whole regiments joining the Confederate line. Soon the whole area was a maelstrom of blue-, gray-, and butternut-colored uniforms, all worn by men trying to kill each other with guns, bayonets, swords, rocks, fists, or whatever else was handy. What little grassy space there was soon disappeared, every man taking advantage of what little cover any tree or stump offered, each man doing whatever was necessary to *kill* the enemy, the *man* he faced.

Grant looked up at the sky. "What time is it, Captain?"

Rawlins fished out his pocket watch, and looked at it. "Just about ten o'clock, Sir."

Grant grunted, his attention fixed on the fight. There was really nothing to be said anyway. They would either win, or they would die right here.

The Kentuckians grudgingly gave ground, the Confederate infantry following. Their goal was the Union artillery. Their hoarse cries of pride suddenly turned to those of shock and pain as the Federal artillery first threw case shot, then turned to firing canister, the giant shotgun-like shells spraying their egg-shaped pellets at the pursuing Confederates. The rebels stopped as if they had slammed into a giant brick wall, men falling by the dozens as the Yankee artillery blew great bloody gaps in the Confederate advance. Now more federal artillery arrived, a section of Regular Army artillery. Battery H, Fifth U. S. Artillery had arrived. The regulars stood to their guns, their highly disciplined ways quickly at work, and soon lent the throaty songs of their Napoleons to the Federal artillery chorus. Their fire swept across the remains of the peach orchard's field, turning what was left of the once fine fruit trees into even more just kindling, the razor-sharp wooden shrapnel punching holes indiscriminately in the bodies of the wavering Confederates. The rebel artillery quickly swung around to try and face the new menace, the Louisiana troops trying desperately to swing around the flanks of the newly arrived Yankee guns. They were met by new waves of Federal infantry that charged out of the woods to meet them. Now the Union men would do the driving, the desperate Confederates caught by the hammer-like blows of Nelson's men.

"General, I do believe that General Nelson's men have arrived!" Rawlins hollered. Grant continued to say nothing, his teeth working hard on the cigar as he watched the slugfest taking shape.

Rawlins was right. The men of the First, Second, and Sixth Kentucky, the Ninth Indiana, and the Twenty-Fourth and Forty-First Ohio was swinging into place, every man-jack of them determined not to let the Confederate troops get the upper hand. The Federal artillery kept up its horrendous rate of fire, canister and grape scything through the cringing Confederate lines. The Yankee infantry quickly prepared to lend their murderous musketry to the defense, even as the Louisianans kept coming. Soon, murderous fusillades erupted from the newly formed Federal lines, waves of globe-like smoke bubbles appearing, streaked with crimson flame, an appalling crash of thunder accompanying each wave of fire. Again and again, the thunder sounded, sending the metallic lightning bolts flashing across the intervening field. It was impossible for anything *human* to stand for long against such a horrific storm.

The battle seesawed back and forth. Three times the incensed, determined Confederates, their savage rebel yells carrying above the din, their war banners carried with equal arrogance and fervor, their weapons already bloodied and looking for fresh victims, charged into the metallic murderous wave of equally pluck-filled Yankee guns, their own flags streaming their own blazing response to the Confederate banners, the rebel yell met with equally ferocity by that of the Federal defenders. The Confederate fire was meeting with some success, dropping Yankee gunners like flies, the battling gun crews refusing to leave their charges, and dying at their posts. Union infantrymen quickly jumped in, picking up where the artillerists fell, and manning their guns in their place. Each time the charging Confederates were slaughtered, and driven back.

Both blue and gray wounded tried desperately to get out of the way of the incredible, many crawling into the ravines and gullies to seek cover from each other's blazing weapons.

Rawlins could hear above the din of the cannonade the piteously heart-rending cries of the wounded, their screams audible above those of the whistling bullets. Everywhere he looked, the gory corpses lay, their ghastly wounds shocking to behold, yet no sound came from any of them. Their sufferings were indeed, over.

Rawlins and Grant watched as another Federal brigade appeared out of the smoke and entered the fray, their drums beating to the charge. Rawlins ducked, an errant missile zipping close by his and Grant's heads. Rawlins again marveled at how his friend could seem so cool even as the cannons bellowed, their shells screaming as they plunged into their targets, or bounded into the air, flying with screech-like hisses around them. Rawlins watched as one nearby soldier suddenly rose up as to flee, only to fly backwards as a series of bullets tattooed his chest. Rawlins pointed at the newcomers.

"That's Hazen's brigade, General."

"Yep." It was all that Grant could say.

The two men continued to watch as the newly arrived Federal troops marched to the attack, bayonets fixed. The additional forces proved to be too much. Even as the Confederate troops rose to meet the new attackers, the exhausted rebels broke, retreating in a headlong race to get away as the Federals drove across the field.

"Go, boys, *go!*" Rawlins cried out. "They're driving them, General! They're driving them!" Rawlins was ecstatic. He whipped around to look behind them. *More* blue troops were arriving, advancing across the blood-soaked fields. He turned to look at Grant, who was still sitting calmly upon his horse. The only sign of agitation was the still moving cigar. There was no sign of a smile on Grant's countenance.

"Steady, Captain, steady. It's not done yet. We have to keep this up." Grant lifted his glasses to his eyes, surveying the field once more. The sound of approaching hoof beats caused both men to turn and look behind them. A courier had arrived. Grant turned to look back at the fight while Rawlins took the message.

"General, good news. The rebels have been forced back to a line along the Purdy-Hamburg Road, and are having a difficult time holding their lines together. General Sherman reports that his men are closing in on Shiloh church. He reports that Wallace, Hurlbut, McClernand, and McCook are all right there as well. The Confederate forces have put up a serious fight, but are now *retreating*. Sounds like we got them, sir."

Grant suddenly put the spyglasses down, letting them drop to the end of their string. He spat out the remains of his cigar, took off his hat, and removing a large handkerchief from his inside coat pocket, wiped his suddenly perspiration-soaked face. He put the handkerchief back into his coat, and replaced his hat upon his head. He looked around the fields again, searching for something, looking to see what was there that he couldn't see, and not seeing it, visibly relaxed.

We're going to win this. Grant thought to himself. I know it, but I can't say it. Not yet.

"General?" Rawlins was watching. A look of concern replaced the elated look on his face. "Are you all right, Sir?"

"I'm fine, Captain. What time is it?"

Rawlins quickly pulled out his watch, his face screwing up with concern. "It's about noon, General." Rawlins peered closely at Grant's face. "Is there something you need, sir? Are you sure you're all right?"

Grant looked at Rawlins, the look of concern on the other man's face touching to Grant's feelings.

"I'm *fine*, Captain. Just a little annoyed with this leg is all. Send a message to Sherman and the others. Continue to press the attacks. They're breaking. Just a little more pressure and I believe we will win this, but *no* premature celebrations." Grant pointed to the retreating Confederates. "*They* made that mistake last night. *We* are *not* going to repeat their error, Captain. No one stops until *I* say so, is that clear? We continue until I am sure that the enemy is defeated. *I* will say when that is. Is that clear?"

Rawlins sat back on his horse. *He will not stop, not Sam.* Rawlins thought to himself. *He's right. We have to make sure.* Rawlins looked back out across the litter-strewn field in front of them. Everywhere lay the flotsam of destruction, the gory field evidence of not one, but two days of savage butchery. Rawlins watched as a group of blue coated soldiers, straggling along behind the pursuing infantry, stopped to claim a prize. One of the men stooped down, and with a whoop of joy, lifted a rebel regimental banner from a pair of lifeless hands for the others to see. Rawlins grinned, his pleasure evident at the sight. His grin faded though as he turned to see Grant had noticed the scene as well. No smile was evident on his leader's face. Rawlins quickly wrote down Grant's orders and handed them to the waiting courier. The man had waited quietly, silently keeping his thoughts to himself. The courier rode away. Rawlins turned back to Grant, an apologetic look on his face.

"Sorry, General. I know we got more to do. It's been a couple of long days, but we all know we're not done yet."

Grant stared at his friend's face for a moment, then looked back at the field in front of him. Both men sat their mounts, listening to the sounds of the fight. The sun reached its pinnacle and began its downward flight toward evening. Gradually it became noticeable that the angry noise emitting from the lines now far out in front of them was beginning to lessen in its intensity. The Federal forces continued to force the pursuit, the Confederates continued to draw back. In time came the word that the Yankee forces had retaken the ground upon which their camps had stood the day before, and that the Confederate forces were quitting the field. Only then did Grant and Rawlins begin the slow careful ride to find Sherman and the other commanders. They carefully picked their way through the remains of the bloodied and destroyed fields, their once lush fresh green grass now ripped and matted with blood. They rode past the ruined peach orchard, its last few trees that still stood completely devoid of blossoms, the rest a monstrous mixture of wood, flowers, and body parts. They rode through the devastated pastures, past the now forever stained pond, its contents colored by the blood of many a brave man. They rode along, until they found Sherman. He sat there on his horse, his uniform and face stained by gun smoke, his bloody bandages now dirty from gunpowder, but his satisfaction evident by the jaunty angle of his cigar, tightly clenched in his grit-covered teeth. No words needed to be said. Sherman's demeanor said it all. Salutes were exchanged, and then handshakes. The three men now rode together, their work completed for the moment.

The Federal army was in the process of forming burial details. They were busy stacking bodies, and preparing them to bury them in the mass graves, the grave diggers were busy digging. The small group of horsemen rode by the remains of the Hornet's Nest. Fire had taken hold in the leaves and grass, and had badly burned many of the corpses, leaving hideous grins on many a newly bared skull. It made it even harder to tell which side the dead had served. Grant shuddered at the sight, and offered up a silent prayer for the souls of the lost, stepping his horse around and through the ghostly sight as quickly as possible. They rode back up toward Sherman's old camp, to where the old Shiloh church still stood, its bullet-scarred walls a witness to perdition that even its most fiery preachers could not have guessed of as they preached their brimstone-filled sermons. Now the wounded filled the pews, the altar, and the choir space. The ground outside was covered with litters, and men sitting, all waiting their turn to be ministered to. As the group rode by, the men watched, some hollering out a greeting, others simply wobbling to their feet to stand and salute. Most just watched silently as they rode by. All of them knew that they had shared in something that *none* of them had ever envisioned in the worst nightmares they had ever had. They had shared in it, and they had survived it, the elephant's mad trampling had missed them, and the survivors would be forged into steel by it, a core of battle-hardened veterans that the Union could count on in the battles ahead. The road ahead would be long, hard, and bloody, but there would be another day. The sun shone down, its rays cutting through the leafless branches of the remaining trees, illuminating the remaining murkiness, the day growing brighter, the gloom of darkness and battle and potential defeat disappearing under the intensity of the bright light of victory. A hard-won victory, one with a cost in human life taken that had never before been seen on this continent, but a victory nonetheless. Grant looked up at the sun, it rays warm upon his uplifted face, then back at Rawlins, trailing along just behind Grant and Sherman.

"What time is it, Captain?"

Rawlins smiled. Again he fished his watch out, and peered at the face of it.

"Just after four o'clock, General."

"Thank you, Captain." Grant looked over at Sherman, riding silently beside him. Grant leaned over to Sherman and quietly mumbled.

"We were lucky, General."

"Yes General, we were, sir." Sherman took the cigar out of his mouth, and eyed it closely. Dissatisfied with what he saw, he dropped the mashed tobacco to the ground, and pulled another out of the inside of his coat. Lighting the stogie, he puffed on it for a few seconds, then spoke.

"General, it seems to me that *luck* favors the *bold,* and General Grant, sir, you are definitely *that*!" Sherman looked back at Rawlins, still riding close behind. "Captain, I believe that a drink might be in order." Sherman looked at Grant and winked. "At least for me anyway!" He roared in laughter, Rawlins nervously joining in.

Grant grinned at his friend's humor. He reached out and patted Sherman's sleeve.

"Maybe one tonight, General, but only one. Tomorrow's another day, and we still have work to do."

"Work, General?"

"Well?" Grant smiled. "Well, we're not quite done *yet.* You don't think I'm just going to let those *people* just go away, do you?"

Sherman whooped again. "No sir. I don't believe you will. I don't believe you will."

BEAUREGARD

The Confederate Lines
April 7, 1862 Mid-Afternoon

The afternoon sun had finally broken through in a shimmering blaze of glory. Everywhere you looked there was a sparkle to the air, the glitter of diamond-shaped water droplets clinging to every surface. The rains of the previous night had washed everything down, cleansing the fields and woods, only to see it all become defiled again by the dirty, smoke-filled activities of the morning and early afternoon. Now Beauregard sat his horse, hatless, his coat opened under the shimmering sky. His Gallic features were pinched in a frown as he gazed upon the lines of his army, and contemplated about what could have been.

The commanding General of the Confederate Army of the Mississippi had experienced another rough day of command. The shocking news that Grant had been reinforced, and that Buell was not many miles away as Beauregard thought, but *right here at Pittsburg Landing,* had taken the New Orleans-born general some time to digest, and it had certainly had not helped his headache or disposition, not at all. It had instead sent a stab of fear through his feverish brow. However, the frightened moment had quickly passed, and once done Beauregard had quickly gotten down to the task of preparing his men to *receive* an attack, rather than deliver the one Beauregard had been dreamed of sending himself.

He had quickly issued instructions to his anxious staff that each member taking a specific message to each corps commander as to what Beauregard expected each to do. It had not been easy to get everyone together, since so many of the army's troops were badly scattered about on the battlefield, out about the destroyed fields and woods, and in the ransacked Yankee camps. Those who had survived the wild melees of the battle by nightfall found themselves in desperate need of food, water, and shelter from the elements of the night's intense storms. These far-flung units had no continuity to them, had in fact some large gaps between units, gaps that could be exploited, and making it difficult to maintain adequate lines of communication between headquarters and the various smaller commands. This had made it difficult for Beauregard to send word to Bragg or Hardee, or even to communicate with *anybody*, so many of the regiments having been wrecked and now intermingled with the remains of other regiments, so much so that commanders were not sure *who* they commanded, or that manner, how many men either. Many a regiment, the bright colors of her flags flying so gaily the morning before, had been reduced to mere company strength from the intense fighting that the previous day had determined would be the rule. Now, many a senior officer slept the sleep of everlasting peace. Junior officers, or even senior enlisted men in some cases, now controlled what remained of their shattered commands. Many of the exhausted men, their abused bodies worn out by the yesterday's horrific fighting, were still sleeping in their captured Yankee tents, the depth of their slumber intensified by the consumption of captured alcoholic spirits from the Federal camps. Now, they were to be awakened much as their federal counterparts had been the day before, the enemy storming out of the woods, the federals anxious for some payback. The morning fog cloaking the movements of the determined Federals as they rolled in and right over many of the unsuspecting Confederate troops. For many who had survived the day before, this was their last morning. For many of them that were unable to answer the clarion call of battle this day, they would pay for it with their lives.

Yet, even though the Federals rolled in and knocked over many of the unsuspecting and groggy Confederates like so many ten-pins, there were many, upon seeing so many Yankee bayonets glistening in the early morning sunlight, with their owners fully prepared to use them, that quickly sobered up and got down to the hard business of repelling the attacks. The rebels had quickly set to their own guns, and even though they were being pushed, and pushed hard, they had settled down, and pushed back. The terrain was helping them some, as it was slowing the Federals down, and thus was giving Beauregard some time to improvise a defense.

"Damn, what a day!" The crusty old Creole had fumed. The morning had started very badly and had looked for a while like the surprised rebels would be destroyed before they could stir from their beds. Yet, the Confederate troops had shown their own gumption, holding on by sheer ornery feistiness to what they had captured.

"The boys gave us just enough time, just enough to hold together what we've got left! Damnation! I wish we had been more ready!" Beauregard swore in manic frustration, his hot Creole temper evident by his angry voice and eyes matched by the crimson color of his neck and forehead.

His anger was communicating itself to his horse, the nervous animal snorting and tossing its head in fear. Beauregard angrily pulled on the reins.

"C'mon old girl, we'll be all right. Easy now, easy!" Beauregard fumbled his field glasses out, and put them to his eyes, peering through the now dirty lenses at the fight in front of him.

"Fight 'em, boys, fight 'em hard!" He hollered. "We can do this! Hold 'em back!"

The early crazy hours of the morning had seen Beauregard busy sending word to the other commanders regarding the situation. Beauregard's message had reached Hardee just as the bewhiskered commander had stormed out of his tent to see what all the commotion was about. Hardee's bushy eyebrows and mustache tips had positively quivered as he impatiently listened to Beauregard's directive. The angry Hardee had offered a few well-chosen cuss words, but had quickly set off to do what Beauregard had requested, that of taking command of what there was of the right flank. His bewildered troops had quickly settled in to defend their positions and to keep a hold onto Breckinridge, who was frantically trying to hold off the determined Federal attacks on his position.

Breckinridge was not having an easy time of it, the Federal regiments swirling around his position in the center of the Confederate line like a swarm of maddened hornets. Bragg, who was in the process of swearing up a frightful storm to match the fight's noise when Beauregard's courier had finally found him, had stormed off to try and take control of the left flank of the Confederate line. His men were fighting desperately to keep their tenuous hold onto Breckinridge's right, with the Federals just as determined to break through. The three Confederate corps commanders had managed to cobble together a defensive posture, gradually pulling their depleted forces back to close the gaps between them. The matter was complicated by the fact that Hardee and Bragg had exchanged wings the day before, and that Hardee now commanded two of Bragg's brigades, and that Bragg now had one of Polk's divisions. The whole thing had become a mess of poor communications and shaky command structure.

Yet there had been some respite, Beauregard and the others grinning with relief when they saw that their own efforts were being helped by the terrain, which had hindered *their* attacks on the Union lines the day before. Now the roles were reversed, and the Yankees were finding it rough going, their own lines being forced to break apart as they were forced to creep and crawl over what was left of the terrain's overgrown vegetation. The smoke-filled dense thickets and grapevine-filled ravines were again witnesses to savage fighting, only today the butternut and gray clad lads were fighting on the defensive, the blue clad troops swearing and screaming as they pushed the attack through the briars and brambles against the dwindling Confederate lines.

Beauregard could see all of this through his glasses, and he knew that at any moment could come the parting of the gray dike, the remaining troops unable to resist the tidal wave of blue coats, the flood unstoppable in its fury as it poured through to sweep away all that the Confederates had accomplished.

"Is Polk up yet?" Beauregard angrily shouted. While desperately attempting to communicate with the clergyman-turned-warrior earlier that morning, Beauregard had found, much to his horror, that the saintly Polk had *misunderstood* the previous night's retirement order, and had marched his surviving soldiers off the battlefield, withdrawing them from their hard-won positions, and had marched them back to their pre-battle camp, some miles back down the Corinth Road. Precious time had been wasted getting word to Polk, who had to turn his men back out, and then march them back to the fight, the weary soldiers double-timing it back to the front.

"Yes, General. I placed him where you said to, between Breckinridge and Bragg's lines, in a straddling position. His men are the reserve." Jordan's wearied voice replied, the tiredness the result of a poor night's rest, his troubled dreams filled with the memories of the slain Johnston. His morning had not started off well either, since upon hearing the sound of the distant cannon, Jordan's tent companion Prentiss, had awakened him with shouts of joy that Grant was on the way, and that the Confederates had better watch out. Then Colonel Jordan had to deal with his angry superior's concerns of the morning. He had to endure the fiery words of both an angry Beauregard, and a condescending Polk, neither man understanding how the communication between them could have been so misunderstood.

"He is there, and his men are going in, or what's left of them." Jordan stopped, the angry look he was receiving proof enough to tell him that he was right as he belatedly realized that in his extremely tired state his poorly chosen uttered words could be misconstrued as a criticism of Beauregard, and his plan, or lack of one.

"Sorry, sir, I didn't mean to imply that . . ."

"Never mind *that*!" Beauregard peevishly snapped, his eyes narrowing angrily. For a quick moment his hot stare focused on the discomforted Jordan, then away. "Let us ride forward!"

Beauregard spurred his horse forward, Jordan riding along, and emitting a silent sigh of relief. The other remaining staff followed behind, a short distance back, so much the better to stay out of the range of their boss's ire. Their horses picked their way through the dense brush, as dirt, leaves, and small branches swirled around them in the angry wind caused by the cannons' hot breath. A tornado of noise, the result of thousands of voices adding their frenzied shouts to that of the muskets and artillery, roared over and around the small party of riders. They had not ridden very far when Beauregard suddenly held up his hand for the group to stop. He pointed off toward a large patch of woods off to one side. There the group could clearly see a large body of troops emerging from the trees, and wearing what appeared to be shiny white silk uniforms. The newcomers were marching into the field, not far from where Beauregard and his staff were now sitting their horses.

"My God, is that the *enemy*?" Beauregard exclaimed. "Have they broached our lines?"

"I don't know, General, sir. I do not recognize them!" Jordan responded. "They certainly don't look like anything I've ever seen the enemy wear, sir." Both men watched as the newcomers rotated their ranks, moved into a line, and then began to fire, their muskets blazing away at some unseen target, in the direction *away* from Beauregard's little group.

"They're firing *north*, General. Those are *our* men!" Jordan exclaimed, for the moment his tiredness all but forgotten.

He's right! Beauregard thought gleefully to himself. They are! Could these men be part of Van Dorn's army? He's got some fifteen thousand veteran troops. I never thought he could possibly get them here in time, but maybe he put some of them on the train at Memphis and sent them east as reinforcements! There sure aren't any uniforms like that in the Army of the Mississippi . . . but you never know what those Elkhorn Tavern veterans might be wearing! The elated Beauregard turned to Jordan.

"Colonel, send someone to find out just who those boys are!" Beauregard shouted. "Whose command are they? Quickly, sir, quickly!"

"Yes sir, General! I'll go myself!' Jordan whooped, and was off in a flash.

"Let's go, boys!" Beauregard shouted. He started his horse forward, heading through the brush toward what appeared to be a group of men trotting toward them, an officer in the lead. Beauregard rode up to the group, and stopped in front of them, blocking their way through the brush, and forcing them to halt. The officer in the lead, a young looking and very dirty captain, looked up at Beauregard and scowled.

"Men, where are you going? The fight is that way! The enemy is *that* way!" Beauregard pointed back in the direction that the tired-looking and disheveled men had just come from. The fighting could clearly be heard just ahead, the glen around them filled with the pop, popping sound of muskets in the near distance.

The dirty-looking captain just stared at Beauregard for a long second, then, realizing his place, and that Beauregard was a superior officer, quickly raised his hand in a half-hearted salute, his arm quickly dropping back to his side as Beauregard acknowledged him. Then the officer spoke, defiance evident in his tired and angry voice.

"Captain Popper, sir. Cleburne's Brigade. General, sir, begging your pardon, but there ain't no *front* to this fight. Hell, General, begging your pardon again, but there's not much more we can do. My boys, they're all shot up, they are exhausted, they need water, and they need ammunition. They have put two hard days of fighting into this here battle and they have never quit! No sir, not once, but now . . . why hell, General, we've even took fire from *our* side! Lost men to it, too. Good men." Popper shook his head, disgust written all over his dirty face. "Those boys up yonder . . ." Popper pointed back in the direction he and his men had come from. "Well sir, there's plenty more of them then there is of us, fresh troops too. Whoever thought the Yankees were done in just plain didn't know what he was talking about! *They* don't think they're done in! *They* ain't ready to quit this fight, no sir, they're not, ah, begging your pardon again, General. No sir, they have got *plenty* of ammunition too, and they are a'using it, plenty. We'uns just can't hold them no more, sir. Not no more." The younger man finished, the defiance still evident in his posture. There was nothing more to say.

Beauregard stared in astonishment at the captain, then looked at the soldiers grouped behind him. It was obvious to him by the angry muttering and dark looks directed at *him* that these men were in complete agreement with their own officer. Beauregard could plainly see their exhaustion, evident plainly in their dejected postures. Their shoulders were slumped, the dash and fire of the previous day's readiness to fight now plainly *gone*. Others were joining the ever-increasingly large group, their voices joining the chorus of despair.

My God, I must do something! Beauregard looked around him, his attention caught by the plight of then men now surrounding him. We can't just fold up like this! This is not our way. These boys must be given something to hold onto. I would have thought they already did, but it must not be enough. Well, I'll give them something to do it with!

He pushed forward on his horse, and reaching out, seized a regimental flag that one of the soldiers held. The standard was propped up on the soldier's shoulder, the drooping colors barely clearing the dirt beneath it. The surprised soldier let go of the standard, and backed away, as did most of the others surrounding Beauregard.

Beauregard stood the standard up, planting the end of the pole into the ground, and letting the folds fall free, the colors draping themselves over the side of his horse and saddle. The sun flashed on the point of the standard, reflecting its light back over the group. Beauregard stood up in his stirrups, looked over the assembled men, and began to speak.

"You think that war is *easy*!" Beauregard stammered, his patriotic anger evident to all. "Did you think that *victory* would be that *simple*? We can't just *let* the enemy win. We have to *fight* them! If it's *leadership* you're looking for, then look no further. *Come, I will lead you!*"

The astounded men looked at him in silence, Beauregard's staff as well shocked into awed silence. Then Jordan, who had ridden back up just as the verbal exchange between Popper and Beauregard was taking place, spoke, a note of caution in his voice.

"General Beauregard, sir, do you think this is wise? Sir . . . you are our commander. General, please, remember General Johnston . . ."

"Colonel, the order must now be *follow,* not *go!*" Beauregard snapped, silencing Jordan. "Follow *me,* boys!" Beauregard snapped his reins, the horse jumping. Pointing the point of the flag like a great lance toward the sound of the fighting, Beauregard began to push forward through the group surrounding him, the men parting to either side to let him pass. As he rode forward others, who had seen or heard the commotion ran up, adding their voices to the chorus of approval of Beauregard's actions. Then Captain Popper pulled his sword and spoke.

"Well boys, are we going to let the General do *our* fighting for us? What are we waiting for? Let's go!" With that Popper pointed his sword at the Yankee advance. The men responded with a roar, and began to pour by Beauregard, screaming their defiance of the enemy, their thirst for combat renewed by Beauregard's plea, as they charged in a mad dash toward the assembled Union troops. Beauregard started forward, and then stopped, feeling a hand tugging on his stirrup. He looked down to see Popper holding on to the leather strap.

"You've done 'nough, General." Popper reached up and took the flag from Beauregard's hand. "We'uns will do the rest. Begging the general's pardon, but that colonel's right." Popper looked at Jordan. "He's right. We *need* you. Go back. This no place for you, sir. You've proven your bravery. We've already lost one good leader. We can't afford to lose you, sir. Ah, begging the General's pardon." Popper stepped back, saluted, then, wrapping the flag around his arm, and then ran off, his voice soon lost in the chorus of others. Beauregard watched his form and all of the soldiers who followed quickly disappearing, lost in the dark, swirling clouds of smoke.

Good man. Beauregard thought. *Brave man.* He turned back to Jordan.

"Well Colonel, what did you find out?" Beauregard spoke, new energy evident in his voice. "*Are* those Van Dorn's men?" He waited for the reply.

Jordan's face darkened. It was obvious he was having trouble speaking. "No sir, they are not." He stopped, the look on Beauregard's face causing him to pause.

"Well then, whom do they belong to?"

"*You*, sir. They are *Louisiana* troops."

"*Louisiana* troops? With white coats? We have no troops equipped like that!"

"Yes sir. I know that, sir." Jordan paused, then began again. "You see, sir, yesterday, those boys were wearing *blue* coats, but when their own troops, other Confederate forces that is, began to fire upon them, well sir, they just *reversed* their coat linings and went back into the fight that way, today. That's what we saw, General."

"So we have no more reinforcements?"

"No sir. I'm sorry, General. *All* our men are in the fight. We have no others."

Beauregard's shoulders slumped, his newfound energy draining from him like through a wide-open wound. His eyes closed in pain, the headache beginning to surge again through his brain. He sighed, the painful reality of the situation beginning to finally sink in.

"General?"

"Yes, Colonel."

"General, do you not think our troops are very much in the condition of a lump of sugar, thoroughly soaked in water, but yet preserving its original shape, though ready to dissolve?" Jordan waved his arm around at the scene surrounding them. There were more men, some running, some walking, all *leaving* what had been the front just moments before.

Both men watched as the soldiers who had left them just minutes before came walking back. One man who was carrying a flag looked strangely familiar to Beauregard, and with a start he realized that it was the soldier he had taken the flag from. It was the same flag, except with a sinking heart Beauregard realized that if this man had it, where was Popper? The soldier walked up to the officers sitting their horses and spoke to Beauregard.

"Sorry, General. Captain Popper won't be back." The soldier fingered some new holes in the fabric. Beauregard realized that they were rimmed with blood, fresh blood.

Popper's blood. Beauregard thought, then offered up a quick prayer. *Lord have mercy on his soul. On all of their souls.* He sighed, tears springing from his eyes.

On my soul, too.

"General . . . would it not be judicious of us to get away with what we have?"

Yes, Colonel, it would be. But we were so close. So close! Yet if we remain on the field those fresh Union troops will pound us to pieces, just pieces. The only recourse is to get the army to safety. I'm afraid a withdrawal is the only thing left for us to do. Now, we will have to start anew. And now, there are so many less of us. Well, there's nothing we can do about it now. We must start again. Start all over.

I am so sorry, Sidney. I thought we could win. I really did.

"General?"

"I intend to withdraw in a few minutes, Colonel. You may make preparations to send to the others to retire, but slowly, and in good order. It would not be proper to allow the enemy to see us run. No, we can't allow that. But, we are finished here, Colonel."

"Yes sir. Shall I give the orders now, sir?'

Beauregard nodded, then took one last look at the field. He looked up at the sun, now more than halfway down on its afternoon course. He sighed, then turned his horse, and headed back the way they had come, back down the road, back towards Corinth. His shoulders were slumping, as silently, he shed his tears. The dream for today was over. Shiloh would not go for him as had Manassas, or as it had gone in Charleston and Fort Sumter. This one would also get his name in the papers, but not for the right reasons. No, no glorious victory here, no spin on the story, no official report could ever hide the fact of all those boys that were now *gone*. Many a new widow or grieving mother would see their loved ones' names on the casualty lists, and the Southern desire for war would be dampened, if only for a while. The facts were plain, and this one hurt Beauregard deep inside. It hurt *bad*. It would hurt for a very long time. The smile would be gone from many a southern face after Shiloh, replaced by a look of grief and fear of what the future would bring.

Beauregard sighed again, his eyes suddenly welling with tears, ones he could no longer control. He could no longer think in dispassionate terms, and his mind could only see one face, one that would never be numbered among the living again. Johnston's face.

I'm sorry, Sidney.

SHERMAN

Fallen Timbers
April 8, 1862 Late Morning

The weather had turned nasty. The days past it had been heavy rains, the downpours thunderous if brief, followed by bouts of steamy sunshine. Now however, the rain had turned earnest, hard and steady. The wind had changed too. It had suddenly veered in from the north, a cold, whistling tempest, as it blew through the boughs of the trees, and coated everything with a fresh crystal blanket of sleet.

Sherman was out in it, riding the Corinth Road. With great relief he took two brigades, backed by a regiment of Illinois cavalry, and with Grant's blessing, had gone out to make a show of pursuit of the retreating Confederates as they fell back toward Corinth. Two more of Buell's brigades under Brigadier General Thomas J. Wood were marching up the frozen road behind Sherman in support of his force.

At least we will make sure that the rebels will not linger. Sherman thought to himself as he rode. The hooves of the horses made a crunching sound on the sleet-covered road as Sherman and his staff rode along. *Don't reckon too many of them are still around, but after the lesson we just got taught we best not be too careless again. I'm sure Sam's going to hear about us not being ready, defensive-like, and that we should have been watching for the Johnnies to try something. Well, he won't make that mistake again, and neither will I.*

"Best be careful up yonder their boys, it looks like the road dips down." Sherman pointed ahead. The pursuing Federal forces had moved about four miles beyond the recaptured camps. The road ahead at first dipped down, then appeared to rise back up, cresting a ridge on the far side. It passed through what appeared to be an old logging project, long since abandoned, stumps, and rotting logs laying everywhere in a half mile wide marshy swale. To the inhabitants of the area it was known as Fallen Timbers.

"Johnny, give me my glasses." Sherman held out his gloved hand to Lieutenant Taylor, who was riding at Sherman's side. Taylor's face had gone through a transformation. He no longer appeared to be the fresh-faced innocent youngster of a few days before. Now, Lieutenant Taylor's face seemed hardened, and there was a certain scruffiness to him now. War had changed him. Johnny Taylor had seen the elephant and had survived its mad charge, but that survival had cost him. Johnny had experienced *hell*, and life would never hold for him a simple sweetness again. The boy was now a *man*, a veteran, and innocence had been lost forever.

"Right here, sir." Taylor slapped the field glasses into Sherman's hand, momentarily forgetting that the outstretched palm contained the injured digits.

"Ow! Easy there, Lieutenant. Them fingers took a powerful beating the other day." Sherman cradled the field glasses against his chest, shaking the damaged hand, the pain still fresh.

"Oh, my, General, I am sorry . . . I did not mean to . . ."

"Forget it son. Do you see what I see up yonder, up on that ridge in front of us?" Sherman pointed with the glasses at the hill up ahead. Taylor peered hard, then shook his head, a quick nod.

"Riders." He replied. "Looks like rebel cavalry to me, sir." The distant horsemen were silhouetted against the sky behind them. "Can't tell how many for sure. Might be more down on the other side of that ridge, just waiting for us, General."

Sherman smiled. *He's learned fast.* Sherman thought to himself. "All right, Lieutenant, I agree with you. We *don't* know how many there are. Send out skirmishers, regimental strength. Use the lead regiment. I want that cavalry with us posted on the skirmishers flanks and backing them up. We'll follow with the rest of the brigade. Attack formation. Let's do this right, Lieutenant, no more mistakes. By the book, Johnny. Go tell the others."

"Yes sir." Taylor spurred his horse away, gesturing to the other officers as he rode back along the line. Immediately the other officers responded, the cavalry splitting and swinging to the flanks on either side of the lead infantry regiment, the horses picking their way through the muddy brush lining the road on either side. Sherman watched as the lead skirmishers made their way forward, quickly at first, then slower as they gingerly picked their way through the remains of the fallen trees, moving toward the ridge ahead with its line of still unmoving men and horses. He watched the skirmishers, nodding in approval of their professional movement, then suddenly frowned. What remained of the wooded field was causing the line of skirmishers to break up, forcing them to spread further and further apart, much more then he wanted them to. Gaps were beginning to appear, large ones here and there between the advancing soldiers.

Suddenly there was the sound of a bugle blowing on the ridge up ahead, and to Sherman's dismay, the entire line of horsemen began to suddenly stampede down the ridge at *him*, with more coming over the crest of the ridge and following along behind their leaders, several hundred in all. A chorus of high-pitched rebel yells could be heard screaming from their throats, their flags and weapons blazing in the bright, brittle sunshine. Out in front rode a large bearded man, sword held high in one hand, a great pistol in the other, reins held tightly in his teeth. Sherman could clearly hear the big officer bellowing as he rode.

"Charge 'em, boys. Charge! Charge!"

"My God, how the hell is he staying on that horse?" Sherman exclaimed as he watched the gray-coated cavalrymen swoop down on the lead regiment, pistols, swords, and muskets flashing in the fight. The skirmishers stood, then broke their ranks, fleeing back toward the assembled blue-coated ranks behind them. The Confederate cavalrymen continued their charge, dashing in among the fleeing infantrymen, swords slashing left and right, pistols and shotguns erupting as well as the gray-coated horsemen carried the fight to the enemy, some perhaps with some thought of getting some revenge for the losses of the past two days. The strength of the charge had carried away the Yankee cavalry as well, and they too were streaming back, hell-bent-for-leather. There were a number of empty saddles now, a testimony to the ferocity of the charge.

"Hell, I can't stay here!" Sherman exclaimed again, turning his horse and riding for the safety of the now drawn up brigades behind him and the rest of his staff. Two thousand bayoneted gun barrels glinted in the sun. He quickly rode through the blue line, the parting to either side to let him and his staff pass through and get behind them, then closing ranks quickly, two thousand rifles now turned on the pursuing rebel cavalry. The awesome sight was enough to bring the pursuing horsemen to an abrupt stop, all that is, but one.

The big, bearded rider, his pistols empty, but his gleaming sword still busy with his butcher's work, had not realized that he was the only gray rider still galloping forward, all alone in his crazed quest. Not until his horse plunged right into the Federal line did the mad officer realize his plight. With a huge roar, he tore his horse's head around, swinging his sword madly to each side as he tried to cut his way out of the swarming Yankees, a solitary, gray coat afloat in a sea of blue.

"Kill him! Kill him! Kill the son of a bitch! Kill that devil!" Sherman heard himself screaming as he watched the Confederate officer, his horse kicking and plunging, the animal screaming in pain as Yankee bayonets stabbed into the frightened animal's flanks, as the bayonets' owners tried to reach the incensed officer, he who hacked and slashed as he desperately tried to free himself from the mass of blue he found himself in.

"Kill him! *Kill the damn rebel!* Knock him off his horse, men! Do it!" Sherman raged. A horrified fascination growing as he watched the other man brutishly slam men down, his sword hacking and slashing a crimson path through the angry Federals.

Suddenly a soldier slammed his musket into the side of the Confederate officer, and pulled the trigger. The muzzle exploded, the force of its discharge lifting the maniacal gray-coated officer clean off his horse's saddle.

"You got him, finish him . . . *finish him!*" Sherman screamed, realizing that the wounded man had somehow miraculously stayed on his horse. Suddenly the Confederate reached down, and with a murderous snarl snatched a soldier up by his collar, and hauled the frightened fellow up onto the back of his now bloody saddle. Sherman watched in speechless amazement as the rebel officer, his wounded body now protected by the body of the terrified infantryman, forced his way through the rest of the Federal line, and galloped away. The other soldiers were forced to withhold their fire, for fear of hitting their fellow infantryman, and killing him instead of the crazed apparition. All watched in amazement as the rebel streaked out of range, then dropped the hapless soldier, the man falling in a tangled heap to the ground. The assembled troops of both sides watched in open mouthed amazement as the wounded officer continued his ride to the top of the ridge where his men had reassembled. None of them had followed their crazed commander in his insane charge into the blue lines. Their faces mirrored their awe, at once both in amazement and fear, as to what kind of *man* could have survived *that*.

"That's no man. That's the *devil!*" Sherman shook his head, both with disgust and amazement. He watched as the assemblage on the ridge turned and rode down the other side of the ridge, and disappeared from sight, their flags last of all.

"Shall we pursue them, General?" Taylor too, was aghast at what he had just seen.

Sherman shook his head. "No, Johnny. Not that one. Have the men collect the wounded and the dead. We are heading back. We have had enough. Three days of this is enough for any man." He pointed at the now empty ridge. "So have they. It's over. Let's go back to camp. Reassemble for the march. I think we should count our blessings."

"Yes sir. I never saw anything like that before." Taylor was still looking back at the ridge. "Hope I never do again."

Sherman grinned as he crammed a cigar into his mouth. Without lighting it, he turned the horse, and headed back down the road, back toward PITTSBURG Landing, back toward Grant and a victorious army, back toward a future meeting with destiny, notoriety, and fame. The stormy weather was beginning to abate, and the immediate threat to them all, was over. Now it was time to rest, rest and regroup. It was also time to rethink the *plan*. The Confederate forces had surely surprised them, and Sherman realized that there would have to be a reevaluation done of the Federal strategy for the conquest of the Confederacy in the west.

As if Sam's not already doing just that! Sherman thought to himself. Well, that's in the future. The future will come soon enough. We will win, at least here in the west, but it sure won't be easy. But we will win. Sam and I will see to that.

He took one last look over his shoulder, back at the now assembled marching soldiers behind them, the cavalry again out riding on the flanks and up ahead on point. He looked again at the ridge behind them, the one the rebels had made their mad dash from, that insane one-man attack. Then he paused for a moment, and pulled a match to light the now damp cigar. He puffed for a long second, looked at Lieutenant Taylor, and gestured back, a thumb pointing in the direction of the ridge receding in the distance.

"You know John, I wouldn't be surprised if we see that devil again."

THE END OF DAWN'S GRAY STEEL

ABOUT THE AUTHOR

Daniel F. Korn was born in 1952 in Rochester, New York. As a young boy he was fascinated by the heroes and stories of our nation's history, with his first hero being Davy Crockett. Dan would grow up in western New York and would follow his love of history by attending the State University of New York at Brockport, (Brockport State), from whom he holds both a bachelor's and a master's degree in History and Education.

As a college student he read and fell in love with Michael Shaara's immortal Civil War novel The Killer Angels. The book inspired Dan to write his own novel, a story about those incredibly horrible days of battle that took place in April, 1862, on the shores of the Tennessee River, near a sleepy little church called Shiloh Meetinghouse.

Dan, his wife Cheri, and their family currently reside in Monroe, North Carolina where Dan teachs high school students in Honors U.S. History and Civil War, and shares a love for Revolutionary War reenacting with his son, Mike. Dawn's Gray Steel is his first book.

Printed in the USA
CPSIA information can be obtained
at www.ICGtesting.com
CBHW081912300324
6067CB00009B/47

9 781959 197843